ALL WRAPPED UP

Ally Bunbury is a bestselling novelist, based in Ireland. Inspired by the TV sitcom *Absolutely Fabulous*, she embarked upon a PR career in New York, London and Dublin. During a personal sabbatical in Paris, Ally wrote the draft of her first novel, *The Inheritance*.

A frequent contributor to *The Irish Times*, Ally lives with her husband, historian Turtle Bunbury, in the countryside.

ALSO BY ALLY BUNBURY

The Inheritance
Infidelity

Facebook: allybunburybooks
Instagram: @allybunburybooks
Twitter: @allybunbury
www.allybunbury.com

Ally Bunbury

All Wrapped Up

HACHETTE
BOOKS
IRELAND

First published in Ireland in 2022 by
HACHETTE BOOKS IRELAND

1

Quotation by Erin Van Vuren is used with kind permission of the author.

Cataloguing in Publication Data is available from the British Library

ISBN 9781399713078

Typeset in Book Antiqua by Bookends Publishing Services, Dublin

Printed and bound in Great Britain by Clays Ltd, Elcograf, S.p.A

Hachette Books Ireland policy is to use papers that are natural, renewable
and recyclable products and made from wood grown in sustainable
forests. The logging and manufacturing processes are expected to conform
to the environmental regulations of the country of origin.

Hachette Books Ireland
8 Castlecourt Centre
Castleknock
Dublin 15, Ireland

A division of Hachette UK Ltd
Carmelite House, 50 Victoria Embankment, EC4Y 0DZ

www.hachettebooksireland.ie

For Jemima and Bay, with all my love

*'Lost and Found
are from the
same box.
Remember this
when you don't know
where you belong.'*

Erin Van Vuren

Prologue

Knightsbridge, London

'I thought we could see my parents next weekend,' said Giles Charter, gazing at his fiancée, oblivious as to what was about to happen. 'They're in a bind about whether or not to convert the Aga.' He reached across the restaurant table and gently pressed his thumb on Holly O'Leary's 18-carat cushion of diamonds. She smiled, curled her fingers away and slid her hand towards her glass. 'All their friends are doing it,' Giles continued. He looked curious as Holly polished off the remains of her Chablis. 'But you know how Ma likes her Victoria sponge to rise.'

Beneath the tablecloth, Holly's restless heel drummed the floor as she turned her ring anticlockwise and pulled it over her knuckle.

'Four months to go,' he said, topping up Holly's glass. 'Or, to be precise, as today is August the twentieth, four months and four days to go.' Dark hair sat neatly across his forehead as he spoke, his brown eyes buoyant with optimism.

'Giles,' she said, feeling awful about what she had to say. 'It isn't that I want to make your life difficult …'

'Sweetheart, how could you make my life difficult? You're the best thing to have happened to me by a country mile.'

He smiled with heart-breaking sincerity and popped a cashew nut into his mouth. She could hear it crunch as his eyes focused on the ring. It now lay on the white tablecloth, next to a smudge of pesto. It looked like a miniature art installation, symbolising freedom for Holly and rejection for Giles. Several seconds passed as they sat in silence, the colour draining from his face.

'I knew it,' he said, taking a large drink of water. He rubbed his forehead and exhaled heavily. 'It was all going too bloody well.'

Holly felt entirely responsible for this mess. For the past three years they had been surrounded by friends, pairing up and hell-bent on outshining one another by Instagramming their elaborate proposals. The wedding flowers, the dresses, the jam jars filled with jelly beans, celebrating newlyweds in one marquee after another. Ever since she began dating Giles, she had been strangely repelled by how he mapped his life out. His Volvo may as well have had car seats for his unborn children. He had already taken steps to put his pharmaceutical research company on the market, responsibly holding on to twenty-five per cent as added security for his future. When they met, Holly had instantly sensed that he liked her but she suspected he'd never dream of asking her for a date. He was a scientist; she, a distracted temp. Giles was modest but self-assured. His sense of purpose was impressive and, slightly hoping some of that would rub off on her, Holly had instigated the whole thing. It was she who asked for his phone number and it was she who suggested a date.

Once he realised she was interested, Giles took control and laid on one romantic gesture after another. Weekly deliveries of hip-high red roses arrived to whichever office Holly was temping at. He asked her to have a weekend bag ready at all times, and every third or fourth weekend he'd whisk them off to a hotel in Europe – Paris, Madrid, Prague, Berlin, Rome. So many cityscapes now flooded her mind. Giles was an excellent travelling companion, always knowledgeable about the population, demography and governance of each new city they approached. It was on the trip to Rome that she had realised with a terrifying clarity that Giles was the perfect friend. Therein lay the problem. Hugs, snuggles and kissing were his forte, but he always seemed nervous about making love. Holly suspected he might have been a virgin when they met, and no matter how enthusiastic she was to climb into bed, he sometimes couldn't quite perform. On their last night in Rome, he had admitted to being a little intimidated by her.

'Is it because I'm not terribly adventurous – you know, as I might be?' Giles almost cringed as his words fluttered across the table.

'Oh God no,' said Holly, but it felt like he was reading her mind. This was a big part of the problem. Mariah, Holly's best friend in London, had been adamant that the marriage could never work unless they sorted out their sleeping arrangements. Holly had thought they could find a way through. She'd read articles, listened to podcasts and even consulted the book *Love Signs* by Linda Goodman. That had been a holy bible for her mother in the seventies – not that it had proved successful in terms of her parents' marriage.

'What will you do?' As was typical, Giles was more concerned about Holly than himself.

'Mariah said I can move my things to her flat and stay there for a while. She spends so much time at the gallery, and she's with Frank every other weekend.'

Giles nodded as if that made sense, but frowned. His eyes were welling up.

'Her flat is rather titchy though.'

'Well, you know Mariah. She says it won't matter if there's a pile of boxes in the sitting room.'

'How kind of her,' he said, wiping his eyes. His face was a combination of shock, hurt and definite sadness. Holly wondered how he was going to cope.

'I suppose Mariah and Frank will move to the country,' he said, 'at some stage.'

'Maybe,' she said, wondering what else she could add. Discussing Mariah and Frank's almost flawless relationship was not going to help either of them.

'I'm not so worried about telling my parents,' said Giles, fiddling with the pepper mill, 'as they are very practical people, but I do worry about your mother.'

'Really?' said Holly, who thought of her mum at home in Dublin, with her wedding folder. Giles had a point. Holly's mother, Juliette O'Leary, had gone on a course of

Valium when she first learned of their plans for a Christmas Eve wedding. The mother who lived for Yuletide for three hundred and sixty-five days a year. She'd already baked the wedding cake, ordered a zillion lights for the reception and drawn up a minute-by-minute itinerary with a wedding planner. A Christmas wedding was to be the ultimate festive event for Juliette. How on earth was she going to take the news?

A week later, having packed and relocated to Mariah's house in Pimlico, Holly sat in the waiting room of the Elizabeth Street dentist with a throbbing wisdom tooth. It felt like she had been dealt a punishment by the universe. How was she going to break the news to her mother that she'd called off the wedding? She'd hit the roof, and definitely the Prosecco. Even worse, Holly's brother had booked the 'incredibly expensive, so it had better be worth it' flight home from Sydney. Her name was about to be mud with her immediate family. To top it all, her mobile was out of battery. A series of outdated magazines lay fanned out on the waiting-room coffee table. The *Dancing Times* led with the cover story of 'Tangoing through the Menopause'. No, thank you, thought Holly. But her eyes widened when she saw the cover of *The Lady*, with the Agony Aunt feature 'Navigating the Crossroads of Life'.

She picked up the copy of *The Lady* and cast her eyes over the dilemmas, problems and quarrels on the Agony Aunt page. One reader was seeking advice on how to tell if her clairvoyant was just making everything up. Holly was musing upon whether she should google an appointment with a clairvoyant and skip the dentist when an advertisement on the opposite page caught her eye.

ENERGETIC PERSON immediately required to declutter remote country house in Ireland. Live in. Short term. I do not use computers and therefore have no email. Please apply to *The Lady* quoting Box 251734.

Chapter One

Foothills of the Wicklow Mountains, Ireland

Knockboden was a magnificent giant of a house, with tall windows and chimneys rising proudly towards the heavens. It had been years since Holly had been in the countryside to breathe in the damp, earthy autumnal air, witnessing the blazing woodland shades of red, yellow and orange. Over the past six weeks, this place had become her sanctuary. She'd deleted her social media apps, removed her nail polish and stopped straightening her hair.

'Whiskey. Over. Are you there? Over.' Lady Serena Harpur's voice bellowed from the walkie-talkie as Holly walked past a row of garden urns, filled with exhausted grasses which had seen better days.

'Soda. Over. I'm on my way. Over,' she said, pressing the button.

Serena had assigned unique names to the walkie-talkies, inspired by her favourite drink. It felt like a 1950s sitcom as her voice crackled into the air, still yelling despite Holly's previous attempts to suggest that the sound from a walkie-talkie was clearer when speaking in a normal tone.

'Whiskey. Over. Tango, Oscar, November, India, Charlie, urgent. Over.'

'Soda. Over. Seriously, Serena, can't you just say *tonic*? Over.'

'Whiskey. Over. Bloody *tonic* then. Over.'

'Soda. Over. With you in five. Over.'

As she approached the front of the house, a pile of logs blocked the doorway. Holly looked through the front hall window; she could see Edwin Duffy hovering over the fireplace.

'Edwin?'

She watched a pair of red hens scratching around the logs. It was anyone's guess whether it was colder inside or outside of the house.

'How are you, Holly?' asked Edwin, wincing as he sidestepped the wheelbarrow in the hall and came to the door. 'I've never known a girl from the city to take to wandering around in the freezing weather.'

'The cold clears my head,' she said, pulling the woolly hat down over the back of her neck. 'Gets the endorphins going.'

'Stacking this wood does it for me,' he said, rubbing his bald head, shimmering with sweat. 'Even if these old bones of mine are creaking, the cod liver oil my Babs has got me on seems to be working.'

Holly watched the hens standing at the hall door, wondering if they were going to venture inside.

'Are you missing London yet?' asked Edwin, shooing the hens out of the way.

'Not really,' she said, but in truth she was, and desperately so. She missed Giles. The phone calls, the Ab Fab comedy sketches he'd send to her of Patsy and Edwina knocking back the Bolly. He had always been a supporter of Holly's friendships and encouraged her to socialise. Giles had even known that Mariah was going to be proposed to before she did. Her now husband had asked Giles to suggest Holly take her on a girls' night out. When Mariah arrived back to her flat, the sitting room was covered in pink roses.

'As long as you're happy in yourself,' said Edwin, 'that's all that matters. Why don't you come in before you turn into an ice block? You're nimble enough to climb over the wood despite the height of you. Grab hold of the architrave as you climb over. That's it ... you're nearly there ... and step carefully onto those logs ... and jump.'

'My mum always says I'm big-boned,' she said.

'And my mam said I was too short. Hard to win, isn't it?'

Even in daylight, the hall was dark and there was a smell of damp rolling in over the logs.

'Edwin, can I check something with you?' Holly made sure the walkie-talkie was switched off before continuing.

'Go on.'

'Any chance you've been paid this month?'

'Now, you'd be better off asking if those hens could talk.'

Holly folded her arms to ease the palpitations brewing inside her.

'Jeepers, there's no need to look so alarmed, love.' Edwin

leaned against the wall. 'I'll grant ye there have been times when it's taken a while to get paid, but I'll have been here fifty years come December. Started when I was sixteen.'

Holly wondered where she'd be in fifty years' time. Maybe sitting alone, overlooking a herd of sheep, with a hairy chin and a bottle of vodka. 'When you think of the life Lady S has had,' said Edwin, 'she is one-of-a-kind, she is.'

'But doesn't your wife mind?'

'Babs? No, she's delighted I'm kept busy, and she has her own busyness minding the rectory for Father Flynn.' Edwin was the picture of contentment. 'I join my Babs in the evenings, when the house is as she likes it. I'm here for the long haul now, Holly; it's something I wouldn't want to walk away from. I've been with her too long to go now. It wouldn't be right.'

'But you do actually get paid by Serena? I've been here for over six weeks, and she hasn't really given me a straight answer as to when I'll receive my salary.'

'I get paid alright, but granted, not always like clockwork,' he said, a little awkwardly. 'But you've no cause to worry. As my old nana used to say, count your blessings and the pennies will look after themselves. It's just the way it is, Holly.'

The door to Serena's study was wide open, and the floor was littered with old magazines. The air smelled of hair spray and smoke.

'There you are.' An unlit cigarette hung from Serena's mouth as she leaned heavily on her desk.

'I'm not sure a stapler can get through a plastic folder,' said Holly.

'To hell with it then.' Serena hurled the stapler across the desk. 'Get me the superglue, would you?'

Holly pulled open the dresser drawer, which was stuffed to capacity with decades' worth of promotional pens. 'I think it's dried out,' she said, holding up a shrivelled tube.

'Drat. Never mind. Did you bring the tonic?'

'Oh no, I'm so sorry. I got distracted in the hall chatting with Edwin; he was busy filling the baskets with logs.'

Serena exhaled noisily and shot out her hand to pick up a sandwich from a chipped plate.

'Don't you want it, darling?' she said, holding the sandwich over Jagger, a silky black labrador. 'No? I can always give it to Daiquiri if you aren't interested.'

Leaping up to retrieve his early lunch, Jagger grunted as he took a mouthful of sandwich and spat out the lettuce. Holly could have sworn she saw Daiquiri, the fat terrier beneath Serena's desk, shudder in disgust. A smell of dog fart invaded the room.

'How about I open a window?' suggested Holly. 'It's quite stuffy, isn't it?'

'I'll tell you what's stuffy. That arse of a man has been on the phone, again.'

'Which one?' asked Holly, pushing up a sash window and wedging an ashtray into the corner to hold up the frame.

'The fellow who wears his tie too long.'

'Kenneth,' said Holly, walking over to the drinks cabinet. She found an old bottle of tonic stashed behind some dusty liqueurs. The bottle hissed its last, flat breath as she twisted open the lid. 'Dead as a dodo. I'll find some more in the kitchen.'

'Don't bother,' said Serena. She was wearing one of her trademark chunky necklaces and a thick leather belt, accentuating her ample bosom and long legs. She had held on to her looks and could still sprawl across sofas and lean against walls like a carefree teenager. 'Flat tonic is one of the few things in life that genuinely doesn't bother me. Pour the gin, then a splash of tonic and a drop of Angostura bitters to pink it up.'

Holly fixed the drink and passed it to Serena.

'Aren't you going to join me?' Serena gave the G and T a stir with the end of her biro and smiled as she took her first sip.

'I'd better not,' said Holly, sitting on the club fender by the fireplace. 'I've got to drive into Turpinstown for supplies and order that bottle of port for you.'

'Thank you for remembering, Holly. This is one area in which I am organised. A round of Stilton and port on Christmas Day is my present to myself,' Serena said, tipping the overflowing ashtray into a wastepaper bin. 'Last year, Daly's Wine stocked the most abysmal port and so this time I want them to import exactly the bottle I want.'

'Who do you usually spend Christmas with?' asked Holly, peering up at the mantelpiece and wondering if she should salute the magpie perched up there in a glass case.

'My dogs, of course. We watch *Dynasty* – the original, obviously – and I dine as if I'm at the Shelbourne. It's the one time I put a lot of effort into my cooking.'

'Turkey?'

'Goose,' she said. 'Mother always insisted on it. And what about you? Will you be with your family?'

'Not this year.' Holly could feel herself tensing up. 'Isn't it a little negative to have a single magpie in here?'

'Certainly not. The ancients believed a magpie to be a sign of opportunity, and that little bird has given me plenty of luck over the years.' Serena lit her cigarette and threw the match away.

'I don't think even the magpie would approve of you dropping a freshly lit match into the bin.'

Serena wrinkled her nose. 'Honestly, your generation, so overly cautious about *everything*. You'll give yourselves ulcers.'

Holly looked around the study. There were stacks of magazines, long-life shopping bags overflowing with letters, moth-eaten felt hats piled on a free-standing radiator and a trunk with its lid open, filled with what looked like old computer wires.

'Now, Holly,' said Serena, holding out her glass for a refill. 'Tell me where we are with the computer site for Knockboden.' She seemed unable to bring herself to use the word *internet*. 'I want to start promoting our B&B for honeymooners. I still think it's a genius idea, don't you?'

'I do,' said Holly, admiring the way her boss commanded so elegantly from her desk.

'And *I do* is precisely what I want people across the world to say, and then to come to Knockboden and test out the bed springs.' Serena squeezed her eyes at Holly. 'Why are you looking like a doubting Thomas?'

'I think it is quite a niche market, that's all.'

'Nonsense,' said Serena. 'Romance is the one good thing which can withstand a recession and my "Knockboden Honeymoon B&B Retreat" is going to bring the lolly.'

'You've added the word *retreat* since we last spoke.'

'Holly, at twenty-nine years of age, do you know nothing? Lynette brought me an article from the *Sunday Business Post*, which said something along the lines of "the more words you include in a commercial offering, the more euro signs you can add".'

'Clever,' said Holly, thinking this may in fact make quite good sense.

'Most of all, we want the B&B venture to shut up the irritating creature that is Karl from that blasted money-lending organisation.'

'You mean Kenneth.'

'Karl, Ken, what does it matter? I just want him off my back.'

'The broadband has been connected, and I've purchased the site knockboden.com,' said Holly, mixing another drink. 'But, Serena, remember, I'm here to declutter and get the bedrooms ready, not to do your online marketing?'

'What's that?'

'We talked about hiring a specialist to do all the promoting.'

Serena held out her hand to receive her drink, like a child awaiting a handful of bon-bons.

'There's no need to be defensive, Holly. I want to bring in some lolly so that I can buy my staff pressies.' She lit another cigarette.

'On that note, Serena, you originally said it might take a few weeks before I get my first pay cheque.'

'And?'

'I've been here since the beginning of September. It's now the twentieth of October.'

'Consider it done.'

'Really? Well that's great.' Holly felt instant relief. She did have savings, but Giles, so good with money, had always advised that it was better to keep them safe for a downpour, rather than a rainy day.

'You know, Holly, once upon a time I was drenched in Chanel, and now I'm drenched in nothing but bills.' Serena was skilled at drifting away from answering questions. 'The thought of having to give up my most beloved bedroom to make way for bonking guests is really quite beyond the imagination.'

It was becoming clear to Holly that Serena was going to take as much managing as the house.

Chapter Two

Manhattan, New York

Tyrone Harpur watched his soon-to-be-ex-wife walk towards him. She was sexy as hell and carrying takeout from the café. He pushed his hands into his cashmere coat and raised his head to acknowledge her. The Conservatory Garden in Central Park had seemed like a sensible location to meet. There were no runners or cyclists, meaning that Kenzie wouldn't be distracted or be a distraction. She was the ultimate flirt, which made his meeting her in person all the more perilous. Her inexplicable ability to make him change his mind – a touch, her breath, her perfume, it didn't take much – but not this time. The sham was over.

'Hey, you,' she said, passing both coffees to Tyrone so she could pull her bouncy curls free from the collar of her coat. 'You look good, darling.' Kenzie would have kissed Tyrone full on the lips if he hadn't offered his cheek. She was not au fait with the proper etiquette once the papers had been served.

'How have you been?' Tyrone took a sip of coffee, which was too sweet. Kenzie always added sugar.

'I was surprised, *obviously*,' she said, when Tyrone passed a coffee back to her. 'I didn't expect you to go legal so quickly.'

Butter would not melt, he thought to himself. 'So you thought I'd just go along with you sleeping with my business partner?'

'Business?' she asked. 'I thought you played squash.' Then she laughed. 'Look, I'm sorry, but you weren't exactly husband of the year.'

'Meaning?'

'In the three years we've been together, not once have you remembered my birthday.'

'I'm hopeless with dates.'

'Yes, those too – when was the last time we actually went on one? If you want your wife to stay, you have to give your wife attention. It's as simple as that.' Kenzie liked to refer to herself in the third person, particularly when she'd got into trouble. 'Sleeping with your wife is also a good tip.'

'That's rich,' said Tyrone, taking the lid off the coffee cup and pouring the contents onto the grass. 'I walked in on *my wife* with another man in my own bed. You have any other tips you'd like to share?'

'How about spending less time with Carl?'

'He's my best friend and he's lonely.'

'Lonely? So was I, and you wonder why I sought out company?'

'Don't be so fucking insensitive. His wife died, in case you've forgotten.'

'Fine,' she said, relenting. 'I did love you, though.' She said it in the same way she might have said she loved a jacket at a fashion show last season. 'But there's a part of me that would like to meet up with your first wife and compare notes.'

'Kenzie,' he said, 'you know I really did love you.'

She reached out to rub the side of his face, which felt almost soothing. 'I worry about you, honey, and I know you don't like it when I say this, but I'm going to say—'

'Please don't—'

'You have Mommy issues and I don't think you're going to make a decent husband until you work them out.' Kenzie's voice was so smooth and extravagant, she could have narrated a self-help book. 'I'd love you to hook up with this therapist I've been seeing.'

For a moment he thought Kenzie was suggesting marriage counselling, but she quickly qualified herself. 'To help you work out whatever it is that's bugging you.'

Tyrone chose to ignore the dig.

They walked towards the entrance to Fifth Avenue. 'Amazing to think these gates were once part of the Vanderbilts' place, isn't it?' Kenzie said. Her appreciation of history had been one of the things that had made him fall for her. 'Do you think the guy who created twenty feet of iron and bronze ever thought they'd welcome New Yorkers and tourists rather than the Vanderbilts and their friends?'

'I think he'd have had a word with Gertrude,' Tyrone said, without thinking.

'Sorry?'

'Gertrude – she was the Vanderbilt who donated the gates to Central Park. But I guess she'd be happy to know that people walking through are looking for solace in the Conservatory Garden—'

'People like us?'

'Sure.' This was what made it annoying. He and Kenzie got on well; conversation had always been easy. 'But can you imagine? Within seventy years of Commodore Vanderbilt's death, all of the Vanderbilt homes along Fifth Avenue had been sold or levelled. There's longevity for you.'

'Maybe some things weren't meant to last.'

Tyrone thought of Ireland and the formal gardens of Knockboden, which he could vaguely remember as a child: the yew walk, the wisteria pergola he used to hide behind when his parents had parties.

Kenzie brushed her arm against him. 'You know, Tyrone, I think if you had taken the trouble to spend more time with me, we could have made it work.'

'I suggested plenty of weekends, but between your facials and fashion shows, Kenzie, you were never around. Always too interested in following the crowd.'

'The crowd? Are you for real, Tyrone, Mr Irish Country Gent? At least I know where I belong and I'm not pretending to be a city slicker.'

'I'm not sure where to begin in my response,' he said, pulling a fake smile across his face, 'but I'm pretty sure that *my therapist* would say turn the other cheek.'

Kenzie pulled the lid off her coffee to scoop up the

cappuccino froth. 'I like to make the most of everything I get,' she said, licking the tip of her finger.

'I'm grateful for the reminder.' Tyrone meant it. Five minutes was all it had taken to assure him that he had made the right decision. Feeling a vibration in his coat pocket, he took out his mobile phone. 'I'm going to take this,' he said, seeing an Irish number flashing up on the screen.

Kenzie squeezed Tyrone's hand. 'Take care of yourself, won't you?' She walked through the gates, waved her hand and within seconds a yellow cab screeched to a halt.

Tyrone watched her go, feeling regret for what he'd hoped and thought could be. He now had two failed marriages and pre-nups behind him.

'Tyrone Harpur?'

'Speaking.'

'Kenneth Gates.'

'What's the latest?'

'There's no point beating around the bush,' he said. 'The clock is ticking on the debt relating to Lady Harpur. We have received precisely no payments to date on her loan.'

'When did you last make contact with her?'

'Last week, by letter, email and phone.'

'Visit one more time, and then call me. I want her to know you mean business.'

The timing couldn't have been more annoying. Tyrone had started a new routine with his personal trainer. That he was co-founder of an investment bank was another aspect, but one that bothered him less. He had given the past twenty years to his clients, advising on acquisitions and restructuring their finances. Increasingly Tyrone felt it was he who needed restructuring. Even when he tried, he couldn't put his finger on what he wanted any more. His ambition had dwindled and it was a dreadful feeling. Then there was the reservation at Jean-Georges on Thursday with Carl. But maybe this divorce could be the impetus to sort all aspects of his life – including the situation with his mother.

Chapter Three

Knockboden, Ireland

Four p.m. November was well underway and already it was getting dark. Holly cranked the ancient Land Rover into gear, and gripping the weighty steering wheel, she felt a pang at the sight of her ring finger. This time last year, she'd had a manicure in anticipation of meeting Giles's parents as their daughter-in-law-to-be. Instagram had been uploaded with a multitude of sparkling engagement photos, Holly with blow-dried hair and lip gloss, believing she was on the right path. But now she was travelling along a track with a grassy centre, flanked by burnt orange and crispy brown leaves in the hedgerow. It was hard to make sense as to why she'd left him, but her intuition had taken over.

On the outskirts of Turpinstown, a large banner advertised for staff to work on a Christmas tree farm. Another sign promoted 'Homemade Puddings & Mince Pies'. The thought of decorating sent Holly into a guilty spin, thinking of her mum's wedding plans. Giles had sent a barrage of messages during the first few weeks following the break-up. He'd offered her a room in his house, 'no-strings attached', for when she returned to London. His parents had wanted to know if they could make direct contact with Holly's mother, but Giles had assured her that he'd keep the cat in the bag until Holly was ready to tell her mother that the wedding had been cancelled rather than postponed.

Holly came to a halt at a roundabout when a WhatsApp call from Mariah flashed up.

'I've got you on loudspeaker,' said Holly, balancing the phone on the dashboard, 'and the coverage isn't great either.'

'Where are you?'

'Turpinstown, trying to find my way into the village. It's my fourth visit and I still find the roundabout confusing.'

'Surely all roads lead to Rome?' said Mariah, her voice confident and reassuring. She and Holly had met at Durham University, both coasting along on arts degrees. Doing the bare minimum had worked for Mariah, but Holly barely scraped a pass in her exams.

'Not sure I can compare Turpinstown to Rome, but maybe once I visit the wine shop I'll feel differently.'

'Bottoms up,' giggled Mariah. 'Once you park, can you put me on FaceTime?'

She always managed to bring levity to a situation. When Holly had arrived in tears after the break-up lunch with Giles, Mariah had comforted her with the words, 'At least you won't have to put up with his mother's baking. Remember the banana-flavoured custard we had to sit through over Sunday lunch?' Missing out on life's pontifications with

Mariah had been the worst part of leaving London. They could spend forty-five minutes discussing night cream. They'd laugh and dream and talk about how their lives might pan out. One propping up the other when the chips were down.

In the carpark, Holly looked down at her filthy jeans and grimaced at her reflection in the rear-view mirror. 'Okay, prepare for rustic vibes,' she said, turning on the camera.

'Hey, Curly Sue, what's with the hair?'

'I didn't bring the straighteners.'

'And your eyebrows could give Cara Delevingne a run for her money,' said Mariah. 'No wonder you haven't wanted to FaceTime.'

'Actually, I'm feeling quite liberated. Giles was so into capturing everything online, I really had to make such an effort to look up to scratch.' It was true: Holly hadn't realised it at the time, but there had been a certain amount of pressure for her to look as well-groomed as he did. This was the first time in a long while that she could forget the mirror. 'The main thing is to make sure that Mum doesn't find out where I am, that's all that matters.'

'She's still buying the idea that you're on some kind of top-secret mission?'

'I had no option but to tell a white lie. I feel terrible about it, but it was the only way out – Mum would hit the roof if I told her the wedding was off, instead of just postponed.'

'God, Holly, she's going to think you're some kind of modern-day James Bond.'

'She even sounded impressed that for once in my life I've found an exciting job, though I haven't told her where or what it is.'

'And is the job exciting?'

'No, but if it takes clearing out fifty years' worth of Tupperware and half-empty shampoo bottles to give me time to work out what's next, then I don't really mind.'

'She's going to find out, Holly, beside the fact that Dublin can't be that far from where you are. I may never have been to Ireland, but I can read Google Maps.' Mariah never let Holly off the hook easily, and that's what made their friendship so crucial.

'Depends on the traffic,' said Holly, knowing full well that her mum's house on the south side of Dublin was no more than thirty minutes away. 'I haven't even started the proper clean-out, or more like *mucking out*, yet. The house is chaos. Everywhere you look, there are boxes, or piles of old clothes, even jam jars. It's like a hoarders' paradise.' A woman walked by, pushing a pram along the pavement, her head bowed to stave off the cold.

'Then maybe it isn't helpful for me to tell you that Giles called again this morning, *and* he's being unusually quiet on Instagram.'

'Really?' Somehow this news was heartening.

'But Holly, even though I'm so fond of Giles, this time you have to work out what it is you really want.'

'What I really want now is to pick up a bottle and pass out in front of Netflix.'

'Fine,' Mariah continued, 'but you and I both know that you escaping Christmas with your mum is about as likely as Kim Kardashian going offline.'

In the wine shop, garlands of red cranberries cris-crossed the ceiling and silver tinsel lined the shelves packed with bottles. Holly's eyes were drawn to a Christmas promotion for artisan vodka.

Behind the counter, the manager looked more interested in pleasure than business as she recited her phone number to a male customer. Holly wondered if the man, forty-something and dressed impeccably in winter layers, was actually typing her number into his mobile phone. This was the kind of behaviour Holly had left behind in London and she had no interest in showing any kind of patience.

'Excuse me,' she said. 'I'm here to collect an order.'

The manager remained deeply engrossed with her customer.

'Sorry to disturb you.' Holly tried again. 'It's literally just a quick transaction.' She reached for a bottle of vodka and put it on the counter.

The man turned and smiled at her. He had short blond curls and a confident mouth. 'Having a party?' he asked in a softly spoken English accent.

'Not tonight,' said Holly, wanting to hibernate.

'I'm fond of that brand myself,' he said, 'and once it's chilled correctly, it's quite enjoyable.' At this point, Holly wouldn't have minded if the vodka was lukewarm. Once she

26

returned to the gate lodge, she was going to imitate Bridget Jones and let loose all by herself. This well-mannered, and handsome, man was getting to her.

Holly turned to the manager. 'I'm here to collect a bottle of vintage port for —'

'I won't make any promises,' said the manager, ignoring Holly as she slipped her phone into the breast pocket of her uniform.

'Then I'll give you due warning before I land back in town,' the man said.

'And if it's a maybe?' she asked, practically batting her eyelids. Holly felt like she was caught up in an episode of *Wine Lovers*.

'Maybes are often full of possibilities,' he said, leaning in.

Holly felt her chest tighten with impatience. 'I'm sorry to interrupt, but do you think I could possibly have my order?'

'You're in a hurry,' said the man.

'I think I'm tired,' said Holly.

'And what was the name?' asked the manager, stepping into managerial mode in front of her conquest.

'Holly O'Leary.'

'Vintage port,' she said, disappearing below the counter and returning with a wooden box.

'That will be rather good at room temperature,' the man said, lifting up the box to inspect the label. 'Thankfully, the Portuguese stick to what they're good at.'

'You can't beat a Portuguese custard tart though, can you?' said the manager, flicking her hair and pouting her lips. 'I love a good pastry.'

Holly retrieved a bank card from her wallet and tapped it on the machine.

'Where are you based?' the manager asked, continuing her flirtation with the other customer.

'New York. Best city in the world as far as I'm concerned.'

The woman practically swooned and then pulled a face at Holly. 'I'm afraid your card's been declined, madam.'

'Oh God,' said Holly, feeling an immediate blush race across her face. She lowered her head and swore at herself for not checking her online banking before going into the shop. 'I'm so sorry,' she said, holding up her phone to the window as she tried to access the app. 'I can't seem to get online.' Holly felt useless.

'Would you like me to try again?' asked the manager, not unkindly.

'I'm not sure there's any point.' She had naively taken Serena at her word when she'd assured Holly that her wages had been paid.

'No, I'm afraid your card has been declined again.' The woman tore the receipt from the card machine and gave it to Holly.

'Let me,' said the man, taking a wallet out of his pocket.

'What? Oh no,' said Holly. 'I really don't want any help.'

'It's no biggie,' he said. 'I'm happy to.'

'Honestly, I just need to re-register my bank app, if I can just get online.' Holly held her phone up to the ceiling, in a last ditch attempt for coverage. 'I don't know why it's logged me out.'

'Such a nightmare,' said the manager. 'Happened to me last week. There I was getting my nails done and the last thing I wanted was to have to use my digits on my phone.'

'I'll have to come back,' said Holly, giving up and pushing her phone into her pocket.

'Then I'll hold on to the order for you, shall I?' asked the manager.

'Actually, hold on.' Holly felt pure relief to find a twenty euro note, folded up with another ten, in her back pocket. Thank God. She unravelled the notes and handed them to the woman. 'I'm really sorry. Will this cover at least some of it?'

'It will take care of the vodka,' said the woman, who looked delighted to have a resolution so she could concentrate on her man. 'Perhaps collect the port another time?'

'Yes, good idea.' Serena could bloody well collect the port herself.

'You must take the port,' said the man. 'I insist.' Before Holly could stop him, he had passed his bank card to the manager.

'You are good,' said the manager as he typed his pin number into the card machine.

'It's nothing,' he said.

'Thank you,' Holly said, begrudgingly and longing to get out of there. 'If you can give me your details, I'll make sure we compensate you.'

He shook his head, walked to the door and opened it for Holly. 'Don't worry about it, these things happen.'

Holly smiled and wished that 'these things' didn't happen to her. Cradling the vodka and port in her arms, she left the shop.

The sky was a deep navy blue now. She looked up at the coloured bulbs winding along the street. What was it about putting up decorations in mid-November? Surely the twelve days of Christmas were more than enough time to get stuck into the excruciating merriment of it all.

Holly crossed the street. Perhaps as a punishment for her 'bah-humbug' thoughts, as she approached the filthy Land Rover, she slipped in her wellies on a build-up of slush. In slow motion, she watched her legs go flying up in front of her. By some miracle, holding up her hands, she managed to hold on to both the port and the vodka without damage. Talk about hitting rock bottom.

Chapter Four

The chaos magnet was at it again, Holly reflected. It was a minor miracle she hadn't been hurt by the fall. An elderly man approached her, offering a hand to get up, but she declined. Knowing her luck, Holly might pull him over and make things ten times worse. Instead, she got onto her knees, feeling the gritty pavement beneath her jeans, and rose up. Her bum was soaking but not too sore as she balanced the port on the roof of the Land Rover to free up a hand. Opening the driver's door, she noticed a small poop next to the gear stick.

'Yuck,' she said, placing the vodka on the passenger seat. She found a tissue in her pocket, wiped it up and dropped it into an empty bag of popcorn she'd munched on her way there. Holly turned around to look for the culprit and found Knockboden's roaming hens perching on the back seats. 'What is this?' she said. 'Are we doing some early Christmas shopping?' They were so cute, Holly swore to herself she would find an alternative to her go-to comfort food: spicy chicken wings. Giles would have found this funny. They'd once driven across southwest France in a tiny car and found a cat snuggled into a jumper on the back seat.

Holly wiped away the condensation on the windscreen, making the sleeve of her fleece jacket wet. She thought about going online to find a Barbour on Vestiaire, but then remembered she was no long receiving weekly cheques from the temping agency. At least she didn't have to pay rent, and she could eat at Knockboden – though Serena seemed to live on expensive pâté, tinned mackerel and a vineyard's worth of red wine. The only way forward was for Holly to ignore materialism, even though she was running out of her favourite bath oil.

It was almost dark as she trundled down the main street of Turpinstown. People strolled along the footpaths, carrying bags of shopping and looking at their mobile phones.

I used to be one of them, Holly thought to herself. As she considered whether she'd mix her vodka with tonic, or have a straight up vodka and soda, she noticed a garda on the pavement, signalling at her to pull over.

'Oh Christ,' she said, 'what now?' She pulled up behind a minibus, and in her wing mirror, she watched the garda walk towards her. Holly rolled down the window as far as it would go.

'Can you put the window down further, please?' he asked.

'I'm afraid it won't go down any further.' Holly thought about cracking a joke about the *down*side of having electric windows that wouldn't actually go down, but he didn't look like he was in the mood for wise cracks.

'Then I'll ask you to step out of the car.' He didn't smile. Opening the door, she slid out of the Land Rover as one of the hens jumped onto the passenger seat and, spreading out her wings, balanced on the bottle of vodka.

'Did I just see a hen?' asked the garda.

'She doesn't usually travel with me,' said Holly, trying to work out why she was being stopped. 'Are my back lights not working?'

'I'm sorry?' asked the garda as the second hen landed into the passenger seat and pooped on the vodka.

'Have I done something wrong?'

'No,' he said, reaching his arms onto the roof of the Land Rover to retrieve the box of port. 'Does this item belong to you?'

'Oh sugar,' said Holly. 'I must have left the port on the roof while I was heaving open the door of the Land Rover. It's a little creaky, as you can probably tell.' She was smiling, but there was no response from the guard as he studied the windscreen.

'Are you aware your tax is out of date and you don't appear to have any insurance?'

'Oh God, I never even thought to check.'

'This is your vehicle?'

'Not mine exactly,' said Holly.

'Meaning?' he asked.

'It belongs to my employer, as in, this Land Rover is for her staff.'

'This is a company car?' he asked, taking out a black notepad and stepping back on to the road. He appeared to take a good look at the Land Rover, with its algae-coloured paint peeling from the doors, missing wing mirror, windowless passenger door and now two hens perching on the back of the driver's seat.

'I'd like to see your driving licence,' he said.

Holly took the wallet from her pocket and held it up like a federal agent might hold up a badge during a raid. It was so freezing, she'd have to stop wearing wellies, or at least buy some thermal socks.

'This vehicle is illegal,' said the garda, straight-faced, 'and you're behind the wheel.' They looked at the Land Rover, where the hens had now relocated themselves onto the driver's seat.

He looked like he was going to smile, almost did, but then straightened his lips.

'You're lucky you caught me in the holiday spirit, Holly O'Leary,' said the guard, taking the driving licence and holding it up to the light. 'Who's your boss?'

'Lady Harpur at Knockboden.'

'Ah, it's herself,' he said, nodding. 'Then you can pass on a message to her ladyship from Garda Tom. She knows who I am. Tell her that she needs to get the tax and insurance sorted before anyone else drives this vehicle.'

'I will,' said Holly.

'And as for you, drive it *straight* back to Knockboden, and don't let me catch you again.'

Holly had to stop herself from reaching out to hug him. Instead, she jumped back into the Land Rover, shooing the hens out of the way.

'Thank you,' she said through the window.

'And next time I suggest you count your chickens before setting off on a journey.' Holly thought she caught a glimpse of a smile from the garda as he spoke.

Chapter Five

Tyrone hadn't expected the convertible Mercedes he'd hired at Dublin airport to make him feel uncomfortable. Clearly his life in New York had slowly become 'full service'. He had a driver and a cleaner who pressed all his shirts; he ate out almost all of the time so he hardly had to wash as much as a cup in his elegant, east midtown apartment in Turtle Bay.

He parked outside Knockboden and let his eyes follow the green hue of weeds across the gravel. A love of trees had been the one thing he'd had in common with his father, apart from their loyalty to Serena, and the sight of beech, oak and lime, their naked branches creating a silhouette against the winter sky, made his heart wrench.

The front door was open: typical of his mother, who was consistently clueless when it came to security and keeping out the cold. Tyrone stepped into the front hall, paved with black and white squares, and fumbled for the light switch. The place looked like a car-boot sale, crammed with picture frames, over-filled boxes and stacks of magazines. As a child, it had seemed completely normal to be surrounded by gazelle and buffalo heads mounted on the walls. With snipe and grouse encased in glass boxes, anyone could be forgiven for mistaking the place for an animal mortuary. Every shot had been taken by an ancestor, choosing the most worthy game as symbols of adventure and bravery. Now, following years of living in New York, his perspective had changed, making him increasingly critical of his heritage.

He looked up at the ceiling, with its rose peppered with greying damp. He had never felt so disillusioned about the future of the house he had once loved. The log baskets were full, as usual, not that his mother would ever light the fire. She likened a fire to a pet dragon, having to keep an eye on it and having to feed it timber.

Still no sign of the dogs. He walked past the main staircase, which was littered with tat. If his father were to see the place, he'd die of heart failure all over again. The corridor leading to the kitchen smelt of damp, and entering the room was no improvement. He touched the Aga, which still sported a thick film of burnt remains encrusted around the hob, and felt gutted that it was stone cold. She couldn't have run out of oil already? Tyrone buttoned up his cashmere-lined gilet to his chin. And there was the clock over the dresser, jammed at XII, appropriately his mother's favourite time to launch into an early lunchtime drink. Knockboden was becoming more like Miss Havisham's house in *Great Expectations* with his every visit. Tyrone had just turned thirteen when his father died and so had only been a spectator to the riot of glamorous people who frequented the house in his childhood. In those days there had been plenty of staff, fresh flowers in the hall, polished furniture and silver at the ready for dinner parties. It had been sheer lack of foresight that Serena had been left without any income. His father's investments had been optimistic, to put it both mildly and kindly.

Tyrone took a glass from the dresser. There were stacks of empty yogurt cartons stacked on the draining board and when he turned the cold tap, yellowing cloudy water came spurting out. Things had massively declined since his last visit in May.

The breaths of anguish he could feel building inside him were thankfully broken by the arrival of Jagger and Daiquiri, skidding in from the boot room and barking in frothy delight.

'Hello, you two,' he said, kneeling down to hug the dogs as they clambered on top of him.

'Home for a doggy facial, are we?' Serena stood in the doorway, holding a white plastic Hellman's mayonnaise bucket in her hands, ear defenders around her neck. She had always been good at emptying the compost bucket. 'It is chilly out there,' she said, sounding put out that he had turned up unannounced. 'I would have thought this weather would put you off visiting.'

'If you'd care to switch on your mobile phone,' he said, trying and failing to keep the irritation out of his voice, 'you'll find I left voicemails and text messages letting you know I was flying in today.'

Serena shrugged her shoulders and landed the compost bucket on the table. 'I find my walkie-talkies are far more reliable.'

'Not when I'm trying to call you from the States.' Tyrone glanced down at his feet and regretted wearing his suede loafers as the dogs circled him. 'And what's with the head-phones?' he said, refocusing on his mother. If she thought he minded about getting his shoes dirty, she'd start shooting arrows.

'Edwin went on a health and safety course and returned with a complimentary pair of these.' Serena took the ear defenders from around her neck and fitted them over Tyrone's head. 'They're especially good when I'm on the ride-on,' she said, looking mischievous. 'If I mow over a rock, I can't hear the din.' She patted her son's cheek. 'Still no greys, darling? Not bad, considering you must be almost fifty.'

'I'm forty-six.'

'And a baby face, just like your father.' It felt like a tender moment, but Serena pulled away before Tyrone could properly connect and find out how things really were.

'Have you lost weight?' he asked. Tyrone suspected that she may not be eating as well as she made out. Usually she'd tell him that she'd had fillet steak for supper the night before or had been at a dinner party with the most elaborate of menus.

'I doubt it,' she said, 'not with all the Roquefort I put away.' Serena brushed her fingers across the table as if sweeping off imaginary crumbs. 'Now, I must change for dinner.'

'And what will you cook on?'

'Sorry?' She looked like someone who was about to get caught out.

'The Aga, it's stone cold.' He stared at his mother. It was time to stop all the messing around.

'How bizarre,' said Serena, elaborately stretching out her hand to tap one of the Aga lids. 'It must have just run out.'

'It takes a good ten hours for an Aga to get that cold and you know it.' What did she take him for? 'Mum, what happened to the money I transferred into your account?'

'At this moment, I have no idea,' she said, walking towards the door. 'Now, if you'll excuse me, I must pop upstairs.'

'Hold on, are you saying that you never received the money?'

She turned around and looked at him unashamedly. 'Details, details, Tyrone, must you constantly nag? I don't need the Aga. Only yesterday, Harry Rose sent over a fillet of beef and a side of smoked salmon from a lunch party.' Serena took a lipstick from her pocket, prised open the lid and applied an immaculate coat. He noticed the lipstick was worn right down. 'I assure you my standards are high. It's simply the case that when one is used to staff, one finds it tiring to keep the kitchen in order, you see?'

Tyrone pressed his lips together. He couldn't think of a polite word to say.

'And speaking of staff, we haven't made up a bed for you,' she said, 'as obviously your visit is unexpected, but there are sheets in the hot press and you'll find pillows and a duvet in the pink room.'

'You expect me to sleep in the east wing after last time?'

Serena glared at him. 'When you screeched like a vixen? And you know I don't like you referring to your father's side of the house as the "east wing". It sounds far too cold.'

'Because it *is far too cold*, and too right I yelled, as would anyone who'd woken up to find a pair of baby rats studying their face.' He shuddered at the thought of their twitching noses. It had taken about five seconds before he registered what was happening and flung off the duvet, sending the twin rats flying.

'Nonsense, they were field mice,' said Serena, as the old cat named Mr Tubbs slunk his way across the top of the kitchen cupboard.

'And Tubbs is still going?' Tyrone had to laugh. 'Christ, that cat has more lives than *Batman* has had remakes.'

'How rude! He controls the vermin, plus he clears out all the spirits.'

'Not all of them,' said Tyrone, nodding in the direction of a cardboard box of bottles. 'But you're off the hook,' he said, sensing his mother was in no mood for a lecture. 'I've booked a room at the Turpinstown Inn.'

'Suit yourself,' she said nonchalantly, and taking a bowl of meat scraps out of the microwave, she presented them to Mr Tubbs, who leaped onto the floor. 'If you want to stay in some low-range hotel, that's your choice.'

'I have to tell you, Mum, I just can't express enough how filthy this house is,' he said, grimacing as Serena took a cigarette from behind her ear and lit it from the toaster.

'Just as I can't express enough that houses like Knockboden were designed to have ten or more full-time servants.' She took a long drag from her cigarette, defiant beyond measure. 'The west wing originally housed the servants, remember – and now I live here alone.'

Tyrone picked up a magazine from a pile of newspapers and began flicking through the pages to calm himself. 'Look, Mum, I feel guilty that you're living here alone, and I worry.'

'I'm not your child, I'm your mother.' It felt like she was taunting him.

He threw the magazine on the table. 'My mother? You don't have a maternal bone in your body.' God, he could have cried at that moment, and by the look on her face, Serena could have done the same. But this wasn't how they operated. Formality had always been an easier option.

'Tyrone, I'm simply pointing out that it's all very well for you to look down from the heights of your New York apartment and criticise me, but it isn't helpful.'

He sat down at the table and tried to tune into the voice of his yoga teacher, breathing down the stress, sweeping it out of his core.

'The cleaning is constant, darling.' Serena tipped her cigarette ash onto a dustpan and brush sitting on top of the microwave. 'Lynette and I are cleaning day in, day out.'

'Lynette who takes a tea break every five minutes?'

'Enough,' said Serena firmly. 'She is a godsend, apart from the fact she is Edwin's niece.'

'She is completely taken advantage of, Mum. You barely pay her.'

'My staff and their wages have nothing to do with you.'

'And I beg to differ,' he said, 'considering I pick up your tab, how many times a year is it? Let me see—'

'Sarcasm does nothing for you, Tyrone. It's an ugly trait.'

'Ugly is a word that fits this situation, and squalor, there's another word.'

'Enough,' shouted Serena, stamping her foot. 'Knockboden is the only place on earth that needs me. What would I do otherwise?' She quickly lowered her voice. 'I'm sorry to shout, Tyrone, but if you'd take the time to tune into my plans – my *big* plans, my *immediate* plans for Knockboden – you'd change your attitude.'

'Dare I ask about your new bathroom?' he said, though he already knew the answer.

'New bathroom?'

'Yes, Mum, your new bathroom – the bathroom *I paid for* so as to give you some creature comforts.'

'You are vulgar, the way you keep bringing up the subject of money, and what is this obsession with comfort? It's all so *American*.'

'And the wood stove in your study?' he asked, eyeballing her intently.

'I decided it wasn't necessary.' Serena avoided his stare.

'Mum, are you going to tell me what you did with the money I gave you?'

'All these questions, darling,' she said, taking his hand. 'Come on, let's go to my study and have a drink. Then you can take me out to supper and I can fill you in on everything.'

'Fine,' he said, in exasperation. He felt himself relenting, like he so often did with her. 'I'll get some ice.'

'I wouldn't bother,' said Serena. 'The freezer packed up months ago.'

Chapter Six

The Land Rover's headlights created a shimmer against the frosted grass either side of the avenue as Holly made her way to Knockboden. She felt shattered, having had her bank card declined and then having been told off by the garda. She passed by the house and drove beneath the archway into the yard. The outhouses were a shambles, with corrugated iron leaning against doorways, grass weighing down gutters and black sheets of plastic heaped into stone troughs.

'After you,' said Holly, jumping out of the Land Rover and holding open the driver's door for the hens, who hopped out like little old ladies. There was little point in trying to coerce them into the hen run, as they seemed to be masters of their own destiny. Holly retrieved the vodka and port. To her disgust, the hens had poohed on the box, giving her little option but to flick it to the ground: the ultimate contrast to her London days, when her fingertips were immaculately clean. Right now, all she wanted was to get back to the gate lodge, light the fire, curl up with a vodka cocktail and watch

The Holiday. This was the film she reserved for times when she was feeling especially lonely and in tune with Kate Winslet, because she escaped the entire façade of Christmas. They had both been accused of being *big-boned* and when Kate scored a contract as the face of Lancôme, it oddly gave Holly a sense of pride. But as Mariah pointed out over FaceTime, Holly's hair had turned into an unruly mop of curls. She barely moisturised, certainly hadn't worn make-up for days and wore two pairs of black jeans on rotation. Hardly the look of a Hollywood doppelgänger.

Using the light on her mobile phone, Holly crossed the yard, her breath visible in the freezing cold. She opened the door into the boot room and switched on the light, immediately getting a whiff of fish. The walls were filled with vintage accessories, including a 'Turpinstown 5 Miles' sign. The stone floor was lined with wellies caked in mud, old runners, a large catering-sized bucket filled with jam jars and another bucket overflowing with lids. Jackets were piled on top of an old chest and paint was flaking from the walls.

'Serena? It's only me,' she said, walking into the kitchen as Mr Tubbs toppled off the top of the fridge and somehow landed on his feet. 'Holy Jesus,' screamed Holly, almost jumping out of her skin. 'Tubbs, do you have to?'

As she placed the port on the kitchen table, Holly heard raised voices coming from the corridor. She followed the sound, and though she didn't mean to snoop, she found herself standing in the doorway of Serena's study. She did a double take when she saw the man from the off licence.

'What kind of syndicate?' he said. 'For Christ's sakes, a hundred grand on the leg of a horse, what were you thinking?'

'Darling, it did seem like a good opportunity at the time.' Serena's voice was the loudest of the two, but she didn't sound angry. It was more of a plea for him to believe her.

'And you think that kind of money just landed in my lap? I don't have a bottomless pot of gold.'

'I do realise, and you know our money might have doubled if the poor love hadn't fallen,' Serena said passionately. 'He really was doing terribly well until a loose horse distracted him.'

'Okay then, great,' he said, staring out the window. 'Let's blame the loose horse.'

'Exactly, and you understand the outcome was quite out of my hands—'

'No, you want to know what's out of your hands? I'll tell you, shall I? My wallet. No more hand-outs.' He turned around, glaring at Serena. 'The money I gave you was meant for renovations.' He didn't seem to notice Holly. 'It was for your comfort, don't you see?'

'Yes, I do see, darling.' Serena got up from her desk and stood square in front of him. They were almost exactly the same height. 'But I'm sorry, I cannot but mention your own misjudgement in selling Great-Uncle Dudley's letter. None of us is perfect.'

'Every time,' he said, 'when the going gets tough, you bring up *Great-Uncle Dudley's letter*.'

'It's true, though, Tyrone, you did make a boo-boo, did you not?'

He threw up his hands and landed them behind his neck. 'Have you ever thought that I might want to raise my own family here?'

'And where is this so-called family, Tyrone? I don't think two childless ex-wives count.'

'You always have to twist the knife.' He turned away from Serena, and his eyes met with Holly's. Why the hell hadn't she ducked away instead of just standing there like a fool?

'Holly,' said Serena, returning to her desk and picking up a pen. 'I didn't expect you back this evening.'

'I'm so sorry, I was just—'

'Stop jabbering,' Serena instructed. 'Your timing is fine, Holly.'

The man looked at Holly for only the briefest moment, his expression neutral.

'Tyrone, I'd like to introduce you to my new private events manager, Holly O'Leary.' Serena gestured for Holly to enter the room. 'And Holly, I would like to introduce you to my son, Tyrone Harpur.'

'Your son?' said Holly, almost exactly as Tyrone said, 'My mum is your boss?'

'Yes, I head-hunted her from London,' Serena said grandly, as she opened the drawer of her desk. 'Damn it. Holly, pick up a pack of twenty for me when you're next in the village?'

'And why do you need an events manager?' said Tyrone disparagingly.

'There's no need sound so negative, darling. Holly is heading up my new honeymooners B&B business.' Serena looked completely defiant as she spoke. 'She's only been here a couple of months and already she's pulled in several bookings, doubling our profits.'

'Bookings for a honeymoon B&B?' Tyrone looked like he was going to blow a fuse. 'Just when I thought things couldn't become any more insane.'

'Serena, I'm only—' Holly attempted to correct her job description, but couldn't get a word in.

'No, Holly, you're far too modest,' she said. 'I think we could do with another drink, don't you, Tyrone?'

'I'm going to need more than a drink to get my head around the fact you two think you can resurrect this place with paying guests.'

'I'm obliged to take every money-making opportunity I can, Tyrone, and I believe Holly may be the key to Knockboden's success.'

Holly stood back as Tyrone walked towards the door with Jagger and Daiquiri in tow and left the room. She wished she had at least washed her hair, and she must have reeked of hens. Talk about first impressions or, rather, second impressions. Worse, though, she felt cross with herself for even caring about how she looked.

'What about supper?' Serena's call was met with silence. She sat at her desk and began scribbling something on the back of an envelope as if Holly wasn't in the room.

After a couple of moments, Holly made a little cough to get Serena's attention.

'Sorry?' Serena looked up from her pen. 'Did you say something?'

'I'm more than a little confused,' said Holly, feeling a sense of panic building. 'You told Tyrone you *head-hunted* me – which obviously isn't true.'

'In what sense?' Serena had a way of widening her eyes, making them look innocent beyond belief.

'I answered your ad in *The Lady.*'

'Of course, and I must say they graciously gave it to me on a complimentary basis, as I promised to subscribe.'

Holly looked at a large silver-framed photograph of Serena in a shimmering gown with a fur around her shoulders, like a young Lauren Bacall. 'It's just that you told your son I'm your private events manager?'

Serena looked bored by Holly's probing. 'It was a figure of speech, Holly,' she said, pulling stems from a geranium on her desk. 'My son has always been sensitive, and no matter that I've tried my best to be a good mother, it isn't easy.' Serena fanned out the pleats of her long skirt in the same way Holly had watched Grace Kelly do in *High Society.* It was her mother's favourite film.

'I think I can understand,' said Holly. 'When my father left, my brother was hard on my mum, and me.'

'What age were you?' The expression on Serena's face changed almost completely.

'I was six years old.' Holly felt her voice break. This was unexpected, out of the ordinary. She couldn't remember the last time she'd said that age out loud, and now that she was twenty-nine, six years of age seemed younger than ever.

Chapter Seven

The morning sun shone through the arched window, leading Serena's focus to the ceiling as she leaned her full weight on the banister. She looked at the cracked plaster where champagne corks had knocked out sections of the cornicing. The upstairs corridors had been turned into an imitation flea market, with piles of moth-eaten blankets, yellowing linen and towels heaved out from bedroom wardrobes. She picked up a red and gold blanket which had once adorned the bedroom where she'd given birth to Tyrone. The bedhead, with its trim of golden bells, had been so exotic and ornate. She remembered thinking, as she lay with the baby in her arms, that she'd had too much gas and air. Spreading the blanket out in front of her now, she found an enormous tear along the fabric's centre. Symbolic of her heart, she thought.

Knockboden was full of *objets d'art*. Like magpies, a long line of Harpurs had gathered collections from their travels across the world. There were bellows from Morocco, carpets from Slovakia, a life-size antique rocking horse from

Russia and curio tables filled with miniature carvings, medals and letters with broken wax seals. It was odd, because she was surrounded by things far more connected to Tyrone than to her. The medieval sword from Sir Reginald Harpur, last used for knocking a plank back into the main hall's supple oak floor, and the bloody racing trophies, all connected to the Harpur family, but not really to her. There was still the outline of a ghastly fox's head, which she and Lynette finally took down when the moths had eaten most of the fur.

'I still remember the dress you wore when I first laid eyes on you.' It had been Desmond's favourite line and the last words he'd uttered before he died. Though his death had been unexpected, when it happened, Serena had felt a strange contentment. They had experienced genuine love, the real thing, the kind of connection to run up the spine, across the shoulders and straight to the heart. They had been lucky.

Serena had always described her education as 'vague' at best, having been taught by a governess at home in County Wicklow, who spent her days reading *Lady Chatterley's Lover* and *The Prime of Miss Jean Brodie*. It wasn't until Serena's mother had found the governess reading *The Country Girls* that she'd given her the boot, fearing a bad influence on her only daughter.

Even though Serena had been stoic about losing Desmond, she still felt empty and irritated on a daily basis. Of course Tyrone would cause more fuss before returning to New York like a diva, but despite his interrogations about her spending, she felt happy to see him. A huge part of her even wished he'd return home and take over the reins to Knockboden, so that she could take her foot off the gas. But determination was at her core, whether she liked it or not. She would beat her son's scepticism and turn Knockboden into a love nest like Ireland had never seen. Couples were going to clamber out of their white dresses and morning suits to spend their honeymoon under Serena's roof. The psychic of Turpinstown had even sent Serena a text message forecasting 'love and rebirth' at Knockboden. The same psychic had written to her when Serena announced she was pregnant. The woman had had the audacity to provide a list of names in line with the Harpur dynasty, one of which 'must be chosen'. Too superstitious to ignore the prophecy, no matter how much Desmond pooh-poohed the idea, Serena had chosen Tyrone.

She toyed with the idea of putting up a tree this year, though there seemed little point if there weren't going to be any presents. She had never blamed Desmond for leaving her so badly off, and the auction houses had been only too happy to swoop in to claw up valuables. But this year, if a handsome Christmas tree would help to attract paying guests, then it may be worth the effort.

Serena was shaken out of her daydreaming by a loud booming sound. Peering downstairs, she saw Lynette, red-faced and out of breath, holding a gong like an ancient warrior about to go into battle.

'What fresh hell is about to rain upon us now?' Serena

shouted down as Holly came running up the corridor with a bin liner in one hand and a walkie-talkie in the other. 'When I hired Lynette to help me in the house, she assured me the double staircase would have her fighting fit and that she'd run up one side and down the other.'

'Shh, Serena, she'll hear you,' said Holly.

'We're coming down,' bellowed Serena, descending the left staircase with Holly behind her.

Serena always made sure to keep her chin parallel to the ground when walking downstairs, as had been instilled in her by her nanny, to maintain the most flattering posture.

'Do tell,' said Serena, standing at the foot of the stairs.

'The gents' loo is overflowing,' said Lynette, holding on tightly to the gong.

'Where is Edwin?' Serena was trying to think of an excuse to send Lynette up to the top of the house, purely for the exercise.

'He's got the day off,' said Holly.

'But Edwin never takes a day off.' Serena turned to Holly, who could do with some rouge to brighten up those pale cheeks. 'You're not going to abandon us to visit your mother, are you, Holly?'

Holly answered without hesitation. 'She doesn't know I'm in Ireland.'

'Where does she think you are?' asked Lynette.

'Travelling.'

'Travelling where?' Lynette looked puzzled.

'This is no time for riddles,' said Serena. 'Lynette, call your Uncle Edwin and ask him to hotfoot it over here and sort out the loo.'

'But that's not the reason I rang the gong, Lady S. It's that lad who wears the same stripy tie on every visit.'

'What about him?' Serena's mind was wandering towards a midday gin and ciggy.

'He's in there,' said Lynette, pointing to the drawing room.

'Is he indeed?' Serena would have to think fast.

'Which one would you like me to deal with?' asked Holly as Serena took a lipstick out of her pocket and applied a fresh coat.

'War paint. What do you think?' Serena pushed up her bosom and balanced her half-moon glasses on the tip of her nose. 'Are the glasses too much, or does it bring the hint of academia?'

'It could work,' said Holly, 'though I think he's more interested in a bank transfer.'

'Can you see through the glasses?' asked Lynette. 'I think they belong to that woman who dropped off the flyers about the donkey sanctuary. She drank most of the sherry in the kitchen, didn't she?'

'Worry not about the sherry,' said Serena, freeing her silver-grey hair to let it tumble down her back. 'And let's hope to God that Mr Gates is in a good mood. '

'Knock 'em dead,' said Lynette, 'and I've left a tea tray for you in the drawing room.'

'My dear girl,' Serena replied. 'At this time of day, I require gin!'

Serena walked into the drawing room and reached out for Kenneth with both hands.

'Dear Kenneth,' she said, 'you couldn't keep away?'

'Lady Harpur,' he said, clutching a brown folder to his chest and tilting his body forward into a subtle bow.

Serena sat on the chaise longue and patted the seat next to her. 'Come sit, Kenny.'

'Kenneth,' he said, 'and I'm fine standing, thank you.'

'Cup of tea?'

'Yes, as long as it isn't a bag.'

'Certainly not,' lied Serena, who only kept tea bags in the house. 'Here,' she said, pouring tea into a china mug. 'I'll give you the crested tit.'

'I beg your pardon?'

'The bird on the side of the mug,' she said, 'it's a crested tit, though maybe you'd prefer a great tit?' The silly man didn't seem to find her jokes at all funny. 'These mugs are rather beautiful, aren't they?' Serena continued with as much enthusiasm as she could muster. 'They came from my postman, who is a great bird lover.'

Kenneth accepted the mug but showed no admiration for the crockery.

'Go on then,' said Serena, taking a sip of tea. 'To what do we owe the pleasure of your — ?'

'I'm here to issue a final demand from my client, on all counts,' he blurted out, heat rising in his face.

'On *all* counts?' said Serena, taking a cigarette from behind her ear. 'Sounds rather dramatic, doesn't it? Would you happen to have a light, Kenny?'

'Again, my name is Kenneth.' Serena noticed his nostrils were beginning to flare, reminding her of a nanny she'd disliked intensely as a child. 'And, as I am a member of the public, I gather it would be against the two thousand and four Tobacco Act for you to ignite a cigarette.'

'What cigarette?' Serena asked innocently, balancing it on the edge of a tarnished silver ashtray. 'Aren't you enjoying your tea?' she asked,

'It's fine,' he said, resting the mug on a side table.

'How about another sort of T? As in a G and T? I have the most splendid artisan gin. *Bertha's Revenge*, have you heard of it? Coriander and sweet orange with just a hint of cumin, it really is quite the —'

'Lady Harpur,' he said, 'might I remind you that I have come here to discuss an important matter?' Kenneth hitched up his trouser leg before sitting on a straight-backed chair. 'And this matter is becoming increasingly serious.' He opened the folder across his knees. 'Simply put, your payments are outstanding.'

Serena realised he was going to be a tougher nut to crack than she'd thought.

'In addition, we, that is, *you*, have interest to deal with, which, I might add, is rising on the daily.'

'On the daily? My, well, I can't say I'm surprised.'

'I suggest we work out a plan as to how you are going to pay, otherwise the options could be catastrophic for the future of this house.'

'Well, my dear Ken Gates, your timing is impeccable. I'm delighted to inform you that, as we speak, I have a skilled team here at Knockboden, coordinating alterations in order to host high-end B&B for honeymooners.'

'Isn't that rather specific?'

'Nonsense, romance is always in fashion and there is nowhere more romantic than Knockboden. Just look at that view.' Serena gestured towards the bay window and marvelled at the hedges laced in icy cobwebs. 'Isn't it dazzling?'

'I suggest you arrange for your windows to be cleaned before promoting the view, Lady Harpur.'

Serena had to steer herself away from barking at this insolent man. Instead, she burst into laughter. 'You are humorous, aren't you, Ken? But rest assured, my private events manager, Holly O'Leary, is currently marketing the Knockboden offering. I feel confident we will soon be raking in the dollars.'

'Dollars? Lady Harpur, firstly my interest is in euros, and secondly I'm not sure bed and breakfast is going to save your bacon this time around, no matter how crispy.'

Serena's expression changed. 'I'll thank you not to refer to *my bacon* and I'll prove you wrong with your most unattractive scepticism.'

'All I want, Lady Harpur, is confirmation that your

proposed income can heave you out of the hot water you are currently steeped in.'

'One step at a time, Ken, I have yet to deal with the immersion tank.' He still wasn't finding Serena's jokes funny. Not so much as a lip curl.

'Would you have a pen, Lady Harpur?'

'You aren't going to ask for my telephone number, are you, naughty fellow? You realise I no longer have a landline?'

Kenneth looked like he'd had enough. Pushing the papers back into his folder, he rose to his feet. 'I'd like you to take down an IBAN, into which account I'd like you to transfer thirty-seven thousand, three hundred and fifty-seven euros and fifty cents, to be precise.' He adjusted his tie, as if to underline his importance.

'Precise indeed,' said Serena, walking towards a painting of her mother. She touched one hand to the gilded frame and brought the other to her forehead for dramatic effect. 'This time of year always brings on nostalgia, don't you think?'

'I do not think,' he said.

'Such a vital time for Christmas preparations. Fattening the goose, plum pudding in the larder, and when I think of the days when we had fires lighting in the majority of rooms, oh, the sheer joy of —'

'Lady Harpur, what is your point?' This man's temperament was almost worse than Tyrone's.

'Allow me to give you an example of seasonal good will,' she said, meeting him eye to eye. 'My late husband would send a live pig to the family of each staff member, which they could sell, eat or keep as a pet.'

'This conversation is going absolutely nowhere, Lady Harpur.' Kenneth closed his pen with a click. 'Therefore you can expect a letter forthwith.' His eyes rose up to the scalloped ceiling. 'I'm heartened to see you have a smoke alarm, but what are those things stuck to it?'

'Mushrooms,' she said, thinking quickly. Pigmy bats had lately become attracted to the heat from the alarm. 'I may even serve mushrooms on toast to my paying guests for breakfast.'

He looked repulsed. 'I take it you are insured?'

'Don't be ridiculous.'

Kenneth looked horrified. 'This is your home, Lady Harpur. Are you prepared to risk losing everything?'

'I tend to follow my nose,' she said, and opening the door, she elegantly gestured for him to leave. 'Risk is a part of life in which I revel.'

Chapter Eight

The charging light appeared on the dashboard of Tyrone's electric car as he drove up the avenue to Knockboden. He'd have to run the cable through the window of his mum's office, which he knew would irk her. He felt inexplicable butterflies. Maybe it was knowing that he alone dictated the future of this family home. Memories of the sweeping landscape had carried him through dark times in New York. He'd close his eyes and visualise a buzzard swooping into the woodland or a pheasant pecking on the front lawn. If only the interior could bring him such peace. In another life, he'd live at Knockboden with someone who'd adore the countryside and love to entertain, maybe even ride and, above all, be a nurturing mum to their children. Carl had emailed earlier from New York with details about a retreat entitled 'Mending Divorced and Grieving Hearts' over Christmas in Mexico. Right now it sounded very tempting. But how could he compare his divorce from Kenzie with Carl losing his wife? They had been devoted to each other, complete soulmates. Tyrone wasn't sure if Carl would ever recover. All he could do now was be there to listen, to have his back and assure him that he would never, ever have to be alone at Christmas time.

'Edwin?' Tyrone called out the car window. 'What in God's name is she up to now?'

A bus was parked in front of the house, having badly reversed over part of the lawn. Why was he surprised? No doubt it was one of his mum's badly organised, last-minute, fast-buck schemes.

'With you in one minute,' said Edwin, dressed in a luminous council vest, as he helped a lady to the front door.

Tyrone turned off the engine and, getting out of the car, fetched the electric cable from the boot.

'Not so steady on her feet,' said Edwin, walking towards him and pulling up the collar of his shirt. 'There's going to be an almighty downpour any time now. November rain, it's a curse when it's already freezing out.'

Tyrone remembered the days when Edwin wore a tweed jacket to work every day. How times had changed.

'Has my mum invited the living dead for morning coffee?'

'Sure, isn't there a great turnout?' Edwin seemed exhilarated. 'A right lot of them piled off the bus, all parched for tea.'

'And who are they?' Navigating a crowd of old women was the opposite of what Tyrone needed, especially when people of his mum's generation told him he looked like his father.

'It's a fundraiser for this year's Christmas parish outing for them less fortunate,' said Edwin. 'My Babs is volunteering.

She's already working on her costume, as Mary Christmas if you don't mind.'

'I see.' Tyrone felt immediately guilty. 'Then I'll make a donation before I go.'

'Back to the Big Apple again?' said Edwin, chuckling. 'My sister, Maeve, well, she went to San Francisco, and do you think she ever came home? Not a chance, she met a fellah there and she never looked back.'

'Good for her,' said Tyrone, with no appetite for one of Edwin's stories of nostalgia. 'Any idea where she is?'

'My sister? Like I told you, she's all loved up in San Fran.'

'My mother.'

'Last time I saw Lady S., she and Lynette were trying to lure Mr Tubbs down from the kitchen counter. Seems he caught a rat and, even though he's only half-eaten the body, he won't let go of it.'

In the ballroom, raffle tickets were being exchanged for five-euro notes as 'O Holy Night' wheezed out of an ancient stereo supplied by the rector's wife.

'We are selling wine by the glass, aren't we?' said Serena, striding across the room in a red dress.

'Yes, by the glass.' Holly knelt down to pick up the cash box she'd stashed behind the velvet curtain.

'And you have used the funnel method?' asked Serena.

'The funnel method?'

'To water down the wine.' There was a wild look on her face.

'You are kidding?'

'Do I look like I'm kidding?' said Serena, twisting her mouth to one side. 'And keep your voice down. It's worked nicely for me in the past, in fact it feels almost heavenly, turning water into wine —'

'It sounds illegal,' interrupted Holly.

'Naturally a percentage will go to the church,' said Serena, picking up one of Holly's pre-poured glasses and taking a large sip. 'When I think back to Desmond and my first Christmas here. He was quite the most elegant creature, pan-frying giblets in his silk dressing gown with quilted collar and cuffs.'

Only Serena could bring romance to the concept of giblets.

'In the early days we had very little money.'

'I know the feeling,' said Holly, hoping for a reaction from her boss.

'Pan-fried giblets with onion, garlic and just a dash of cognac.' Serena kissed her finger and thumb like an Italian chef before vanishing through the baize door.

'Would her ladyship be interested in selling any firewood?' said a man coming in from the other side of the table, pulling out the straps of his braces. 'I noticed a pile of wood at the front of the house. Nicely chopped.'

'Maybe,' said Holly, sensing an opportunity to bring in some cash, which could filter down to her wage packet.

'If you have birch, then I'd take a trailer-load,' he said, licking what looked like meringue from his lips.

'Paying in cash?' asked Holly.

'Certainly. I'll give you my number and you can let me

know.' Putting on his glasses, he took a biro out of his pocket and scribbled on the back of a scrap of paper.

'Bob or Rob?' asked Holly, trying to make out his writing.

'Bob Duffy.'

Holly looked at him. 'Why does your name sound familiar?'

'Minister for Transport,' he said.

'You're the Minister for Transport?'

'I have the same name as the Minister, Bob Duffy,' he said with a cackle. 'You wouldn't believe the number of calls I get, people with problems mostly, and by the time I can get a word in to tell them I'm not *that* Bob, they're crying down the phone.'

Holly wished she could click her heels together and escape to literally *anywhere*. She felt like she was in a dark comedy sketch on loop when Tyrone made his way towards her.

'This is rather like a déjà vu,' he said, picking up a bottle of wine and, clearly unimpressed, putting it back on the table. 'Except this time you're selling wine rather than buying vodka.'

Holly pushed her hair behind her shoulders and planned to completely ignore him.

'This is typical of my mother,' he said, looking stone-faced. 'She thinks a Christmas party fundraiser is going to save the place. It's a joke.'

'No,' said Holly, 'what's a joke is your lack of compassion.' And she walked away feeling pleased with her one-liner.

Chapter Nine

In the kitchen, Holly turned on the mixer tap and began rubbing washing-up liquid between her palms, wondering if the wood sale could happen so that Serena could pay her at least something.

'Have you seen my mother?' Tyrone stood in the doorway just as the kitchen tap came flying off, hurling itself into the Belfast sink. The water exploded upwards like a fountain, immediately drenching Holly, who stepped back in shock. Tyrone rushed to the sink, retrieved the tap and squeezed it back into its socket. The water stopped and Holly couldn't tell if Tyrone was going to follow suit and explode like the tap.

His blond hair had turned brown from the water, and the shirt beneath his jacket looked wet. To her surprise, he started laughing.

'The Knockboden Falls,' said Holly, grabbing a tea towel from the Aga and passing it to him. She had to laugh too.

Tyrone ruffled the towel across his hair and Holly felt

unsettled as he smiled back at her. No way was she going to find this guy attractive. Not for a single second. She'd have to call an emergency FaceTime with Mariah.

'Who's manning the wine table?' boomed Serena's voice as she came into the kitchen holding Daiquiri in one hand and a chocolate eclair in the other. 'Holly, you know it doesn't take a lot for the parish to tuck into the wine, be it holy or otherwise. And what are you two doing looking like drowned rats?'

'Mum, I want to talk to you.' Tyrone looked briefly at Holly before pulling out a couple of chairs at the table.

'How flattering,' said Serena. 'I do wish they could remove the cream element from these fundraisers, it simply won't do for my waistline.' She put Daiquiri onto the bed next to Jagger, cut the eclair in two with a bread knife and fed it to the dogs. 'Holly, be a sweetie and fetch the white wine, would you?' She reached for a glass from the dresser behind her and placed it on the table. 'What?' she said, looking at them both. 'It's lunchtime, isn't it?'

'I'm just going to go back to the lodge to change,' said Holly, taking a bottle of white wine out of the fridge and putting it on the table. 'And by the way, Edwin is looking after the wine table inside.'

'Fine, Holly,' said Serena, relaxing back into chair.

'Hold on a moment, Holly, please,' said Tyrone, laying his hands palms down on the kitchen table. 'I'd like you to witness my mum's response when I ask her why in hell's name she is attempting to sell the woods from under my nose.'

'What?' said Serena, looking genuinely surprised.

'And, well—'

'Darling, I have no idea as to *what* you're talking about.'

'You are selling a part of Knockboden with zero consultation with me and you claim to have no recollection?'

Serena got up from the table, retrieved a cigarette from behind her ear and, pressing down the toaster, she lit up. 'Even if I were to sell my woodland, why on earth should I consult you?'

'Because the land is mine. Bob Duffy said you were selling wood to him.'

Holly suddenly realised what was happening. 'Oh God, hold on, Tyrone, I think there's been a misunderstanding,' she said. 'Bob Duffy asked me if he could buy the birch which Edwin had chopped at the front of the house.'

'And?' said Serena and Tyrone in unison.

'I said yes, or that I'd look into it, at least.'

'You what?' said Tyrone. 'Is that your wood?'

'Holly, how dare you sell wood from under my nose?'

'I only said I'd look into it, Serena, and would you blame me? I don't see how you're going to pay my wages any other way?'

'Holly, how dare you!'

'I guess that's your number called,' Tyrone said to his mother.

'And on top of that, Holly, you were under strict instructions to water down the wine,' snapped Serena.

'Christ, watering down the wine?' said Tyrone.

'And you, Tyrone, can stop picking up fag ends. Not that I have to explain *anything to you*, but I am *not* selling woodland to Bob Duffy, or to anyone for that matter.'

When Holly got told off as a child, she'd climb into her tree house, and that was exactly where she wanted to be now. She needed to think, time out to work out what she was doing. She followed the stone corridor towards the winding back stairs, not caring where she was walking to. Stamping her feet on every step, the higher she climbed, the more confused she felt, and taking the final step to the top landing, her foot went through a floorboard.

'Christ,' she screamed, with one leg dangling and the other crouched up to her chest. She could hear the wood creaking. Was the entire staircase going to collapse?

'Holly?'

'Tyrone, something's slipping,' she called back. 'I think the step is going to fall through.'

Lying back on her elbows, Holly felt like a baby bird waiting to grow wings to escape.

'Don't move,' said Tyrone, who had run up the main staircase to reach the landing from the other side.

'It's not as if I have a choice, considering my leg is jammed into the floorboards.' Holly felt humiliated. The kitchen was meant to have been the last place she'd ever see him, as she had been planning to resign as soon as she got Serena to herself.

'Take my hand,' he said, reaching towards her. 'Do you think you've broken anything?'

'Only my pride,' she said, meaning it. At least her black jeans had protected her skin. Accepting his hand, she carefully pulled her leg out of the hole until she was standing upright.

'You're shaking,' he said. 'I'd give you my jacket, but it's damp from the kitchen tap.'

'It's okay, I'm going to the lodge.' Holly turned around and thanked the gods that her leg felt in one piece.

'What the hell were you thinking, coming up here?' he called after her.

'I don't know,' she said, trying to stop trembling. 'I was just wandering.'

'You could have broken your damn leg and then, knowing you, we'd be landed with a lawsuit.'

'Knowing me?' Holly felt so cross she could barely get the words out. 'You don't know me, and what's more, I don't want you to know me.'

'Okay, fine, I'm sorry, but Holly, just hold on, I think you're in shock,' he said.

But choosing to ignore him, she walked along the corridor to the main staircase and descended the stairs with her hair wet and her jeans torn.

Chapter Ten

Holly woke up on the floor next to an empty packet of custard creams. She was still in her clothes from the night before, and her mouth tasted like burnt popcorn. The vodka bottle was more than half empty. Or half full, depending on which way you looked at it. She smiled, almost laughed, finding herself funny, and then realised she must still be drunk. Oh God, the flashbacks were coming.

She'd started the evening with a highball or three of vodka cocktails, and she remembered scrolling through Giles's Instagram page. Oh God, that was it. She remembered the photos of them at the Snow Ball last year. Holly had won a Christmas tree and he'd insisted on carrying it all the way back to his flat. They had been to restaurants, gallery openings and antique shops and gone on walks through Hyde Park. 'Please tell me I didn't make any comments.' Pressing her hands against her forehead, she felt she was going to be sick.

Holly tried to talk herself away from a downward

spiral. She realised that she must have been on some kind of automatic pilot when she'd applied for the job at Knockboden. Well, she'd have to duck out. It wasn't working; nothing was working. She would, however, have to follow through on her vow not to spend Christmas with her mother this year. Goodbye golden baubles and over-seasoned sausage rolls. Toodle-oo to obsessions with throws, lights and winter berries. Farewell to carrying trays of Prosecco, while her mum handed out double-edged compliments about an outfit doing 'wonders' for Holly's figure, or how Holly could be 'surprisingly' helpful, or prompt, or pretty, or clever 'when she put her mind to it'. Every compliment tainted with a punishing snideness. Her mum could take her itinerary and stuff it up the Christmas roast. And her brother, Gabe, who would no doubt put Holly on a massive guilt trip because he'd booked his flight home from Australia specially for the wedding, could bloody well greet the guests and help eat the turkey leftovers.

This moment had to be the lowest of the low in her life, deeper than rock bottom, perhaps as close as one can get to the earth's centre. Getting to her knees, she crawled across the sitting-room floor and scraped her finger through a thin layer of ice on the window pane. She was overwhelmed by a feeling of wanting to be looked after, for a loving hand to press her forehead and for someone to tell her everything was going to work out.

'I don't know where I'm supposed to be,' she said out loud. 'Where is it? Where do I belong?'

Outside the gate lodge, fuzzy headed and dehydrated, her breath appeared like tiny white feathers. She almost slipped on a flagstone, which was a good reminder to be careful. She pulled her woolly hat down over her ears and zipped her Puffa jacket up to her chin. Her mobile phone was in her pocket; there'd be no need for the walkie-talkies from now on. Serena wouldn't be surprised to receive Holly's resignation, and judging by the way she'd looked at Holly after yesterday's fundraiser, the relief would be mutual. Her senses heightened by her hangover, Holly could hear what sounded like a chainsaw in the distance. Funny how noise seemed to travel further in the frozen air. The driver's door to the Land Rover seemed to be frozen; she had to press her foot against the tyre and heave like a sailor pulling on a rope at sea to open it.

By the time she was seated at the steering wheel, the water she'd poured across the windscreen had already frozen. She got out of the Land Rover, but this time kept the windscreen wipers going as she emptied the remainder of the water bottle. Nobody had taught her that and so she felt quite pleased with herself.

She set off down the drive. Nearing the last bend before Knockboden, the stony avenue crunched and groaned beneath the tyres. The thermometer in the Land Rover wasn't working, but it was definitely below freezing. The house looked so beautiful with its roof white and glistening, along with the hedging and lawns, as if they had all been sprinkled in icing sugar.

Turning through the archway into the yard, Holly came to an abrupt halt. She jumped out and tried to scream but no sound came, her voice empty with fear. Running across the yard, she slid on the icy cobblestones, landing on her hands. Everything turned into slow motion from then on. Pulling off her hat, she forced herself to walk towards the yard tap and then slid to her knees.

Serena lay on her side in her silk leopard-print dressing gown. Her body was stone cold. The hose pipe, frozen, lay in front of her.

'Serena,' Holly shouted, crouching down to cocoon Serena's head on her lap in an attempt to bring some warmth. There was no response. 'We need to get up,' said Holly, choking on fear, and using every ounce of strength, she tried to lift Serena's shoulders, but it felt an impossible task. She unzipped her pocket, found the mobile phone and dialled 999. By some miracle she managed to recall Knockboden's postcode before the woman from the call centre asked Holly to describe the scene.

'It's Serena,' Holly screamed, 'she's blue, her lips are blue.'

Calm and matter of fact, the woman urged Holly to take a breath. 'If your friend is unconscious but still breathing, let's get her into the recovery position with her head lower than her body.'

'But I don't know if she's breathing.' Holly felt so

inadequate. She didn't know how to help; her hands shook; her entire body seemed to have been over taken by fear. Dropping the mobile phone, Holly put her arms around Serena. 'You have to wake up,' she said through tears, choking her speech.

The last thing she remembered was looking up at the house, with its black iron bars protecting the ground-floor windows, and the sound of a siren in the distance.

Chapter Eleven

'Tyrone?' Serena opened one eye, then the other. Her legs ...
she could feel them. She wiggled her toes and stretched out
her fingers. She could taste a sort of bitterness at the back
of her throat, and catching sight of the drip, she realised it
must be the morphine running through her veins.

'Mum,' he said, turning away to wipe his eyes. 'How are
you feeling?' His voice was unusually tender.

'Aren't lilies usually reserved for coffins?' she said,
reaching to touch the flowers and wincing as the IV tube
pulled on her hand. Her speech felt like it was slurring.
'What's going on?' She pushed herself up in the bed.

'Can I help?' he asked.

'No, thank you, I'm perfectly well, in fact that was quite
the best sleep I've had in a long time.' In truth she was feeling
awful. Her mind was groggy and she felt a sense of lethargy
that was entirely foreign to her.

'Mum, you're going to have to take it slowly. You've had
a major concussion and hypothermia.'

'Concussion my eye.' Serena rubbed the back of her head. 'It'll take more than a knock on the noggin to do me in.' She glanced around the room, which looked like one of those airport hotels on television. There was a modern sofa beneath the window and pastel-coloured walls. 'My private healthcare finally paid off, by the looks of it.'

Tyrone was unusually quiet.

'Schoolgirl error.' She shrugged. 'I must have left my ciggy somewhere, is that what happened?'

He nodded. 'Yes, a small fire in the kitchen. The Fire Chief suspects that you must have thought the best solution would be to go out into the freezing cold to procure a hose.'

'The water from the kitchen tap was coming out at a trickle—'

'That damn tap, why didn't I do something about it? I should have fixed it.'

'That's beside the point, Tyrone. I went to the yard to find the hose, but the blasted thing was frozen solid.' All Serena wanted right now was sympathy. 'I got it wrong. Badly judged.'

'And what if they hadn't found you? You would have frozen to death. Don't you realise what a liability you are?'

'Oh, piffle-paffle.' But in truth, for the first time in her life, she felt frightened.

'Come on darling,' she said, trying to charm him. 'And who called the emergencies?'

'Holly,' he said, 'and if it wasn't for her, it is very unlikely you and I would be having this conversation.'

Damn it, this was awkward. More than awkward: it was

embarrassing. 'It was clearly a slip-up on my part, and most probably Holly overreacted.'

'Mum, you were unconscious for seven hours following your admission to hospital. Of course she called the ambulance.' Tyrone looked exasperated.

'Then you can be thrilled with yourself.' She could feel her heart race as she spoke. 'You've won.'

'What do you mean?' Tyrone moved closer.

'I know you want me out.'

'Sorry?'

'Why should I trust you? After all, you've been perfectly happy to steal from me.'

'Oh, here we go. When the going gets tough, you have to bring it up.'

'It was unforgivable. Your father's Great-Uncle Dudley wrote the letter the day before he sailed on the *Titanic*. He was born at Knockboden. The letter was addressed to Knockboden. It belonged to the house, and that is where the letter should have stayed.'

'We all know I messed up in the early days.' Tyrone fiddled with the cuffs of his shirt, like he always did when feeling agitated. 'I've told you a million times, putting the letter up for auction was my single mistake. How many times do I have to say it? What do you want me to do? Slit my wrists and write an apology in my own blood?'

'Don't be so vulgar,' she snapped.

They had been over and over it. Serena knew only too well that if Tyrone hadn't sold out to Christie's, they would have lost Knockboden years ago. That money had given her independence, for a time, but now she was tired of fighting against it all. The leaks and dust, having to walk a marathon every time she left her reading glasses upstairs. Was this the universe telling her that it was time to throw in the towel? She was only seventy-six; could she really give in so soon?

Tyrone lifted his overcoat from the sofa and put it on. He always looked so well-tailored, so in control. 'I'm not sure what's next, Mum,' he said, and leaning forward, he kissed her forehead as if she were his child. 'We're going to have to make some hard decisions.'

Chapter Twelve

Despite his attempts to breathe deeply, Tyrone's chest felt tight. His mother had always been a force, an unrelenting wave of determination. This was the first time he had thought of her as being vulnerable. However, she still played the game. He knew she had stopped her health insurance years ago, even though she continued to send him annual requests to cover the elusive bill, amongst others. It was his fault for not confronting her, and now things were beginning to snowball.

In the beige corridor, a nurse with tinsel dangling around her neck balanced on a wooden ladder. 'The decorations go up earlier every year, don't they?'

Tyrone made an effort to smile and thought about offering to hold the ladder, but she looked very competent.

'My gang at home would have the tree up if I let them, but I've told them not until *The Late Late Toy Show*.' The nurse's expression was so cheery, it made Tyrone feel even more depressed. 'There's only three days to go, and they're on at me every waking minute.'

He was about to send a message to Carl, letting him know his return to New York would be delayed, when Holly appeared on the corridor. She looked as tired as he felt.

'Holly.' He slipped his phone into his jacket pocket. 'I was told you had gone home.'

She pulled her hair back into a ponytail before she spoke. 'I had, but I wanted to see Serena, just to make sure she's okay, so I came back.' He wondered if she was going to cry, though it was hard to tell as she wasn't making eye contact.

'How are you feeling?' he asked, to fill the silence. He looked down at his shoes. It was unusual for him to wear the same pair two days in a row. He thought of the board meeting he was meant to be chairing tomorrow morning and knew he'd have to reschedule for a second time.

'I may as well tell you that I'm going to resign,' she said, pushing her hands into the pockets of her jeans. 'I wanted to let Serena know, just to manage her expectations because, you know, she has plans and —'

'Don't you think it would be kinder to my mother to stay and help her to recuperate?'

'Kinder? If you want to talk about kindness, then we may as well talk about gratitude?' she said, feeling defensive.

'I'm sorry?'

'You say *thank you*, and I say *you're welcome*.'

'For?'

'For calling the ambulance.'

Tyrone wanted to turn around, jump in a taxi and fly to New York. He didn't have time for this. Maybe he should just offer to pay her wages to date and hire a professional carer to accompany his mother home.

'You're not the only one who's had a shock,' she said.

'I'm not shocked.' Tyrone checked his watch. 'In fact, I think Mum's fall was a blessing.'

'A blessing? How would that be exactly?' Holly asked. Her lips looked very dry, and he would have been almost tempted to offer her lip balm if he hadn't been so fed up.

'This might jolt her into realising her days as the grand madam of the big house are over.'

She let the silence stretch for as long as she could, maybe twenty long seconds, and then she broke it. 'I'd like to see Serena.' She made sure not to look at him.

'Be my guest,' he said, stepping out of the way.

Chapter Thirteen

Holly's bones felt cold, despite all the attention the paramedics had given her, wrapping her in shiny foil and plying her with sweet tea. It must have seemed odd that Holly had given Lynette's name as next of kin, but her mum would have arrived like a torpedo if she'd found out what had happened. Edwin had collected Holly from hospital, and back at the lodge, Lynette had lit the stove, put a shepherd's pie in the oven and a hot-water bottle in the bed. Simple kindnesses were making Holly's plan to resign all the harder, especially as she had no idea where she'd go next. Mariah had sent a bundle of messages, strongly suggesting that this was the time to come clean with her mum about being in Ireland, but the thought of bringing in that element was an instant head-fry. And to top it all, how typical to have found Tyrone standing in the corridor. What was going on with the Law of Attraction? It was as if the universe was continually throwing mud at her.

Holly closed the door behind her, scrunching up her face to try to stop herself from bursting into tears. Without makeup, Serena eyes looked smaller and her mouth wizened without lipstick.

'I'm sorry,' said Holly, fanning her eyes.

'Surprisingly sensitive, aren't you?' Serena held out her arms. 'I suppose you can give me a hug, if you must, but stop crying.'

The hug was brief, and not at all maternal, but then why should it be? They'd only known each other for a couple of months and it had hardly been a successful venture. All Holly had achieved was building a basic website for Knockboden and mucking out several wardrobes so deeply cluttered they would have stretched the imagination of C. S. Lewis.

More tears came as Holly carried a plastic chair next to the bed.

'Surely this is an overreaction?'

'I know,' said Holly, reaching for a tissue on the overbed table and blowing her nose. 'I just keep thinking of you lying in the yard.'

'Thank you for calling the paramedics. I do hope they were strong and handsome.' Serena was putting on a brave face; she must have known this was a blow to her plans. Holly had expected an immediate request for gin, or for notes to be taken, but there was nothing. It was as if the light in her eyes had gone. The best thing Holly could do now was to rip off the bandage, quickly and painlessly, flattening out all the bad news at once by resigning. Serena and Tyrone could then work things out between the two of them, one way or another.

'The thing is, Serena, even before your fall, I don't think my position at Knockboden was working out.'

'In what way was it not working out?' Serena didn't sound very bothered; it felt more like she was making polite conversation.

'I'm thinking of signing up to an agency and maybe cooking on a yacht or something.'

'But I thought you couldn't cook?' Serena had closed her eyes.

'I sort of can,' said Holly. 'I completed almost half of a cookery course, and I spent a few seasons as a chalet girl in Verbier, and Giles—'

'Giles?'

'My ex-fiancé.'

'When it comes to romance, Holly, like the slopes, the learning curves can be steep.'

She moved her long legs further down the bed before turning on her side.

Serena said nothing for a while, and Holly began to wonder if she'd fallen asleep.

'Holly.'

'Yes, Serena, what can I do?'

'Can you help me to get used to this sort of place?'

'What do you mean?' Holly had never imagined Serena defeated.

'I'm going to be confined to one of *these places*, aren't I? That's what Tyrone is gunning for.'

Holly lifted the chair to the other side of the bed to face Serena, except her eyes were still closed and her lips were pursed together. It was as if she was signalling the show was over.

'My mother used to say, "We've been over higher fences than these,"' Serena whispered. 'But this fence is too high.'

Holly gently pulled the top sheet and blanket over Serena's shoulders. Just like that, everything was over. There barely seemed any need to resign. It was all too obvious.

Turning to the window, Holly caught sight of an old man walking next to someone who might have been his daughter. Her arm was looped in his, gently guiding him towards a car. It was something Holly knew she would never experience with her own father.

Quietly, she crossed the room. As she reached for the door handle, a vibration came from her mobile phone and she fumbled to switch off the sound before it woke Serena. An American number flashed up on the screen – most likely Tyrone's mobile phone. Reluctantly, she answered.

'Knockboden Castle?' It was the voice of a young American woman.

'Sorry?'

'Is this the castle in Ireland?'

'I'm sorry,' said Holly, again, 'but where did you find this number?'

'It's listed on your site.' The woman sounded impatient, then Holly realised she had put the number of her Irish mobile on Knockboden.com as a filler until Serena decided what phone number to use.

'Actually, yes, this is Knockboden, but it's not a great time, could you possibly — ?'

'We've picked up the story on Reuters about Lady Harpur and the castle, and we'd like to discuss dates with you.'

'And who is this?'

'Valentina Lewis,' the woman said, chewing gum between breaths. 'We're in pre-production for the Christmas special of *Insta-Love* and our producer wants to film at your castle.'

'But, you know, it's not a castle —'

'Yes, we're certain Knockboden Castle is a fit for our show,' said Valentina, interrupting Holly. 'We feel the location is exactly the vibe we're seeking.'

'I'm not sure I understand what you're saying. Is this some kind of book or something?'

'No, sweetie,' said Valentina, '*Insta-Love* is a reality TV show, created by Mindeflicks.'

'And you are saying a show airing on Mindeflicks wants to film its actual Christmas special at Knockboden?' Holly felt such a rush she purposely repeated Valentina's words to catch Serena's attention.

And it worked. Serena sat almost bolt upright in bed.

'But it's only five weeks to Christmas,' said Holly, putting the phone on loudspeaker.

'I know, jeez, it's so crazy.' Valentina laughed. 'The thing is,' she continued, 'we had a castle in the Scottish Highlands, but there was a last-minute hitch with the booking, and then we read about your castle and Lady Harpur's history in terms of the "open marriage" and we thought *Bingo* —'

'You read about Knockboden and Serena online?'

'Sure, on our socials and so, how do you pronounce it? Knock–boo–den?'

'Knock–bo–den,' said Holly, as Serena twisted her hair into a high bun and popped in a biro to keep it in place, 'and sorry, but what kind of socials?'

'Sweetie, just go online.'

'And where in America are you calling from?' Holly did a little party dance as she spoke, and Serena joined in from her bed.

'LA, sweetie,' she said, 'and if Lady Harpur's castle —'

'Sorry, Valentina, but just to double confirm, Knockboden isn't actually a castle.'

Serena waved both hands over her head. 'If they want Knockboden to be a castle,' she whispered, 'it can bloody well be a castle.'

This phone call was like divine inspiration.

'How much?' asked Serena, trying to keep her voice hushed.

'Do you have an idea on the location fee?' Holly asked, unsure what exactly was happening. She was feeling dizzy and realised she hadn't eaten all day.

'The standard deposit is ten thousand dollars.'

'Ten grand,' whispered Holly to Serena, covering the mouthpiece to her mobile phone. 'Right.' She was amazed to see how the sheer mention of cash seemed to pink up the colour of Serena's complexion.

'And three thousand dollars per day —' said Valentina.

'Three thousand dollars?' repeated Holly.

'Per week?' asked Serena, sitting up straight.

'Per day,' Holly mouthed to Serena.

'Are you still there?' asked Valentina.

'Sorry, Valentina, yes, I'm still here.'

'Then can we firm up dates?'

'What sort of timeline are we looking at?' Holly was trying to play it cool, but knew that was ludicrous.

'Okay, sweetie, you've watched reality shows before, right?' She didn't wait for Holly to reply. 'The finalists of this year's *Insta-Love* will arrive on December twentieth, and as long as they avoid kissing beneath the mistletoe, they will marry at Knockboden on December twenty-third.'

'Okay, so you mean—'

'I mean they'll be checking in to single beds, and if they are tempted to take it to the four-poster, they lose the prize money and the sponsorship opportunities and we get to eat the cake.'

'I'll have to discuss this with my boss,' said Holly.

'Then I'll ping over an email to the address on knockboden.com, okay?'

'And if we say yes, what sort of timing are you thinking of?'

'Three weeks.'

'As in, you'll stay for three weeks?'

'No, we'll be on location with you in three weeks.'

Holly held her hand over the phone again. 'They want to come to Knockboden in three weeks?'

'Fine,' said Serena, sucking in her nostrils as she breathed deeply, recharging herself like a Duracell bunny.

'Fine,' repeated Holly.

'The *Insta-Love* film crew will land in Ireland on December sixteenth. Allowing a day for jet lag, we'll start filming background on December seventeenth, and then we'll film our Insta couple through to the wedding on December twenty-third.'

Stunned, Holly listened to a few other details Valentina rattled off, only able to offer a dazed 'Goodbye' as the call ended.

Meanwhile, Serena removed the intravenous tube from the back of her hand, kicked off the blankets and swung her legs over the side of the bed.

'Hold on,' said Holly, rushing towards her. 'You've got to take it easy.'

'Take my hand if you must,' she said, 'but don't smother me.'

'Serena, you're on medication and you've had proper concussion. I'm sure you aren't meant to move a muscle without the hospital's say-so.'

'Rubbish,' she said, 'Hollywood is nigh.'

'I guess it is,' agreed Holly.

'Failure is not an option, Holly. It's time to buck up and sweep a comb through our hair.'

Chapter Fourteen

Mindeflicks, Los Angeles

The air-con was turned up so high, Farrah Fox could feel tiny bumps on her arms. Unlike the age spots on her hands, at least they'd disappear once she pulled on her jacket. She couldn't stop thinking about her housekeeper's ashes. Arranging the cremation had been a call above duty, but at least the compassionate leave had got Farrah's fasting schedule on track, plus her specialist had listened when she'd asked him to 'botox the hell out of my face'.

In the board room, Diane Striker, producer of the *Insta-Love* franchise, crossed her legs and took a sip of coffee. While Farrah spent a fortune on keeping the grey out of her hair, Diane dyed her hair silver on purpose.

'When the Scottish castle backed out, I got in a sweat, but this place in Ireland? A romantic Irish castle at the height of winter is going to turn the *Insta-Love Christmas Special* into TV gold.'

'I've scheduled a FaceTime tour of the castle so we can visualise the shots,' said Valentina, *Insta-Love* location scout and makeup artist.

'Good, and obviously we'd usually do a recce, but, as we're up against it time-wise, we don't have the luxury.'

'What did you say the prize money was?' asked Farrah, wishing she could turn back the clock and be a reality TV star rather than a presenter.

'A hundred K for the Insta-Lovers when they say I do and camera footage shows there hasn't been any physical contact between them,' said Diane. 'It's tough, but if they want to be winners, they've got to think of their finances before getting frisky.' She stood up, twisting her waist from side to side. 'I missed my workout this morning, so I'm making up for it.' Her body was so toned she could keep a printer running. 'The heat between this couple is insane,' she said, moving on to squats. 'He's from Chicago, she's from New York, and when they met in person, holy jingle bells, they were like magnets. I saw it with my own eyes.'

'Except magnets who can't connect until they say I do at the altar, right?' asked Farrah.

'You got it,' said Preston Minde, the network owner's son. 'Sorry I'm late.' He pulled out a chair and sat down.

Diane pushed her thumbs and forefingers together to make a heart shape while rotating her hips. 'It's okay. I'm going to recap the show's concept, though I'm sure you've done your homework, Farrah?'

'Of course,' she said, giving a reassuring smile. She had meant to watch previous episodes but she'd been distracted by her beauty prep.

'Our love gurus scrupulously matched Insta-Lovers online,' said Diane, now air-punching. 'The couples who formed genuine connections were flown to a deluxe historic hacienda in Mexico for a month of romance and dating, but absolutely no sex allowed. Tough or what?'

'You bet,' said Preston. Cute and freckle-faced, he must have been at least twenty years younger than Farrah.

'Not even holding hands is permitted.' Diane disappeared from view as she moved into plank position. 'The Insta-Lovers were under constant surveillance, even when the cameras were off. There was no way these guys could *get it on* without our knowing.'

'They fell like dominoes,' said Valentina, 'except for Jake and Olivia.'

'Which is why Knockboden Castle has got to have temptation at every turn.' Diane, now standing upright, spoke almost entirely in the direction of Valentina, whose fingers moved at lightning speed on her MacBook, logging her boss's brainstorm. 'I'm talking log fires, romantic poetry recitals, candlelit dinners, the whole works.'

Farrah could have sworn Preston winked at her.

'Ireland is famous for its cold, damp weather,' said Diane, signalling to Valentina for a coffee refill. 'Throw in some Irish whiskey and they'll be between the sheets before Santa can say *Ho, ho, ho.*'

'And if the couple manage to resist?' asked Farrah.

'As long as the Insta-Lovers keep their hands off each other during the three-day build-up to the live wedding, once they say "I do" at the altar, they get the hundred K prize money and seriously lucrative sponsorship deals, including a beach house in Florida.'

'I kind of wish I'd entered myself,' said Preston, lazing back on his chair.

'So do I,' said Valentina, dreamily.

Diane zeroed in on Farrah. 'You still with us, honey?'

'Oh yes,' she said, tilting her hips forward to show off her miniature waist. 'I'm absorbing every word.'

'As your co-host, Farrah, we're bringing in Eric Rimmel.'

'You wouldn't prefer a little fresh blood?' suggested Preston.

'Eric pulls in the over-fifties. I want everyone we can get watching this show. The Instagrammers will pull in the TikTok followers, and Farrah, you'll pull in the—'

'Under forties,' she said, flicking back her hair.

Farrah saw Valentina splutter into her cappuccino. Goddammit, she only turned fifty a couple of years ago.

'As I was saying, Farrah, you'll take the lead,' said Diane, 'and Eric will follow—'

'Your ass,' muttered Preston.

'Sorry?' Farrah looked at him, so sweet with his freckly face. The detox must be affecting her concentration. He merely grinned by way of a reply.

'Lastly,' said Diane, clicking her fingers at Valentina for

a Santa Claus hat. *'It may be* Insta-Love, *but can they resist unwrapping each other until they say, "I do"?* This is our updated logline for the show. I added *unwrapping*, you know, just to add a holiday sizzle.'

'And what happens if they do *unwrap* each other?' asked Farrah.

'They still leave with hundreds of thousands of followers, but they won't get the cash or the Florida beach house and the brand partnerships won't be as lucrative.'

There's a reason why 'power couples' exist, Farrah decided. It doubles everything.

'Anyone fancy a seasonal muffin?' asked Valentina, as a guy in flip-flops arrived with a basket trimmed in red tinsel. 'Seventy per cent dark chocolate, as promised, with a dash of cinnamon.'

Diane picked up a cricket-ball-sized muffin and ate it like an apple. She was so damned skinny, thought Farrah. Where did her calories go? It must be nervous energy burning off the fat.

'Let's just hope our Insta-Lovers rip each other's clothes off, with consent of course, live on air just before the wedding, and we end up with running mascara and hot tempers at the altar – that will make our ratings soar.'

'It's horribly mercenary,' said Preston, rubbing his hands across his chest, 'and I like it.'

'Obviously the couples have separate bedrooms, but let's encourage them to fail. Mistletoe, mulled wine, red ginseng in their soup, oysters, asparagus, strawberries dipped in chocolate, whatever it takes so long as its legal – I want footage of corridor-creeping.'

'Can you imagine having all those empty bedrooms?' said Valentina, cutting a muffin in half.

'And it goes without saying, for this *Insta-Love Christmas Special* to be a success, I need all of you to stay off Santa's naughty list,' said Diane, stretching out her calf muscles.

'Yes, ma'am,' said Preston, rubbing his hands together.

Chapter Fifteen

In the hospital carpark, Holly pulled the sleeve of her jacket over her hands as she scraped away the ice on the windshield. The air was heavy with moisture and the sky looked heavy, suggesting snow was on its way.

Less than an hour ago, she had been on the brink of leaving Serena and Knockboden forever, but one phone call had changed her direction completely.

Here was her boss, in her seventies, most likely still semi-concussed, who had discharged herself from hospital and was now sitting in the passenger seat puffing on a cigarette.

In a bid to disperse the smoke, Holly pressed the button to put down her window. As the glass struggled to go down, she realised that was how she felt about returning to Knockboden. She'd have to say something. This was a ridiculous charade. For all Holly knew, the call could have been a hoax. The moment they returned to the house, she was going to get online and find out if *Insta-Love* was even a thing.

'Serena …' Holly spoke in her kindest voice. 'I'm just not sure this is going to be possible?'

'What isn't possible? Having a few guests to stay?'

Maybe Serena was still in shock, or the medication was making her feel invincible. There was no way they could turn the house around in time; Serena was completely delusional about what they were taking on.

'This glorious Christmas-themed opportunity has landed on Knockboden's doorstep,' said Serena, fishing out a hip flask from the glove compartment, 'and I for one intend to celebrate accordingly. Let us drive on!'

The combination of cigarettes and whiskey was making Holly nauseous. Tyrone was the only person who was going to talk any sense into Serena. The sooner they got home the better.

'This call from Hollywood is the one we've been waiting for, Holly. The more we can do ourselves, the stronger our margins.' Serena twisted the lid off the hip flask and raised a toast. 'Here's to saying *up yours* to the loan shark, and *hello healthy bank account*.' She took a large gulp and offered it to Holly.

'No thanks,' she said. 'Honestly, I'm feeling a little delicate. And I'm driving.'

'Suit yourself,' said Serena, lighting another ciggy.

'Does Tyrone really not know about the money you owe?' They were on the outskirts of Turpinstown, and the sight of Christmas lights on neighbouring houses was oddly comforting.

'I had no option but to take out the loan,' she said defensively. 'The Kenneth route was simpler than the bloody bank. We even had a whiskey together before he transferred the thirty grand. When was the last time anyone drank whiskey with a bank manager? Those days are rare now.'

'But wouldn't it just be easier to ask Tyrone for help?'

'I wouldn't give him the satisfaction.' Serena sounded adamant. 'Besides, I've got myself out of worse pickles before now. When Desmond flew through his inheritance, I was the one who ended up paying the bills.'

'By modelling?'

'Yes. For example, my shoot with *Playboy* went a long way towards Tyrone's school fees.'

'What else?' Holly was completely intrigued.

'There was a top-notch dealer in Dublin, slimy character. He'd choose a painting, have a copy made, take out the canvas and do a discreet swap.'

'You're saying the paintings at Knockboden are copies?' Holly's mind began racing through the various portraits and landscapes she'd admired in the house. It was a pretty clever solution to a cash-flow crisis.

'Only the ones of value, and I suppose I also sold the occasional piece of silver, a gravy boat or candlestick.' Though the light was fading, Holly noticed that the colour of Serena's face was looking paler by the minute. 'When I ran out of paintings to sell, I had to brace myself and ask my son for a top-up.'

'Was that when you bought the race horse?'

'You are a smart one, aren't you?' Serena waggled her finger. 'Well, yes, I may have spent Tyrone's money on the horse. It was risky and foolish, but I felt too embarrassed to let him know, and so, damn fool me, after that I went to a loan shark. Plain and salty.'

The smoke circulating around the car mingled with the freezing air was making Holly feel more sick. She turned on the heating but the noise made the car sound like a Cessna. Risky and foolish were the words. And she hadn't even been paid yet. What was she doing?

'And Holly, speaking of money ...' It was as if Serena could read her mind. 'I really am so sorry that I haven't paid you as yet. I feel bad about it.' She took another sip from the flask. 'But I promise there'll be a healthy wedge of reality TV pie with your name on it. Deal?'

'Serena, honestly, don't worry. We'll sort something out.' It was like when Holly said yes to Giles's marriage proposal. She hadn't wanted to disappoint him. He was so nice, and kind, and it was the same with Serena. Her resignation now seemed unthinkable. She thought of Tyrone, his judgement, and her options. She didn't have any. It was twenty-one days until Christmas. Couldn't she take this on and then move in the new year?

'And it seems obvious for you to move into the house during the filming, Holly, don't you think?'

'I suppose I could,' said Holly, turning through the gates of Knockboden. 'I'll de-clutter the house, help prepare for the crew but then I'm going to have to work out what on earth it is I'm going to do with my life.'

'That's the girl,' said Serena. 'Now, let's win the moment in front of us! I heard those words from a handsome, red-headed rugby player once. Rather good, don't you think?'

Chapter Sixteen

Serena's ancient Mercedes, exhaust rattling, pulled up by the front door, and there she was again. Holly, the female version of a boomerang who kept on returning. He could see her through the car window, with hair shaggier than a Spanish water dog. Tyrone found it odd how she made literally no effort with her looks. Not an ounce of makeup, oversized and filthy jeans. Was it arrogance? Rebellion? Or did she truly not realise she was rather beautiful? In New York, Tyrone hung out with women who even on their days off had a blow dry and wore lip gloss, his ex-wives included.

For several minutes he waited for Holly and his mother to get out of the car, but neither of them budged. They were no doubt hatching a plan.

'Mum, let me help you,' he said, opening the passenger door to be met by a waft of smoke and booze.

Serena got out of the car and held up her handbag as if it were a shield. 'I can manage perfectly well.'

'You know the hospital wanted to keep you in for longer?' he said, feeling some relief when Serena took his arm.

'More like you wanted to keep me there and most probably transfer me to a loony bin.'

'Of course,' he said, planting a kiss on her cheek as they walked towards the front door.

'I'm surprised there isn't a "For Sale" sign hanging on the gates.'

'There wasn't time,' he said, managing to make his mother smile. 'You're still here, I see?' Tyrone nodded at Holly, but no witty remark was forthcoming.

'So, Mum …' He felt awkward saying it. 'I've had Lynette make up the bed in the flat for you.'

'No, thank you,' said Serena, full of her usual stoicism. 'I'll climb the stairs like I've always done. Besides, what would the dogs do? You know they only sleep properly on the four-poster.'

Holly laughed but he did not find it funny. It seemed impossible to get anyone to take this situation seriously.

'Didn't the hospital discharge you with a cane?' he asked.

'They attempted and I declined,' said Serena.

Anyone else might have thought his mother was a little drunk, but it took more than a hip flask to get her tipsy. She most probably didn't realise he knew about her stash in the car, and the one in the boot room; there was even one in the greenhouse. But this was Serena. This was how she functioned and, strangely, how she thrived.

'I spoke with the hospital registrar,' said Tyrone, persisting. 'He said level ground would be best, giving your knees time to heal.'

'So that's how it works, is it?' Serena reached out her hand and clutched Holly's shoulder for support. 'Those nosy parkers at the hospital, telling tales out of school.'

'They're concerned for you.' Tyrone tried to keep the disapproval out of his voice but it wasn't easy.

Serena walked to the front door with Holly and paused before entering the hallway. 'Tyrone, I think it's time for you to return to New York,' she said, clearing her throat. 'I've got Holly firmly on my team, and she's going to move to the house to keep me company.' She was looking guilty about something. What was it?

'And?' he asked. 'Come on, I know there's something more. I can tell by the way your eyes move.'

'Hollywood is relocating to Knockboden,' she said, moving into the hall and sitting on the fender.

Tyrone felt mildly sorry for Holly, who was caught in the crossfire.

'Three thousand dollars per day for lights … camera … action, right here.' Serena mimicked a clapper board with her hands.

'I can help to explain, if you like?' said Holly.

'Please,' he said, just as the dogs went flying outside to bark at a taxi.

'And who's this?' asked Serena, walking over to the front door, still using Holly as a crutch. 'I'll deal with them, Tyrone. You can go and book your flight.'

'You are kidding, Mum, I'm not going anywhere until someone tells me what the hell you've signed up to.'

'Hollywood, Tyrone. Hollywood is coming to Knockboden,' Serena said proudly.

'It's a reality TV show,' explained Holly.

'Just when I thought things couldn't become any more ridiculous.'

'It seems my petite adventure going to hospital was an early Christmas gift.' Serena balanced herself against the door. 'The production company in Los Angeles read about me online and they've completely fallen for Knockboden.'

'And is this so-called *production company* aware that Knockboden is a like a set for a jumble sale?'

'I hope I'm not disturbing you?' said a woman dressed in a full-length Puffa jacket as Tyrone opened the front door. 'I'm from the hospital,' she said, nervously looking at the dogs.

'Do shut up,' Serena shrieked.

'She means the dogs,' said Tyrone, inviting the woman into the hall. 'What can we do for you?'

'I'm Jan. I'm a public health nurse, specialising in geriatric patients.'

Tyrone had to laugh as his mother, right on cue, lit up a cigarette.

'What's that?' said Serena, returning to sit on the fender with Holly.

'This lady is from the hospital,' said Holly.

'She doesn't look like a public health nurse,' said Serena,

as if the nurse couldn't hear what she was saying. 'She looks like she's off to the North Pole.'

The taxi driver arrived at the door carrying a silver Zimmer frame.

'You're very good,' said the nurse, taking the frame. 'The occupational therapists want you to have this,' she said to Serena, 'just for five or so days.'

'Good idea,' said Tyrone.

'And while I'm here, I can help you with a bath or shower, if you'd prefer.'

Serena looked utterly shocked. 'Are you actually serious?'

'A bath, to freshen you up.' The nurse was very jolly.

'My dear girl, unless you are six foot two, male and with Paul Newman-like features, there shall be no baths, in bed or otherwise.'

'Ah God, if I'd have known we could have arranged for one of our male models to come over,' said the nurse with a large grin. 'We dress them up from time to time in doctors' outfits.'

Even Tyrone found himself smiling, but then remembered the insane suggestion of a reality TV show being filmed at Knockboden.

'Holly,' he said, 'the first thing I'm going to do is boost the broadband so that I can work from here. There is no way I'm going back to New York – you two are not to be trusted.'

Chapter Seventeen

If it hadn't been for the stench in the Land Rover, due to Mr Tubbs regurgitating some kippers on the back seat, Holly might have stayed behind the wheel. Tyrone stood outside Knockboden, looking as if he was checking his phone signal.

She opened the driver's door, jumped out and heaved out a large rucksack from the passenger seat.

'Is that it?' Tyrone asked as she carried the rucksack like a sack of potatoes.

'I've learned not to be sentimental,' she said. 'Besides, it's so freezing, I'm wearing half my clothes.' She'd have to buy some thermal leggings online.

Reluctantly, she let him carry the rucksack and tried not to find the scent of his aftershave attractive. He had annoyingly good taste, with his earthy toned jumpers, probably cashmere, his Barbour perfectly worn in and his blond hair merging into soft scarves around his neck.

'Go on, then,' she said, as they walked towards the front door. 'I know you want to say something.'

'I'm just wondering why you came back?' He turned his head briefly to look at her.

'Serena asked me to.' All Holly wanted was to get into the house and start clearing out cupboards. She had to get on with the job and ignore the pointless politics.

Entering the hallway, Tyrone put the rucksack on the fender by the fireplace.

'I'm fairly sure, at the hospital, you told me things weren't working out and you were going to resign,' he said.

'I can change my mind, can't I?' She tried to keep her voice strong and steady.

'How do I know you aren't mucking her around?'

She felt like swinging for him. 'Serena asked me to stay on while the film crew are here—'

'And sensing a fast buck, you agreed.' He folded his arms and stared at her.

'I don't know what kind of person you think I am, Tyrone, but I've been at your mother's beck and call for almost eight weeks and I have received zero payment.'

'Do you expect me to be surprised? Holly, it wouldn't take a genius to work out that this place will inevitably be put on the market. I refuse to put a single cent into a property that's soon to be out of my hands.'

'A property? This isn't a property, it's Serena's home. It's your family's home.'

'What would you know? What about your family? I don't see you rushing off to see them. Or them coming to see you.' He looked like he knew he'd gone too far. 'Typical millennial,' he said, 'unable to handle criticism.'

'Millennials? Only old people use that term.' She'd hit a nerve and couldn't help but smile as his eyes narrowed. 'You talk about my generation? Let me tell you about *your* generation, Mr Born-in-Nineteen-Seventy.'

'I was born in seventy-six.'

'Okay, then, *Born-in-Seventy-Six*. You lot are obsessed with pensions and ownership. It's all so dated.'

'Maybe you're right,' he said, walking to the fireplace and resting his elbow on the mantel. To Holly's delight, there was a chalky mark on his jumper.

Their row was thankfully interrupted by the sound of squeaky wheels coming along the corridor.

'Has anyone seen my leopard-print lighter?' asked Serena, arriving into the hall. The light from the fan window above bounced off the stainless-steel Zimmer frame.

'Aren't you meant to be resting?' asked Tyrone in his usual bossy tone.

'If you had your way, you'd have me stuffed and mounted.' Serena pointed to the stuffed head of a gazelle above the drawing-room door. 'Now, Holly, I want to run through sleeping arrangements.'

'What sort of arrangements?' said Tyrone. 'Is she going to sleep in a bath? Because you sure as hell won't find a bed in the house that doesn't have decades of clothes, magazines and wires all over it.'

'*She* is going to sleep in your father's dressing room. There's a perfectly adequate day bed.'

'But it's next door to my room.'

'Yes, and there will be a door between you. Holly, I'm sure

you'll resist,' said Serena, using her best tone of sarcasm. 'But now, I'd like you to fix me a pre-lunch spritzer to help pass the time while I'm expected to use this monstrosity of a walker.'

'I smell trouble,' said Tyrone. 'This month is going to be like *Fawlty Towers* on acid.'

'Certainly not,' said Serena. 'Rather than Sybil Fawlty, I prefer to think of myself as a younger version of Sophia Loren, and I'll be channelling Sophia's energy when they interview me for the show.'

'Hold on a second,' he said. 'You never mentioned anything about being involved in filming. You aren't going to be part of the show.'

'Naturally they're going to want to give me airtime, darling. I was an icon in my day. There were even rumours that Joan Collins modelled Alexis Carrington on me when filming *Dynasty* in the eighties.'

Tyrone turned to Holly. 'Could you give us a moment please?'

Tyrone looked down at the *Daily Express* tucked beneath his arm and reminded himself that, above all else, he was livid with his mother. He shook the newspaper open and held up a page in front of Serena.

'Unless you're going to give me a pair of binoculars, Tyrone, you shall have to come closer.'

He angled the newspaper in front of her. There was a large, glamorous photograph of Serena, wrapped in fur and clutching an evening bag in the doorway of what appeared to be a smart hotel.

'How exciting,' she said, wiggling her toes and thinking back to the heady partying days in London when she and Desmond regularly appeared in the pages of *Tatler* and *Hello* magazine. They'd even appeared in *Page Six* a few times.

'I must say, it's not a bad picture.' She looked up at her son, with his flaring nostrils, and wondered where his straight-laced genes came from.

'Aren't you going to tell me what the article is about?'

He shook his head as if he knew the answer to *everything*. Even before he opened his mouth, she knew he'd put on that patronising voice which got right up her nose. 'I'll read it out to you, shall I?' he said. 'Although the words came from you in the first place, apparently.'

'What words?'

'Somehow you spoke to the press while you were high as a kite on benzodiazepines.'

'I was high on benzowhatty-what? Is there more?'

'Seriously, Mum, I've spoken with your consultant. She gave you a tranquilliser when you were admitted, and somehow a journalist reached you.'

'I'm feeling a little groggy,' she said.

The past twenty-four hours began to resurface. Serena recalled the nurse giving her a dose. She remembered taking a call from a cousin, who'd asked all sorts of questions, bringing her back to the days when she and Desmond had hosted parties at Knockboden. Who was the cousin again? No, she literally couldn't recall, but she could vaguely remember a fabulous chat about those exotic days of partying at Knockboden, shaking the house down with their antics. It was such fun, all so endlessly exciting: champagne, guitars, singsongs and the nocturnal antics. Bedrooms merging into bedrooms.

The cousin had been such a delight to talk with, but now, looking at the deep frown on her only son's face, she wondered just what else she'd told her cousin, and whether he'd actually been her *cousin* at all.

'You have no idea about the fun your father and I used to have at Knockboden,' she said defensively. 'They were the glory days.'

'Oh I do,' replied Tyrone, severely lacking in humour. 'Believe me, I have every idea, because you've told the entire world.' He looked upset.

'I haven't the foggiest what you're talking about, Tyrone.'

He turned his eyes to the newspaper and began reading. '*Society queen of Irish castle tells all following near-death experience.*' He looked up at her, and she waved at him to continue reading. '*According to local sources, Lady Serena Harpur is "lucky to be alive" after being forced to flee a fire at her historic home.*'

'And?'

Serena attempted to appear innocent. The journalist had obviously become carried away with his story regarding the fire. She remembered explaining how the tea towel had caught the flame of the camping stove and how the kitchen tap had ceased to work. Her only option had been to fetch the yard hose. In hindsight it hadn't been the finest decision of her life. Fortunately, the tea towel must have tumbled to the stone floor and extinguished itself.

'With the blessing of her late husband, Sir Desmond, Serena Harpur was best known for being the first Irish woman to pose for Penthouse *magazine in the 1960s, and the couple were well known for their open marriage. In her latest interview, Harpur claims to have had three-in-a-bed romps with her celebrity guests at Knockboden Castle.'*

'I can see you're upset,' said Serena soothingly. 'I know how much you hate it when they call Knockboden a *castle*, and I quite agree, when it so clearly is not a castle. It is a fine Georgian mansion.'

'And that's all you have to say?' exploded Tyrone. 'What the hell were you thinking? You clearly gave an interview when you were trolleyed.'

'What else am I to say?' Serena's mind began racing to cover her tracks.

Tyrone continued reading. *'Talking about her son, heir to her juicy pile, Harpur says, "Sometimes I'm not even sure who his real father is."'*

'Oh, don't be silly,' she said. 'I was only teasing. Of course he's your father. Only a son of Desmond's could look so handsome when furious.'

Chapter Eighteen

As the first of December struck, whatever about 'Silent Night' and all being calm, Holly thought ironically, it certainly didn't feel that way as she lay in bed after midnight, scrolling through her phone. She had put her mother's WhatsApp messages on mute, which made things easier, sending a friendly acknowledgement every other day so as not to hurt her mum's feelings. But the barrage of messages from her brother Gabe, in response to her email explanation about postponing the wedding, were on a whole other level. He'd fired insult after insult, calling her selfish and asking if she didn't know that coordinating flights from Sydney was a nightmare.

Mariah also messaged, saying she had met Giles for coffee and he was missing Holly like crazy. At moments like that, she couldn't help but second-guess herself. What if she really had made the worst decision of her life? Right now, she could be in London with Giles, planning the honeymoon, mapping out the placement. Laying on the guilt, Gabe had also messaged to say their mother had booked a choir of twenty-one singers for the marquee reception in her garden; each singer had been meant to wear a white T-shirt to spell B-E-S-T C-H-R-I-S-T-M-A-S E-V-E-R. This was the kind of reminder that Holly needed. She didn't want to get married. Not to Giles, not to anyone. And she certainly didn't want Christmas.

Yet it was Valentina, of the *Insta-Love* team, who surpassed all three of them in her prolific use of WhatsApp. In the space of a single morning, Valentina sent fifteen instructions, from dietary requirements and exercise regimes to specific Christmas decorations they'd like at 'the castle'. The FaceTime walk was being scheduled for Friday morning, which gave Holly four days to make the dining room, the library and at least one bedroom presentable, to steady expectations from Los Angeles. She desperately hoped the absence of castle turrets and towers wouldn't put them off. At least they wouldn't feel the cold over a screen.

When Holly awoke, her nose was the only cold part of her body, having cocooned herself in heavy blankets. Sleeping in a large country house in the height of winter was going to take practice. Lying in bed, with the pale light of morning coming through the crack in the shutters, the pretty wallpaper on the sloped walls beneath the eaves made it feel like the bedroom of Beatrix Potter. She considered the bathtub across the hall from her bedroom, which may once have been white but presently was grey. There was no way she was going to risk taking a dip until it had been thoroughly scrubbed.

In the drawing room, Holly took a last mouthful of coffee and stepped onto the marble surround of the fireplace. She surveyed the room: Tyrone by the window, scrolling through his iPad; Serena, who lay like a large whippet across the sofa, smoking and turning pages of *Vogue*; Edwin warming his hands around a mug of tea, while Lynette, wearing Christmas-tree earrings, offered everyone cinnamon rice cakes. If Holly was leading a charge into battle with this lot, she'd most certainly write a farewell letter to her family beforehand.

'I've put an Advent calendar in the kitchen, in case anyone's interested,' said Holly, trying to get their attention.

'Don't tell me it's chocolate?' said Lynette. 'I've just started a new diet.'

'Pictures only,' said Holly, throwing another log on the fire. She thought of her mum's Advent calendar last Christmas, filled with solid silver ornaments, and couldn't help but feel completely guilty for lying to her mum about the wedding. She feared her reaction, the look of disappointment on her mother's face. When they'd discussed having the wedding at home in Dublin, it had been the project her mother had been waiting for. Her honed Christmas decorating techniques, the drinks party canapé recipes she knew off by heart. Juliette O'Leary had told Holly that this was the opportunity for her to create a happy-ever-after for her daughter, when her own marriage had been so abysmal.

'Serena, before we get started on who's doing what, can I have a quick word?'

'Really, Holly, I'm quietly enjoying my morning ciggy.'

'Valentina of Mindeflicks has sent an email to say …' Holly quoted directly from her mobile phone. 'She's "delighted Knockboden can provide their talent with five-star treatment, including Egyptian cotton sheets, organic menus – Farrah Fox is hyper allergic to garlic – and massage on demand".'

'And?' said Serena, eyes wide and looking only slightly sheepish.

'Not only do we not have hot water for our guests,' said Holly, 'where is the linen coming from, and do you have a masseur on speed dial?' She could see Tyrone smirking over his iPad.

'Lynette is our resident masseur, aren't you, darling?' Serena turned another page of *Vogue*.

'I feel a cold sweat coming on,' said Lynette, zipping up her hoodie.

'Nonsense,' said Serena. 'You'll be delighted with the extra money, won't you?'

'Are you qualified?' asked Holly.

'I worked at the beauty salon in Turpinstown until it closed down,' Lynette said, 'but my clients definitely used to comment on my strong thumbs.'

'That's the spirit, Lynette, always full of initiative,' said Serena. 'So come on, Holly, boss us all about and get the house in order. I want to catch the twelve-fifteen at Aintree on telly.'

Spreading the flipchart across a pile of books on the coffee table, Holly looked down at her childlike map of the bedrooms and bathrooms, allocating guests and highlighting problems to be sorted. She felt way out of her comfort zone, but had decided to use Tyrone's scepticism as an impetus to succeed.

'I might as well state the obvious and tell you we have a mountain to climb.'

Lynette started to sing the opening bars of 'Ain't No Mountain High Enough', handing out yellow Marigolds.

'There's no way I'll be putting on these,' said Serena. 'My ciggies would almost certainly burn through the plastic.'

'Serena, you're off the hook,' said Holly, 'but not the rest of us. We have exactly fourteen days to get the house into shape.'

'Which brings us to?' asked Serena.

'December the fifteenth,' said Holly, 'if you can believe it's that time of year already.'

'I believe it alright,' said Edwin. 'My Babs gets chilblains this time of year.'

'Declutter, clean, and then we'll decorate,' said Holly, slightly horrified to hear herself sounding like her mum. 'We'll start with the bathrooms and Lynette has brilliantly created a chemical-free batch of cleaning agent.'

'White-wine vinegar, lemon juice and water,' said Lynette, proudly holding up a spray bottle like an assistant on a game show.

'This is like a remake of *Ghostbusters Goes Organic*,' said Tyrone. It was doubtful if he'd ever worn rubber gloves in his life before, or had ever done the washing-up, for that matter.

'If you can each choose a bathroom,' said Holly, circling the rooms on her flipchart with a Sharpie, 'we can move on to clearing out the bedrooms.'

'I agree,' Tyrone said. 'We've got to tackle the filth or the crew will turn around so fast they won't have time to say "action", let alone "cut".'

'Yes, you must listen to Holly,' said Serena, lighting another cigarette.

'That's rich, coming from you, and by the way, you look exhausted,' said Tyrone.

'Nonsense,' said Serena. 'It's the smoke blocking your vision.'

'Lynette and I will sprinkle baking soda on the carpets,' said Holly, drawing a red circle around the drawing room and the dining room.

'I'll sort out boosters for the broadband,' said Tyrone, 'and the Aga is being serviced, and I've had the oil tank filled to the brim. The hall stove will have to be lit twenty-four hours a day to at least create a feeling of warmth.'

'Good idea,' said Holly, 'and we'll have to buy bed linen and bath towels in a local shop.'

'We can cut off the labels and pretend they're from a posh organic place!' Lynette's eyes were shining at the prospect.

'That's all fine,' said Serena. 'No need to get bogged down in the detail. Let's cover the basics and to hell with the rest. I'm purely interested in getting the weekly bank transfer into my account.'

Chapter Nineteen

The sight of snow made Tyrone's childhood feel so recent. He had forgotten the ethereal beauty of Knockboden's parkland in December: the bone structure of the trees, the winter sunshine landing on frosty lawns. In the butler's pantry, he came across a cardboard box of baubles with a thick gold ribbon around it. Dappled silvers and faded pinks, which he'd hang on the Christmas tree branches within his reach, until his father lifted him onto his broad shoulders. Accumulated memories, which had been hidden until this enormous house-tidy.

Tyrone rubbed the back of his neck. He was feeling old and the damp mattress wasn't helping. Pulling on a jumper, he walked to the kitchen to make a cup of tea, but was quickly turned off by the incessant smell of fish. There had to be an alternative to what his mother fed Mr Tubbs for breakfast.

'Goodie,' said Serena, wrapped in what looked like a throw around her shoulders and raising her mobile phone like a trophy.

'What are we celebrating?' he asked flatly.

'I've got a buyer for the horsebox.'

His mother was on the loose again.

'What are you selling the horsebox for, and without as much as a whisper to me?'

'Holly took pictures and uploaded them, and now I'm about to be cash rich.' Serena's cheeks flushed with excitement as she showed her mobile phone to Tyrone.

'Are you telling me Holly took these pictures?'

'Rather good, aren't they? She's included Jagger and Daiquiri in one of them, looking so adorable in the snow, and look, I even put a little red bow around their collars.'

'Nobody in their right mind would buy that box. Look at the state of it. Does it even have a floor?'

'It may require a little work here and there, but overall I'd say it's a solid buy.'

Tyrone looked out the window and saw Holly crossing the yard towards the skip. She carried a bin liner over her shoulder like Santa Claus.

'What's in the bag?' asked Serena, joining Tyrone's view. 'I've told Holly nothing is going into the skip without my say-so.'

'I'll find out.' He was going to give Holly a piece of his mind. What the hell was she thinking, introducing his mother of all people to eBay? She'd flog everything in sight. The dogs followed him into the boot room and out into the yard. 'Come on, you two,' he said. 'Holly?'

She stopped by a wheelbarrow and dropped the bin liner into it.

'That's easier,' she said. 'I'll use this from now on.'

Tyrone had been ready to tell her off, to call her irresponsible, to point out that his mother was the perfect target for online scammers, but something stopped him. Her eyes were shining, brighter than before. She looked motivated, as if even enjoying the clean-out.

'Did you want something?' she asked.

'It's nothing,' he said, 'just letting out Jagger and Daiquiri.'

'The stars of the horsebox ad!' she said, grinning.

Tyrone nodded, and turning away, he felt furious with himself. He had to toughen up.

Returning to the kitchen, he found Serena rummaging through a cupboard.

'Darling, you aren't being tough with Holly, are you?' she asked, stacking reindeer-shaped egg cups onto the worktop. 'I haven't seen these little fellows for years. You and your father loved your runny boiled eggs and soldier toast on Christmas morning.'

Tyrone found himself laughing. 'I do remember those little guys. That's so bizarre. I can almost taste the breakfast. Thanks, Mum.' His mobile phone started ringing, and for the first time in a long time, Tyrone had to think twice about leaving his mother. Usually he'd make phone calls to get away from her.

'Carl, how are you?' he asked, stepping out the back door to take the call.

'Bored, mostly, but I guess that's my fault for losing my wife.' Making jokes had always been Carl's way of coping.

'Look, I'm sorry I had to miss our reservation at Jean-

Georges. They promised to put us on priority listing in the spring.'

'Thank God for that,' said Carl, 'though I might starve in the meantime.'

'Seriously, though, how are you?' Tyrone looked up at the bell tower and imagined how lovely it would be to restore it one day. But then what was he thinking? He was going to sell the place. He had to stay grounded.

'Hell on earth without her,' said Carl. 'But like the books say, I'm getting out of bed in the morning. I'm having breakfast like a goddamn robot, but I'm alive. That's got to be something.'

'Yes it has.' They laughed. What else could they do?

'So is that Holly girl still getting on your nerves?' asked Carl.

Tyrone hesitated. 'Not so much.'

'Go on, tell me more.' There was very little that got past Carl.

Chapter Twenty

Holly opened a photo album and looked through a series of Polaroids of a young man, maybe in his early twenties. In every picture he looked straight at the camera, no qualms, as if he knew he was beautiful and was doing the photographer a favour. His cheeks were slender, leading towards that mouth, lips like rosebuds when he wasn't smiling. Dark eyebrows, open shirts, girls hanging out of his arms as he held a champagne flute by the stem or a pint of Guinness with effortless elegance.

Turning the page, she checked again. In some photos, he had long hair; in others, his hair was tied back. Was it Tyrone? It could only have been him. She studied the pictures. How could a photo album from what must have been twenty years ago give her butterflies? Those achingly cool parties she hadn't been at: beautiful people in polished urban clubs, shabby country pubs and wood-panelled dining rooms, breakfasting after the night before. She closed the album and almost wished she hadn't seen it. She couldn't have been much more than seven or eight when these pictures were taken.

Annoyingly, Tyrone arrived just before she put the album away, though he didn't seem to notice.

'Here we go,' said Lynette from beneath the four-poster, her feet peeking out beneath the bed skirt.

'Another mouse?' asked Holly.

'No, it's a jackdaw. Looks like it's been here for a long time; it's totally hollow.' Lynette reversed from beneath the bed. 'These houses are meant to have servants keeping the rooms spotless, like in *Downton Abbey*,' she said, 'and now it's flipping well left up to us.'

Holly's hair felt like straw, with dust and sweat gluing the strands together. She didn't mind looking like this in front of Tyrone, but her mind did wander to Giles and what he'd think of her now. She felt she had changed, in a few short months, and even though her wrists were scratched from pulling up old carpets, her toes hadn't been painted for weeks and she hadn't so much as touched an inch of makeup, things felt better in some odd way. It was only natural that she'd think of Giles: he had, after all, been going to be her husband, to love and to cherish, till death do us part. That was enough for Holly's wake-up call. As Serena said, she had to win the moment in front of her and stop dawdling over old ground.

'We'll get through it,' said Holly, holding up an old lamp with precarious-looking wiring.

'Let's bin it,' said Tyrone.

'I can hear you,' came Serena's voice from the corridor.

122

'Ears like a bat,' said Tyrone.

'What's going on in here?' said Serena, arriving in the room and making a beeline for the Tupperware. 'Aer Lingus,' she said, opening up a container and fishing out a teaspoon. 'From the days we dressed up to travel by air, when afternoon tea was served in crockery.' Serena held what looked like a sherry glass up to the light. 'Your father always said this set of glasses belonged to Napoleon.'

'And how about this tray?' asked Tyrone. 'I suppose this belonged to Louis the fourteenth?'

'Definitely keep,' said Serena, who was sounding quite upset. 'Selling a horsebox is one thing, but don't you see? These things are all part of my life; I can't just bin them. How will I remember what's happened? It may seem like junk to you lot, but to me these items are like a memory map.'

Tyrone put his hands on his mother's shoulders, as if to reassure her that it was all going to work out. 'Mum,' he said, calmly, 'you have got to let this stuff go. It's Holly's job to get the place ready for the TV crew and if you say no to everything, how can things progress?'

Serena shook her head in resignation.

Tyrone dangled a dead mouse by its tail. 'I think we're safe with this, Holly,' he said, and to everyone's relief, Serena had a good laugh.

'Fine, but I'm warning you lot,' said Serena. 'As much as necessary and as little as possible when it comes to clearing out.'

Lynette waved a duster over her head in a show of support.

The moment Serena left the room, Tyrone shot his hand into the air and clicked his fingers. 'I've got it,' he said.

'Got what?' asked Lynette, who was trying on a riding hat.

'I'm booking Mum into the Stephen's Green Club. My father used to call the club his great escape. I think it's in all of our interests. And Holly, I'll give you my credit card to buy linen and Christmas decorations, but on the proviso that this stays *out* of my mother's hands.'

Chapter Twenty-One

The feeling of grandeur at Knockboden was undeniable, even though the banister wobbled beneath Holly's fingers and every third step creaked as she walked downstairs. She imagined a Christmas tree in the hallway, reaching right up to the ceiling, branches fluffed out, baubles on every branch and a multitude of tiny white lights. But then, Holly was not celebrating Christmas this year – she had to remember that. Mariah had sweetly invited Holly to spend Christmas with her in-laws when her contract finished in Knockboden, but this was her best friend's first Christmas with her new family. The last thing Holly wanted to do was play the role of the lost friend, who had no place to call home, no career and definitely no sign of romance. All in all, Interrailing around Europe was looking like the best option.

Her mind returned to the problem of electricity supply for filming. She'd sent several emails to Valentina at Mindeflicks to ask if they could hire a generator for high-voltage equipment, but rather than supplying answers,

Valentina had responded with questions, chiefly to do with bedroom comforts for the reality stars.

Holly had some experience with trip switches, due to her mum overloading the fuse board with outdoor features, including a small herd of life-size reindeer, but to be safe, she called the one and only electrician of Turpinstown.

'It all starts with the equation P equals IV,' said Lionel, over the phone. 'I'm sure you know that from physics at school?'

'Um, afraid not.'

'Power equals current x voltage,' he continued. 'Basically, you want to keep an eye on kettles and them hairdryers and straighteners. I know from my daughters that them things are as power-hungry as bejesus and classics for tripping the board.'

Holly was about to send a WhatsApp to Valentina about the 'electricity etiquette' at Knockboden, when Serena walked into the hall dressed in a long green coat and a fur hat. Tyrone was behind her, with a case in each hand.

'What on earth have you packed in here, Mum? It's a lead weight.'

'Women like to have options,' she said, taking out a compact from her handbag and powdering her face. 'It may even snow, and you know I prepare for every eventuality.'

In the hall, there were piles of magazines, saucepans without handles and broken ornaments awaiting transit to the skip. There was even a porcelain chamber pot at the foot of the stairs, but Serena didn't seem to notice. She was far more interested in her mini city break.

'I am looking forward to the Stephen's Green Club, and I do hope they still mix my favourite cocktail – I can't remember the name.'

'I'm sure Russell will remember,' said Tyrone, pulling on his coat. 'He's under strict instructions to wine and dine you like the old days.'

'And remind me why must I meet my dreadful drunk of a cousin, who is famous for handling waitresses and falling out of taxis?'

'I want you to have company, that's why, and Russell is into Pilates these days. I wouldn't worry.'

'And you know this how?'

'We've spoken. That's how.'

'Russell was always a compulsive liar.'

'Say goodbye, Mum.' Tyrone gave Holly a knowing look and carried the suitcases outside, where Edwin stood beneath the frosty night sky, holding open the rear door of Serena's Mercedes.

'Alright, Holly?' asked Edwin.

'Great, thanks. I've just got a quick thing to run by Serena.' Holly pulled the sleeves of her jumper over her freezing hands. 'It's just to prepare you that there'll be a smoking ban in the house while the crew are here.'

'A ban in my own home?' Serena looked disgusted.

'It's literally for eight days, Mum,' Tyrone said. 'I think you can handle it.'

'Then I'll blow the smoke up the chimney, like in my school days.' Holly admired Serena's twinkling eyes; she had a way of making things fun. 'And that reminds me,

Holly, and damn, I meant to tell you earlier.' Serena paused by the open car door. 'Darling Harry and Freddie Rose, dear friends from Farley Hall, not far from here —'

'Mum, could you get on with it? We've got a lot to do, in case you hadn't noticed.'

'So impatient, Tyrone.' She took a cigarette from behind her ear and held it out for Edwin to light. 'Harry and Freddie Rose have a couple of youngsters staying at Farley Hall, nice and strong apparently, and they're keen to keep them busy.'

The last thing they needed was a couple of high-maintenance teenagers to deal with. 'Good,' said Holly, letting Serena's suggestion go in one ear and out the other. 'Have fun, let your hair down.'

'I can't remember the last time I wore my hair down in public.' And as if she had rehearsed it, Serena released a leopard-print clip from below her hat and a wave of silver hair tumbled down her back.

'Serena, your hair is incredible,' said Holly, meaning it.

'My lovers always liked it down,' she said, looking into the middle distance for dramatic effect before climbing into the car. 'And Holly, I am trusting you to be highly discerning in what you clear from the house., Keep it to an absolute minimum.'

Chapter Twenty-Two

The mural of fish, seaweed and shells in the coral bathroom was incredibly well preserved, considering it had been painted by Tyrone's great-aunt in the 1930s. The same could not be said for the bath, with its ingrained tidemark.

Holly sat cross-legged, holding her mobile phone in front of her. 'What's with the internet?' she said, without looking up at him.

'Well, good morning to you too.'

'Sorry, but I'm trying to download a spirit level and it's just so slow.'

'For what purpose, throwing a séance?'

'Funny, ha, ha,' she said, looking unamused. 'We've got five days to go until the film crew arrive and I'm beyond stressed.'

'And what's the spirit level for?'

'I got the Land Rover jack to hike up the bath so we can tile beneath it.'

Tyrone was more than a little fascinated by Holly's eccentric approach to DIY.

'You're like the Bear Grylls of the interior world.'

'If Bear's hands are stained with oil and his hips ache from pushing a four-poster bed across a room, then yes, maybe there are similarities.'

'Morning, you lot,' said Lynette, arriving in the bathroom out of breath and red-cheeked. 'Edwin gave me a lift in from town and it's that slippery, we may as well have ice-skated.' She raised her eyebrows at Tyrone. 'And no need for you to look at me like that. It isn't easy to look dignified carrying a twenty-four pack of bog roll.'

'Did I say anything?' Tyrone, having downloaded a spirit level, passed his mobile phone to Holly and lifted the loo roll out of Lynette's arms.

Holly grumbled a sort of thank you, while Tyrone got onto his knees and began turning the jack lever clockwise.

'Lord of the manor, rolling up his sleeves,' said Lynette, patting Holly's back. 'Quite the sight, isn't it?'

Tyrone wasn't sure if this was praise or ridicule, but as the jack made contact with the bath and it began to rise, he felt an unfamiliar sense of satisfaction.

Ten minutes later, Lynette was cleaning the mirror over the bathroom sink when she suddenly dropped her cloth.

'Oh flip,' she said, 'I forgot to say Harry and Freddie Rose are waiting in the hall, and there's a pair of French lads too.'

'Oh God,' said Holly, looking at Tyrone, 'they must be the guys coming to help with the clear-out.'

'And there was I thinking they were the reality TV stars,' said Lynette.

'I think we'd better go and greet our neighbours,' said Tyrone. 'Come on, Holly.'

'Do I have to?'

'Yes, you can't turn into a hermit,' he said. 'Beside, you're going to be playing host to Hollywood. You'd better get some practice in.'

The last thing Holly wanted was to babysit teenagers. Walking downstairs to the hall, though, she saw that Serena's suggested helpers were not only identical twins, but very good-looking young men.

'Darling Tyrone, heaven to see you,' said a glamorous woman in a fur coat. She gave Tyrone an enormous hug before turning to Holly. 'We're sorry to arrive so early, and here you are,' she said, reaching out a hand adorned with rings and gold bracelets to Holly. 'Aren't you just gorgeous?'

Holly didn't quite know what to say.

'You are a dark horse, Tyrone,' said Freddie, speaking very loudly. 'We had no idea you had a new girl on the scene.'

Tyrone looked at Holly with an almost panicked expression.

'What? God no,' he said, laughing. 'Holly is only an employee; she's here to declutter the place in prep for the TV crew.'

'Ah, I see,' said Freddie, clapping her hands in Holly's direction. 'Well, aren't you marvellous?'

'Whereas I may not be marvellous, but I am Harry Rose,' said the lovely man dressed in a yellow polo neck, bearing an uncanny resemblance to Jack Nicholson. 'I'd better apologise for my wife, who can get her wires crossed from time to time.'

'I'm so embarrassed, Holly. I do apologise,' said Freddie.

'It's fine,' laughed Holly. 'After all, I am the employee, as Tyrone said.'

'And these boys are the mighty Gold brothers, Benoît et François,' said Harry, keeping everything light. 'Say *bonjour* boys.'

'Hello,' they said, with beautiful smiles.

'They're fresh from Paris, where they narrowly avoided being snowed in with their formidable *grandmère* for Christmas.'

'Naturally, we insist the boys stay with us,' said Freddie, 'but we feel the young like to be kept busy.'

'Exactly right,' said Harry, 'and when we heard from Serena about Hollywood coming to town, we thought what a good idea for these strapping lads to muck in and help.'

'Not to mention the fact our hot water supply is rather shaky at Farley this time of year,' added Freddie.

Holly smiled along. She had been about to point out that it wasn't much better at Knockboden, but why bring reality in when things were already so nuts? Soon they were inevitably going to be faced with high-maintenance reality stars.

'Parlez-vous anglais?' asked Holly, scrambling to find her school French.

'Oh yes,' they both said, literally at the same time, and everybody laughed.

'I'm Benoît,' one said. 'You know me by my little tail' – he turned around and pinged his ponytail, neatly bound – 'and my T-shirt,' which featured Santa Claus carrying a large bottle of champagne.

'I have freckles across my nose, but my brother's English is not so good.' François, whose hair flopped over his forehead, playfully punched his brother's arm.

'No, don't worry, he's joking,' said Benoît. 'We both speak well and we help you.'

'We'll put them in the lodge,' said Tyrone, 'and we'll give them the Land Rover, now that it's actually insured.'

'Damn red tape,' said Harry, 'I didn't even have to do a driving test in my day.'

Freddie walked around the hall, humming 'The Twelve Days of Christmas'. 'I can't imagine a more beautiful hallway for a Christmas tree than here,' she said. 'Once you decorate, Holly, this place will be transformed.'

'You really think so?' she asked.

'Of course, darling.' Freddie linked her arm into Holly's and Tyrone's.

'We can do it, don't worry,' said Tyrone, giving her a reassuring look.

Chapter Twenty-Three

The Trojan work in the kitchen seemed complete. Holly and Lynette had emptied the cupboards and removed the archaic appliances, including a 1960s Kenwood with exposed wiring. All the surfaces looked immaculately clean.

'The Gold twins are getting on well,' said Tyrone, feeling in the mood for a chat. 'I've just been to the top floor. Benoît is emptying the chests and François is flipping the mattresses.' And the twins were impressive. They'd had summer work experience at Christie's and had learned how to move furniture and paintings properly. Holly looked up briefly and then returned to wiping place mats.

'It's an old-fashioned thing,' he said, 'but rotating mattresses can give them a new lease of life.' He wondered what was up. Holly seemed cold.

He filled up the electric kettle, being faster than the Aga, and turned it on.

'Shall I make a pot?'

'Not for me,' said Holly.

'Lynette?' She seemed distracted by her mobile phone.

'No thanks, I've got to call my sister about Christmas dinner,' she said. 'I've said it's her turn to do the veg, and as usual she tries to worm her way out.'

'I've never had any siblings,' he said, 'but if I did, I imagine we'd be having similar debates.'

'Family,' said Lynette. 'Not so bad, really.' She looked at Tyrone, then at Holly, and then back to Tyrone.

'Thanks, Lynette,' he said, and once she had left the room, he sat back on a chair at the table. 'Holly, is there a problem?'

'A problem?' She raised her eyebrows, as women always did when there *was* a problem.

'Yes,' he said. 'Am I meant to have done something?'

'How would I know? I'm *only* an employee,' she said quickly. 'I'm here to decorate, like some kind of Christmas elf.' She threw down the dishcloth and folded her arms.

'Alright,' he said, realising what she was talking about. 'I'm, well, I'm obviously totally out of practice.'

'Out of practice?' she said. 'Sorry, when you say "out of practice", is this in terms of being respectful to people who are doing their best to help your mother?'

He tried to speak, but she jumped back in.

'Because for some reason that only the universe seems to know about, I've become very fond of Serena and I want to help fulfil her dream of making this house sustainable.'

Tyrone didn't know what to say. The situation was certainly unpredictable and at every turn things seemed to be changing. Maybe that was it; maybe he wasn't sure what her role was.

'I'm sorry,' he said, 'if I made you feel uncomfortable. It's just that sometimes, if I'm unsure of what I'm saying, I just say something stupid, or annoying – or insulting.'

Holly nodded in agreement, which wasn't helpful.

'At least that's what my ex-wife said in the cover note on my divorce papers.'

Holly laughed. Tyrone hadn't worked so hard to get out of a tense situation since explaining to his very sweet secretary that he had no option but to give her notice, because she was too disorganised. He'd sent her on courses and given her carte blanche to order any gadget that could help her, but she just wasn't cut out for the job. But Holly had exceeded expectation. She was a diligent, hard worker, mostly polite, and she had a vision for Knockboden that he had never had, or even wished to have.

'Shall we?' he said, unplugging the American-style fridge freezer, relieved the moment had passed.

'I guess it's beyond cleaning,' said Holly, 'but Serena is going to miss this filthy brute.'

'Well, an even larger fridge is due for delivery tomorrow,' said Tyrone, 'and I should compliment you on your bed and bathroom linen orders. Even the scatter cushions, rugs and mirrors. You have good taste.'

'Let's hope Serena thinks so too,' said Holly. 'Shall we?'

One, two, three, and together they pulled the fridge away from the wall where it had been for years.

'Do you think the reality stars will want skinny lattes?' asked Lynette, who'd clearly been out for a smoke. She began pulling the fridge towards her. 'Or maybe they won't be so precious,' she continued. 'I think the media hypes it all up.'

'We can't take any chances,' said Holly, pushing her shoulder against the fridge. 'Once we've got this out, we can mop the hell out of the floor.'

'Hello?' said Lynette.

'Hold on, we need to get this through the door,' said Tyrone, from the other side.

'No,' said Lynette, with some urgency. 'Holly, I'm actually properly trapped between the fridge and the door. Did no one think to open it?'

'Oh God, can't you squeeze out?' asked Holly, peering around the back of the fridge to catch sight of her.

'No, I can't, and before you say anything, it isn't my fault Weight Watchers increased their annual subscription.'

Holly pulled a kitchen chair to the fridge, and stepping on it, she hoisted herself on top of the fridge. 'The grime up here is unbelievable.'

'I feel a sweat coming on,' said Lynette. 'You know I have claustrophobic tendencies?'

'Don't panic,' said Tyrone. He looked up at Holly, who was giving encouraging smiles to Lynette. 'Let's try sliding it the other way,' he said. He put his hand around Holly's waist as he helped her to climb down. 'We'll have to stop meeting like this.'

'Oy, you two,' said Lynette. 'In case you haven't noticed, I'm still behind this blooming fridge.'

With a swift shove, Tyrone pulled back the fridge and angled it through the door.

'Thank you,' said Lynette, taking her coat from behind the kitchen chair. 'Edwin's about to arrive, so you two can blooming well move that fridge without me.'

'Come on, Lynette,' called Edwin, from the boot room, 'my car's about to freeze over.'

'Coming,' she yelled. 'Bye, you two.'

'Thanks, Lynette,' said Tyrone, checking his watch. 'How about we get this outside and open a bottle to recuperate?'

Chapter Twenty-Four

'It's a dog's life by the Aga,' said Tyrone, as Holly twirled her fork into a bowl of spaghetti. 'Sometimes, I think I'd quite happily join Jagger and Daiquiri's uncomplicated lives.'

From the kitchen table, Holly watched the dogs who were sound asleep. She felt exhausted, having heaved and cleared what felt like mountains of clutter from the house.

'It was kind of you to cook,' she said. 'I don't think I could have even poached as much as an egg.'

'I'm not surprised. You and Lynette have played a complete blinder.'

Holly looked at the clock, which she'd got working after what must have been years, according to Lynette. 'It can't be midnight already? That's crazy. Sometimes I feel like we're in a bubble at Knockboden.'

'That's one way of looking at it,' he said, leaning across the table to top up her glass.

Holly took another sip of wine and felt oddly like her old self, the version she liked.

'I'm sorry again,' he said, 'calling you the *employee* and everything. It's just you seem to cover a myriad of roles here,' he said. 'I promise you will be paid properly, I'll make sure. You've been so kind to Mum.'

'Why wouldn't I be?' said Holly. 'If only I was so kind to my own.'

'Aren't you?'

'I'm not sure,' she said, taking another sip. 'I can remember sticking to her like glue as a little child. We were inseparable, and then Dad left.'

'And?'

'Mum went into overdrive, there's no other way of explaining her reaction. She turned into the great entertainer. The queen of canapés, the drinks party goddess. Any excuse, she'd throw a party, and Christmas became bigger and bigger.'

'Really?' Tyrone looked genuinely intrigued.

'Our house went from having a Christmas wreath on the front door to being covered in lights of every possible shade and size, and she moved things into the front garden, and then the media became interested and that upped the game.' Holly rubbed Jagger's head as she spoke. 'Mum brought in entertainers, like a choir, Santa Claus, Mrs Claus, and one year we even had a live reindeer eating carrots for a photoshoot with Mum dressed as Mrs Claus.' Holly hadn't spoken about that for so long, and it felt heartbreaking. Her mother must have been devastated when her husband left; she had clearly been trying to make up for Holly and Gabe losing their father. Every Christmas the pain must have been raked up for her, and her over-the-top decorating must have been her way of working through it. Holly took her mobile phone from her pocket. It was like she knew when her mum was about to text, some kind of weird sixth sense. 'There she goes,' she said, and passed her phone to him.

Darling, the cater hire people have returned the deposit, re postponement of your wedding. I'm spending the money on more decorations, including another 4 strands of lights over the front door, and I've commissioned a willow sleigh to go next to the elves' house in front of the house in time for Christmas Eve. The Brooks will love it. Love you darling, Mum XXX.

Tyrone smiled politely and passed the phone back to her.

'The Brooks?' he asked. 'Some kind of bird I'm not familiar with?'

'Mum's neighbours.'

'And this is why you're here?'

'To avoid Christmas? Yes.'

'And the postponed wedding your mum mentioned?'

She had felt so relaxed she missed her mother's mention about the wedding in the text. But it felt okay: whatever it was about the kitchen, at that moment, Holly felt on a new level with Tyrone. She held the warm glass of wine and drank deeply.

'Cancelled wedding. I haven't told my mum that I've called the whole thing off.' Holly paused. 'I was engaged,' she said, putting down her glass, 'and then I don't know what happened, but something inside me just said it wasn't right. I pictured my life with him, or something, but it just didn't add up.'

'How did it look?'

'Tidy,' she said. 'Very tidy. He was kind and good. Everything was – I don't know, tidy. It's the only word I can think of. Maybe the wine has stalled my vocabulary.'

'No, I get it,' he said, uncorking the bottle. 'I'd say it was very brave of you to call it off.'

'It didn't feel brave. I felt like a chicken, and even more so leaving London. I ran from him, from having to face what I'd done, and how I'd hurt him.'

'And your dad, is he around?'

Holly shook her head. 'Would you like the short or the long answer?'

'I'm open to either.'

'He left when I was little,' she said, pressing her palms together. 'I see him now and then, he sends me a cheque, I tear it up, and that's our sort of pattern.'

'I'm sorry.'

'No need,' she said. 'I'm fine without him.'

Their eyes met, and Holly knew this was the moment where she had to show Tyrone that she was no victim.

'And tomorrow, I'm Christmas-tree shopping for this place.' Holly started laughing, and almost couldn't stop. 'But can I tell you something?'

'Go on.'

'For the first time, I think I'm feeling proper job satisfaction. Is that awful?'

'How could that be awful?' he said. 'It's a good thing. Anything related to satisfaction is a good thing.'

'Sounds boring, though, doesn't it?'

'Boring? No, and I'll tell you what else isn't boring: how my bedroom door almost collapsed on me this morning, and ...' Tyrone paused.

'What is it?'

'I had a call from my lawyer earlier this evening to say the papers have come through for my divorce.'

'I see,' said Holly, not knowing what to say.

'My second divorce – it's become something of a habit.' Jagger wandered over and put his head on Tyrone's knee.

'Did you love her a lot?'

'My first wife? Boy, I did, beyond all expectation, but when it came down to the practicalities, how we both wanted to live, it was never going to work.'

Keeping up with Tyrone, Holly finished her drink.

'But the second time, to Kenzie? I married on the rebound. I just found that out too late.' He got up from the table to fetch another bottle of wine and pulled the cork. 'I should be used to it by now, but it still hurts like hell.'

Tyrone poured the wine, and spilt a little down the side of her glass.

'Sorry,' he said, 'I'm a lousy shot when it comes to pouring, drunk or sober, but I would like to officially thank you for rescuing Mum, and for bringing this whole crazy operation together.' He raised his glass to her. 'Thank you, and even better, my mother hasn't called to complain from the club, so that's a good sign.'

'I hope she's having fun. She deserves it, like I'll deserve my hangover in the morning.' She wondered if it was the alcohol making her feel that he was studying every inch of her face.

'I've got to fly out first thing to New York and catch up in the office.'

'Tomorrow?'

'You'll be fine,' he said. 'I'll only be gone for a few days.' Tyrone leaned forward to top up Holly's wine again. Slowly, their heads drew towards each other and, closing her eyes, Holly felt their lips meet. Warm, perfect and melting for a single moment, before the spell broke with the sound of the wine bottle toppling over. Daiquiri, his tail wagging, looked up at them both, almost smiling.

'Holly,' said Tyrone, standing up and retrieving the bottle from the floor. 'I don't know what I was thinking. I'm so sorry. It's the divorce and the wine – I just lost it for a second.'

'It's fine,' she said, feeling like a complete idiot as she backed towards the door. 'I'm going to just head off now.' She heard him say good night but she didn't look at him as she left the room. Why was it that men were so fast to make excuses? It felt like she had fallen into a failed speed date.

Chapter Twenty-Five

Rory's Cracking Christmas Emporium was an unexpected treasure on the outskirts of Turpinstown. A huge wooden barn had been converted into a magnificently decorated festive haven, filled with garlands of pomegranates and ivy, golden and silver paper stars, and barrels upon barrels overflowing with wooden ornaments. Compostable Christmas wrapping lay in sheets on a long table, with long silks of green, red and pink. Tubs of environmentally friendly glitter lay next to colourful cardboard gingerbread men. Staff, dressed as 'eco elves', wore home-dyed aprons and served moon-shaped 'I can't believe it's not turkey or ham' sandwiches.

'I really can't believe this isn't turkey or ham,' said Lynette, taking another bite. 'It's delicious.'

Holly was thinking about the card Tyrone had left for her in the kitchen, along with a Swiss Army knife, wrapped in navy paper.

Just in case you need a little help – the corkscrew may be the
most essential item. See you in a few days,
Tyrone x

It was a goodwill gesture, a peace offering, and she'd decided to accept. She was still cringing at the thought of the kiss. What if he'd thought she had made a pass at him? It was a massive relief he had left. Giles in London, Tyrone in New York. City boys. It was time to leave them to it.

'Would you like a sandwich, miss?' asked one of the elves.

'No, thank you,' said Holly.

'Then how about coming over to our Christmas pudding demonstration? Cindy Christmas is our special guest and she knows all there is to know when it comes to cooking up a smile in the kitchen.'

Holly grabbed a basket and pretended to immerse herself in the display of Christmas-themed wild swimming accessories. There were mistletoe swimming hats, plum pudding dry robes and reindeer booties. In the camping section, sleeping bags looked like sausage rolls and tents were covered in bright pink stars. They were all rather lovely, and not even Holly, feeling a little down, could resist the magic of it all.

'We want to be healthy turkeys, fit fajitas this year, people,' said one of the elves from the loudspeakers. 'Cindy Christmas will be demonstrating her favourite winter vegetable smoothie recipe, so we can keep Santa Claus and his taste buds happy, and why not try our sleigh-shaped bread-making machine, the perfect gift for the person you loaf?'

Lynette had filled a trolley with stars and garlands of mandarins and cherries, and bright yellow and pink striped candles.

'This is fun, Holly, I've even found Pawfect Puppy spray for Jagger and Daiquiri. And Serena will love the Christmas cookie scent.'

They wandered to a 'Jolly Zen' area, with bean bags and dimmed lights, therapists offering massage and facials, and even relationship counselling. Holly could have pitched a star tent, jumped into a sausage-roll sleeping bag and spent a month there. She loved the sign for 'Elegant Meltdowns', beneath which there was an array of chocolate fountains and fondue makers.

'What about this one?' asked Lynette, holding up a reindeer outfit for terriers. 'Do you think this would fit Daiquiri?'

Holly giggled. She was beginning to feel better; she even liked the look of a long table with candy-cane red-striped tablecloth and napkins. There was a most gorgeous assortment of quirky vintage ornaments, alongside hand-painted glass mushroom ornaments for a woodland wonderland theme and Santa Claus bathrobes.

'Farewell, tinsel, your time is over,' said Holly, running her hands through a wooden barrel overflowing with gold and silver papier-mâché stars. 'I think there is more than enough inspiration here for us to create our magic at Knockboden.'

'We'll have Knockboden looking like Santa's kingdom in no time,' said Lynette, taking a hot chocolate shot from a passing elf.

'Glad to hear it,' said a man with a deep, rustic voice, stretching out his hand to Holly. His hair, pure white, was tightly shorn, with a white beard; he wore a check shirt and braces, and his eyes shone behind small wire-rimmed glasses.

'Santa?' Holly couldn't believe the words coming out of her mouth.

'Rory,' he said. 'This is my emporium, but I must say, you've made my Christmas.'

Chapter Twenty-Six

Outside Knockboden, the front door was festooned with pine boughs and bows, which led down to two giant log baskets hung with ribbon. The principal fireplaces had been lit; brass urns had been filled with branches of yew, sprayed with gold paint; silver stars had been hung at their tips. Ivy with red velvet ribbon weaved around the staircase banister, and an infusion of fairy lights adorned the portraits, including the one of Great-Uncle Dudley.

In the hallway, gold baubles were suspended with green ribbon, and as Serena walked through the front door, the candles on the hall mantel flickered.

Briefly touching the stove, she moved to the central table and ran her finger along the side, as if checking for dust. Holly breathed in the spicy, festive scent from the gold fish bowl of pot-pourri and awaited a reaction, but none was forthcoming. There was no reaction to the silver urn filled with abundant branches of berries, nor to the fairy lights discreetly wrapped around the glass cabinets, nor the enormous Christmas tree, topped by an angel, homemade by Holly. The romantic staircase of ivy was met with silence, as was the dining room, where lights twinkled around the polished table, laid with shining silverware. It wasn't until Serena arrived in the drawing room and stood in front of the tree that she made a sneezing sound.

'Bless you,' said Holly. 'Or wasn't that a sneeze? Serena, do you not like it? Is it all too over the top? Maybe I'm no better than my mum. Oh God, I'm sorry.'

'I knew you could do it.' Serena beamed her gorgeous smile and hugged Holly. 'You've even got mistletoe over the doorways.'

'But you looked upset?'

'No, I'm not upset. I'm overwhelmed, because I brought you to this house of mayhem and you turned it around, I don't know how, and maybe you don't either? But I think, by some miracle, it's happened.'

In her entire life, Holly didn't think she had ever received a compliment like that. She wanted to cry, but she chose to laugh instead.

'I think I had my midday gin too late today,' Serena said, with tears in her eyes, 'but it's funny, isn't it? How things can hit you, just like that – quite out of the blue.'

Seeing her watery blue eyes and full mouth, so regal, so beautiful, Holly was aware of a melancholy in Serena that she hadn't seen before.

'He may be back in New York, but he wants me out, like a lion poised to pounce.'

'Tyrone?'

'I had a realisation when I was away, and by the way, I might tell you that the Stephen's Green Club is as *glorious* as ever, and even the dreaded Russell behaved himself.'

'Good,' said Holly, wondering what Serena was going to say about Tyrone.

'Because my son has made it, he thinks it gives him a licence to come back and take Knockboden from me.'

'Do you think he loves the house, deep down?'

'Love? I'm afraid I'm the one to blame for his lack of understanding on that score, Holly. I fear I didn't give him enough love as a child and he has punished me ever since.'

She sat down on the sofa and, fumbling around her jacket pocket, she pulled out a lighter.

'You know, the coffin was just over there,' she said as she lit up her cigarette, pointing towards the fireplace. 'Desmond lay inside it like a cold Sunday roast. A piece of meat. I can hardly bear to think of it, and yet—'

'Yes?'

'And yet, somehow, knowing the house was being freed of its deluge from the past, I felt you were clearing the ghosts away, Holly, do you know that?'

'Ever heard of a séance with a skip? Maybe this can be the new approach to exorcism.'

Serena smiled, and taking a handkerchief out of her sleeve, she dabbed her eyes. 'You know my parents never sent me to school?'

'Then it just shows how naturally clever you are,' said Holly.

'I know somebody must have taught me to read and

write,' she said. 'Maybe it was the cook, but you know if I were to change any aspect of the past, I would have made sure to have had Tyrone's nursery in the same wing as our bedroom. It wasn't until he was in his teenage years that he told me what had happened.'

'What kind of thing?' Holly's mind began to race.

'He'd be vomiting in the night, from crying so intensely, and as a comfort, the bitch of a nanny spanked him with a fish slice, and when he wet the bed, the cycle continued.'

Holly felt instantly different towards Tyrone having heard this.

'If the nanny hadn't already died by then, I would have visited her with her own fish slice to give her a taste of her own medicine.'

The gravity was lifted by the glorious arrival of Jagger and Daiquiri, cornering the doorway and barking in ecstasy at having Serena home again.

'Hello,' said Benoît and François as they too appeared, armed with a bottle of wine, glasses and a corkscrew.

'Brilliant timing,' said Holly. 'Serena, I'd like to introduce Benoît and François Gold.'

'Enchanté, Lady Harpur,' they said.

'How about that?' Serena clasped her hands with joy. 'Talk about bringing home a double gold for Christmas.'

Chapter Twenty-Seven

Since the *Insta-Love* booking, Holly had been waking in the night with visions of bedrooms filled with glittering reindeer and snowmen. Idea after idea kept landing on her. She had promised Tyrone that she'd keep the spend to a minimum. Edwin's wife Babs volunteered to make gingerbread stars to hang on the tree, and enthused by the prospect of their craftmanship being aired on TV, her knitting circle got to work on Christmas stockings for the reality stars. For their bedrooms, Holly kept the scheme warm and cosy, buying discount velvet throws and twinkly sequinned cushions in pale pink. Fairy lights and silk-star pillows with pom-pom edging would light up the headboards, and she tied red ribbons on the handles of the wardrobes and drawers. She'd filled silver vases with red anemones, hellebores and eucalyptus pods, and she and Lynette had unearthed the best china for the table.

'It looks like one of those posh hotels you'd see on Instagram,' said Lynette, with tears in her eyes. 'I'm dead proud of you, honey.'

Edwin had cut down three Christmas trees. The biggest was in the drawing room, with middle-size trees in the hall and the dining room, all decorated with cream lights and gold and silver baubles. As popcorn was on Lynette's list of treats that she could consume within her diet, she was happy to make garlands to string around the trees and was mostly successful in not eating the popcorn as she went along.

The fires in the main reception rooms had been lighting since early morning in a bid to heat up the house. As a show of festive enthusiasm, Serena wore a red cashmere beanie and Holly had a platter ready for hot crumpets next to the china tea service in the drawing room.

'Where on earth are they?' said Serena, circling a folded newspaper with biro. 'I've had a flutter on the 2.30p.m. at Chepstow and I'll be damned if I'm going to miss it.'

'Maybe they're still in the air,' said Holly, checking her phone again.

'Can't you send another one of those text thingies?' asked Serena. 'What time were they meant to be here?'

'Three hours ago,' said Holly, pulling off her woolly gloves to send another WhatsApp to Valentina.

'Keep your hair on,' said Lynette. 'Sure isn't there a huge jeep outside?'

'Lynette, how long has it been there?'

'Never mind that,' said Serena, elbowing Holly out of the way. 'Those wretched electric cars are more silent than an unresponsive lover.'

A pair of white snow boots were first to emerge from the

Range Rover, followed by leopard-print leggings and an oversized silver Puffa jacket.

'What is that?' said Serena. 'Some kind of Yeti?'

'I think it's Farrah Fox,' said Lynette, in awe.

'You're late,' said Serena, walking with a wooden cane, having thrown her Zimmer frame on the skip. 'We had an afternoon tea of hot crumpets and scones prepared.'

'And I'm excited to be here,' said Farrah, oblivious to Serena's reprimand. 'Please don't feel nervous around me. People tend to get jittery when they recognise me.'

'I have no idea who you are,' said Serena, almost poking her stick into Farrah as she spoke.

'You're Farrah Fox,' said Lynette, pulling down the hood of her coat. 'I watched you on *Pancake Flipping with the Stars* in the nineties.'

'I've actually done a lot since then,' said Farrah, smiling nervously.

'It's great that you're here, Farrah,' said Holly diplomatically, 'and we really hope that—'

'Farrah, sweetie, it's time for you to rehydrate,' came a voice from across the bonnet.

'This is Valentina, my makeup artist,' said Farrah. They all looked at the woman with long peroxide hair, who removed her sunglasses just long enough to reveal smudged mascara and bloodshot eyes.

'We spoke on the phone,' said Holly, passing a bottle of what looked like swamp water from Valentina to Farrah.

'I'm so happy to be here,' said Valentina, watching as Farrah obediently squeezed her lips around the paper straw, sipping the swamp water. 'I've been in the industry for, like, ten years and this is my first time shooting in Ireland.'

'More guests?' said Serena, as a blue Golf drove up the avenue at speed.

'That's our producer, Diane Striker, and Preston Minde,' said Valentina, holding her phone in front of her face and running her tongue across her teeth. 'Damn that spinach I had for lunch.'

'Preston … is that a male or female?' asked Serena.

'Most definitely male,' said Valentina, patting her bustline as the car pulled up.

A man with tightly shorn red hair stepped out of the driver's seat. Giving a friendly wink to them all, he turned his back and leaned against the car.

'Preston's always on the phone,' said Valentina, smiling dreamily in his direction. 'He's connecting with the camera crew. They'll be here any second to position secret cameras around the house.'

'Then let it be known my bedroom is out of bounds, unless Hugh Grant has become a camera technician,' said Serena, 'in which case he may enter.'

'Good taste,' said Valentina before turning to give Preston a thumbs up as a jeep rolled up. 'These guys will be in out and in a couple of hours. Like the cameras they install, they are very discreet.'

'Farrah, catch a nap before dinner,' ordered Diane,

pressing an iPad against her chest like a shield. 'I need you looking fresh.'

'Don't worry if Diane is sharp with you.' Valentina lowered her voice to Serena and Holly. 'It hasn't been the smoothest of journeys.'

'Lynette, can you show Farrah to her room, please?' said Holly, who was more concerned by the arrival of Preston.

'Thanks,' said Farrah, 'and can you bring my Pilates mat?'

'Sure I can,' said Lynette, 'and I'll be handling your massage, in case you fancy one?'

'That's kind,' said Farrah, in a questioning sort of way. 'I'll stick with Pilates for now, and if you can find my bamboo cane too, please?'

'Bamboo?' asked Serena.

'Yes, I tap to maintain self-awareness,' said Farrah, patting her behind.

'This it?' Lynette held up a green bamboo cane over her head.

'You're a doll,' said Farrah, taking the cane and following Lynette to the house.

'My, oh my,' said Diane, removing her sunglasses, eyes blinking. 'What do we have here?'

'It's not a what, it's a house,' said Serena, noting that Diane reminded her of a pony she had as a child.

Stretching her hands over her head, Diane showed off a toned midriff. 'This place is just what we need. Neglect at this level is hard to find.'

'Sorry?' said Serena.

'Don't be. This place is just we've been looking for. It's all about making our reality stars shine out from the old building, you know?'

'And is this it?' said Serena. 'Only four in your crew?'

'Just one more to arrive,' said Diane.

'A human, I take it?'

'Yes, I suppose Eric Rimmel is human. Last seen being frisked at LAX,' said Diane, looking at her phone. 'We're a tight team for this shoot.'

'And that young man, what is his role?' Serena looked sideways at Preston, who was wearing more wool than a sheep in the height of winter.

'He's our camera guy. Preston's father owns the company,' said Diane, 'but don't be fooled by the silver spoon or the baby face – he's good at what he does.'

'I can't see his face, he's so wrapped up,' said Serena.

Relations improved when Diane announced that a hefty deposit had been lodged into Knockboden's bank account that morning.

'Then let's warm you up with a glass of something sticky and I'll give you a very brief history of the house,' said Serena. She checked her watch, hell-bent on getting to her race.

'Whatever we're drinking,' said Diane, pulling down the collar of her leather jacket, 'I like it neat and on the rocks, like our couples on *Insta-Love*.'

Chapter Twenty-Eight

Mougins, France, that was it. The moment Preston saw Holly O'Leary, he knew they'd met before. She was still cute. He watched Diane stalking the drawing room like a panther. She seemed remarkably cool, given that the ratings of last season's *Insta-Love* were right down. One of the many benefits of being son to the network boss was having access to data, and he knew how important it was for the *Insta-Love Christmas Special* to reignite public interest in the show.

'Gin or vodka?' the old lady asked him, though it sounded more like an order.

'How kind,' he said. 'Vodka, please.'

'Are you sure?' The old bat looked put out by his choice. 'How about gin?'

'A good choice,' she said, 'and you may call me Serena. I'm not one for airs and graces.'

Preston took a step back as Valentina came striding into the room and marched towards Holly.

'I'm Valentina,' she said, shaking Holly's hand. 'I wasn't sure if you caught my name before.'

'Thanks, yes I did,' said Holly, who had noticeably been avoiding eye contact with Preston. 'Is your drink okay?'

'Water is really as far as it goes with me,' said Valentina. 'Our schedule is tight and I want to be on it at every moment of our shoot.' Valentina looked at Preston, just as he'd guessed she would. He nodded at her and smiled, making no promises.

'So, Holly, has our shipment arrived?' Valentina asked.

'Shipment of ...?'

'Oh really? It hasn't arrived?' Valentina looked around the room in panic. 'Diane, did you get that? Our shipment, you know, the goblets and multiple sponsors' products, it was due Tuesday, wasn't it?'

'Which Tuesday was that now?'

'Lynette, do you know anything about a delivery?' interjected Holly.

'Well now,' said Lynette. 'There was this fellah who arrived a number of days ago, in a big van—'

'And?' asked Holly. Everyone was listening, including Serena, who took a pause from mixing another drink for herself.

'I think—'

'Yes, Lynette, go on,' said Valentina.

'A box or two were delivered into the yard, but we were that busy with filling the skip and clearing out all the—'

'Thanks,' Holly cut in, with a huge smile. That gorgeous smile he remembered. Oh my god, her lips. That was it: he could place Holly completely. Beneath the mimosa, which was like a golden tree of flowers in his memory. 'Valentina, Lynette and I will go to the yard and check on the delivery.'

'Or Preston and I can go?' suggested Valentina.

'What's so crucial?' asked Serena, settling down on the sofa.

'Our *Insta-Love* finalists drink exclusively from gold-plated goblets,' explained Valentina.

Serena instinctively pulled a face and the diplomatic Holly stepped in. 'How festive,' she said.

'Though as part of the contract, Jake and Olivia, our finalists, don't drink alcohol,' said Valentina, 'so the non-alcoholic Prosecco is key.'

'Winterbottom's Prosecco is the best, isn't it?' said Diane, who looked like she was enjoying her gin and tonic. 'We only have premium brands as dedicated show sponsors.'

'Anything to do with that PR fireball Gilda Winterbottom?' asked Serena

'No idea,' said Diane, who had little interest in the people behind her show sponsors as long as they coughed up the dough. 'I'm glad to say the no-alcohol rule does not apply to me.'

'Indeed, there's nothing like a warm brandy in the winter to set pulses racing,' said Serena, with a fabulously naughty smile.

'And while we're on the subject, the bedrooms aren't heated, are they?' asked Diane. 'I want to make sure Jake and Olivia are desperate for body heat.'

'With certainty,' said Holly, 'I can assure you that warmth

in the bedrooms is something you won't have to worry about.'

Preston noticed the shaggy-haired terrier hovering around his feet. Dogs had always liked him, even his grandma's mutt, who literally refused to let anyone else pet him.

'Do you have dogs, Preston? Daiquiri looks interested in your scent,' said Serena.

'I don't,' he said, looking down at his feet, 'but I love this little guy.' He bent down to pat Daiquiri on the head. Maybe he'd ask Holly for a tour of the house. Putting a piece of gum into his mouth, he felt a warm sensation on his ankle, reminiscent of a stepping into a puddle during a tropical storm. The warmth then turned to a sticky, wet feeling on his sock and he noticed everyone was giggling and staring at his feet.

'You've got to be kidding me?' Preston realised he'd been peed on and began to laugh.

'My poor darling,' said Serena sympathetically, welcoming Daiquiri to her arms. 'It's his little way of welcoming you. If you're lucky, Mr Tubbs will visit your room.'

'Mr Tubbs?' asked Preston, moving towards the fireplace to unlace his shoe.

'A cat,' said Holly.

'And not just any cat,' said Serena. 'He knows all that goes on here, and for him to leave a mouse at your door is the highest praise anyone can receive at Knockboden.'

Chapter Twenty-Nine

Apart from the bat droppings on the boxes, the cardboard was thankfully in good condition. Edwin said that having Benoît and François help had been like an early Christmas present. They were 'dab hands with the timber' and had already mended much of the fencing on the land. Within twenty minutes, under Edwin's instruction, they had moved several heavy boxes, emblazoned with *Insta-Love* sticky tape, from the coach house to the kitchen. Holly wondered about inviting the twins to dinner, but with the *Insta-Love* couple on the verge of arriving, perhaps one heartthrob at a time was better for all concerned at Knockboden.

In the kitchen, she couldn't resist taking a peek inside a few of the boxes. There were jars of Plum's Luxury Pudding Truffles in the first, boxes of Christmas Miracle Crunch in the second and the goldiest, gaudiest-looking goblets imaginable. Holly held up a flute and pretended to take a sip. 'Oh, you're a dream come true,' she said to the fridge, and then felt utterly ridiculous. Her mum would have loved the goblets; in fact, if she were here, she would have ordered a ton of them for her Christmas Eve drinks party. An immediate pang of guilt hit her stomach. Maybe she should tell Gabe the truth and ask him to gently break the news to their mother that the wedding had been cancelled, rather than postponed. But then Holly would have to rework her story about the amazing job in a secret location. This must be what people meant when they talked about a 'web of lies'.

'Aren't they quite something?' said a tall man, standing in the doorway and holding a brown suitcase similar to that of Paddington Bear.

Holly yelped and dropped the flute, which bounced onto the floor.

'They are plastic on purpose,' he said, pointing to the flute lying on its side intact. 'In case the Insta-Lovers have words and decide to hurl objects.'

This man had the most gorgeous aura. 'You must be Eric Rimmel,' she said, guessing he must be in his early seventies.

'Guilty as charged, ma'am,' he said, and popping his heels together, he gave a salute.

'I seem to have arrived either earlier than the crew,' he said, 'or later. Either of which is typical of me. I never could tell the time.'

Chapter Thirty

Eric walked into the drawing room and moved towards the fireplace, his hands extended to soak up the heat.

'My apologies for the delay,' he said, 'I hired the most beautiful Jag and couldn't resist stopping off at a village to meet the locals.' He looked from left to right. 'Has there been a murder or something? I feel like I've just landed into a scene from *Poirot*.'

'Eric, take a look behind you,' said Diane.

'Whoops,' he said. 'I'm terribly sorry, these boots seem to pick up grime. I think it's just earth from the avenue's edging, rather than doggie doo-doo.'

'Doggie doo-doo?' said Serena, looking amused.

'Perhaps doggie *don't* would be more appropriate,' he said, eyes widening.

'It took me ages to shampoo that carpet,' said Lynette, who was slicing a lemon at the drinks table. 'The beige colour came up lovely on it.'

'Don't worry,' said Holly, trying not to notice that

Preston was laughing. 'We'll let it dry, and then we can brush it off.'

'You'll forgive me staying glued to the spot,' said Eric, waving at Serena, 'but my feet are like icebergs. In fact, would you mind if I pulled off my boots?'

'Good idea,' said Lynette. 'Save me from more carpet-cleaning.'

'Holly, aren't you going to introduce Eric and Serena?' asked Preston.

'I'm so sorry.' She was feeling very put off by Preston. 'Eric, this is —'

'Lady Harpur's younger sister, I presume,' said Eric, gratefully handing his footwear to Lynette.

Serena seemed to visibly melt. 'I expected you to be American,' she said.

'I'm Irish to my cotton socks,' he said. 'Twenty years of LA and not a crack in my accent, though I am partial to an egg-white omelette, for my sins.'

'Which might explain why you are dressed in sportswear,' she said.

'This isn't sportswear, it's designer,' he said, unzipping the front of his shiny tracksuit.

'It looks like sportswear to me.'

'You're formal, aren't you? Mind you, you are a lady after all.'

'If you say so.'

'Don't worry, I like it,' he said.

'Like what?'

'Formality,' said Eric, focusing on Serena. It was like

166

watching an episode of *Insta-Love* for oldies. Holly could almost feel the chemistry between them. 'There's very little of it in LA, formality, it's all bare flesh and sneakers.'

'I think that's extreme, Eric,' said Diane, who had begun swiping through her phone.

'I don't think so,' he said.

'What's extreme?' said Farrah, flowing through the door in wide-leg woollen trousers and a tight jumper. 'The charm levels of my handsome co-presenter, perhaps?'

Eric embraced Farrah, double-kissing like a pro. 'Doesn't time just stop when you walk in the room?' he said. 'And haven't you had some lovely work done since I last saw you?'

'Eric, you are funny,' said Farrah, trying to laugh off Eric's suggestion. 'I'm on a new aloe vera regime – it's very effective.'

'Are you feeling rested?' Serena asked, eyes on Eric.

'Certainly,' said Farrah. 'I've been practising my plank.'

'Farrah's obsessed with Pilates,' said Diane.

'Is that so?' said Serena. 'What's that you're spraying?'

'I'm balancing my chakra,' said Farrah, who began spritzing orange-smelling blossom over Serena. 'Now, close your eyes and breathe it in.'

'Yes, I'm breathing,' she said.

'And what can you smell?' Farrah seemed to have transitioned into interview mode.

'I'd say it smells like something in the garden,' said Serena.

'That must be the orange blossom.'

'No, I mean the mushroom compost.' Serena opened her eyes and smiled at Holly.

'But you do like the smell?' asked Farrah.

'Like it? No, not particularly. Why don't you have a drink? Surely that will be better for your balance?'

'Thank you, but I'm full of aloe vera juice.'

'Nice,' said Diane, running her finger along the wood of the billiards table.

'Can you believe it's resting on a plinth of chalk?' asked Serena, who was longing for a ciggy. She'd have to belt outside in the next few minutes, but first she wanted to get a handle on the head of operations and make sure she was in love with Knockboden.

'Beats the hell out of the classroom chalk I knew growing up,' said Diane.

'The Victorians were practical people,' said Serena. 'To chalk the cue, you simply rub it on the plinth.'

Diane nodded; she seemed to know the game.

'That's my late husband, Desmond.' Serena pointed to a vast portrait of him, standing by his favourite dog, Smudge, before they married. The original had been long sold but Serena was satisfied with the copy. 'He frequently passed out on this table.' Serena leaned both hands on the green felt. 'It would be remiss of me not to tell you —'

'Go on,' said Diane.

'I've had a triangle full of lovers on this table.' Serena knew it was early to divulge, but she couldn't resist. It was a breath of fresh air having fresh blood in the house and she hoped they could bring joie de vivre to Holly; the thought of her wasting romantic opportunities really bothered Serena. She had been engaged at least once herself, if not twice, before actually going through with it. That was the whole point of being engaged: having time to work out if 'yes' really was the correct answer. If Serena could relive her twenties, and her thirties – bloody hell, that went for her forties, fifties and sixties too – she would do it all again, and again, and again.

'I love that,' said Diane. 'Would you be happy to tell that story to Farrah on film?'

'Delighted, and tell me, have you found Insta-Love?'

'Insta and Love are two words I intend to keep out of my private life,' said Diane. 'I'm all in for the show, and I'm full of hope that it's my retirement fund, because I sure as hell can't keep going at this pace for much longer.'

'I know the feeling,' said Serena, who realised they both needed this show to work.

Chapter Thirty-One

Holly stood by the Aga as Lynette whipped up a full Irish breakfast with unexpected precision. She claimed the secret was to fry everything in the same pan, at the same time, except for the baked beans.

'Whatever about *Insta-Love*, it's like *Love Island* in Turpinstown with the French twins on the loose,' said Lynette, shaking a pan of mushrooms into a dish. 'I hear there's more mistletoe than mascara in the pub, and that's saying something.'

Holly cringed at the thought of Preston. The first and last time they'd met was at Mariah's twenty-first birthday party in France. Whether it was the moonlight or champagne, there had been very little talking between them and a huge amount of kissing.

While Lynette piled sausages into another dish, Holly sent a text message to Mariah, who replied instantly.

'OMG, Preston?' wrote Mariah. 'The guy who crashed

my party when he got bored of his dad at the film thing in Cannes?'

'Yes! What were the chances of him landing here?'

'Still handsome?'

'Maybe.'

'And?'

'No comment,' Holly wrote, adding an emoji of a face with blushing cheeks.

Managing to avoid being crowned by Lynette with a 'Head Elf' sweatband, Holly carried an impressive platter of rashers, sausages, mushrooms and eggs along the corridor to the dining room. Even with oven gloves, she could feel the blistering heat coming through the material.

'Good morning, Holly, or should I say *bonjour*?'

Preston stood in the doorway, looking like a catalogue model in a cream Aran sweater with a beanie covering his tightly cut red hair.

'Good morning,' she said, wishing she had at least tweezed her eyebrows.

'Baby, it's cold outside,' he said, picking up a sausage in his fingers and then dropping it back onto the platter. 'Unlike that sausage.'

Holly sensed where this was going and cut to the chase.

'We did,' she said, 'briefly.'

'Did what exactly?'

She'd met his type before, he liked to stir the pot. 'We've met before,' she said. 'At the festival in Cannes and you scored a last-minute invitation to the twenty-first birthday party.'

Preston nodded in agreement. 'I'm impressed. And what was her name again? The birthday girl of Mougins?'

'Mariah,' said Holly. 'We were at uni together.'

'She wasn't as sweet as you, if my memory serves me.'

That was enough. Holly walked into the dining room and landed the platter on the sideboard hotplate.

'How about a cooked breakfast?' she said. Valentina and Eric were already seated, working their way through bowls of muesli.

Yes, he was good-looking, in a cheeky sort of way, and so what if they had snogged, but nothing more. Well, maybe a little more, but 'the line', as her mum liked to call it, had not been crossed. Holly's mum had encouraged her to have lots of boyfriends, most likely because she'd married her one and only relationship, who had turned into an ex-husband.

'I've got beans here,' said Lynette, arriving into the dining room red-cheeked and looking in her element with a tea towel over her shoulder.

'Yes, please,' said Preston, helping himself.

'Only two sausages?' said Lynette. 'That's a bit of a feeble attempt, but anyway.'

'What's with the half-drawn curtains?' asked Preston, getting back on Lynette's good side by accepting a large portion of baked beans.

'I gather it's to keep in the heat. It's a battle of wits between the draughts going up the chimney and those coming in through the old thin glass,' said Eric, who was delighted for Lynette to dish up 'whatever it is I deserve' for breakfast. By the looks of it, Eric deserved a lot, as he accepted three sausages and enough bacon to fill several BLTs before sitting back down at the dining-room table.

'The works for me, please, Lynette, and a glass of milk,' said Valentina. 'I've got to keep my strength up for the unexpected.'

'Morning, team,' said Diane, wearing a sleeveless Puffa jacket with a scarf wrapped around her midriff. 'Is this place like the North Pole or am I Mary Christmas?'

'The fire has been lighting since 6 a.m.,' said Holly apologetically. 'I'm sure things will warm up now there are more people in the house.'

'And not to bombard you with complaints,' said Diane, turning around and holding a navy towel in front of her. 'But this towel, from my bathroom, is wet.'

Lynette stepped forward and ran her hand around the edges. 'Sure, that's only damp.'

'The towel is damp?' asked Diane, her tattooed eyebrows raised to maximum capacity.

'You see, in Ireland, there's a difference between damp and wet, and that towel is definitely damp.'

'You are kidding?' Diane was not amused.

'Damp is very normal at this time of year, and it's mighty good for the immune system,' said Lynette, full of admirable gusto. 'How about a cuppa, or something stronger?'

'I'll help myself,' said Diane, heading straight for the coffee pot.

Even though she felt flattered, Holly chose to ignore Preston's ongoing stares from where he had perched himself at the table. 'Toast?' she asked Diane.

'Not for me, I'm part Italian, only coffee before 11 a.m.'

'And I'm part Danish,' giggled Valentina, 'so I'd love more bacon, please.'

'Would you pass the mustard, please, Valentina?' asked Eric. 'I want to create more heat on the plate.'

Next came Farrah, wearing a full-length orange velvet coat and gloves. 'Damn it, I forgot my spritzer,' she said, rummaging through her handbag.

'Going somewhere?' asked Diane.

'No, why?'

'Because you look like Joseph in his technicoloured dream coat.'

'I like to stay warm, that's all.'

Holly, topping up coffee, decided that Farrah was sweet. Her voice was gentle; she looked like she took her job seriously and wanted to please.

'Lucky for you, Farrah, wrinkles are less likely to puff up in the cold,' said Diane, with a thick layer of condescension. 'Valentina, this will make your job easier – makeup time can be halved.'

'You bet,' said Valentina, revelling in her boss's observations.

'Don't worry,' said Preston. 'These days we have filters on the camera, so the viewers will never see the reality – that's the irony of reality TV.' Cackling with laughter, he picked up a piece of bacon in his fingers and ate it all in one.

Holly noticed Eric studying Preston's face, and quickly realised why.

'Oh no,' winced Preston, spitting out his mouthful into a napkin. 'What was that?'

Valentina dutifully handed over her glass of milk, which he drank in one.

Eric was laughing his head off and slamming his hands with glee on the table. 'It's my favourite trick,' he said, wiping his eyes. 'Coating the reverse of the bacon with mustard.'

Preston seemed to find it funny. 'If I wasn't such a gent, I'd get you back.'

'Just getting into the festive spirit,' said Eric, still laughing.

'Boys will be boys,' said Diane, showing no sympathy for Preston. 'I'm taking my coffee to the drawing room, and Holly, make sure to give Valentina signed copies of the NDAs by lunchtime, please.'

'Sorry, NDAs?' asked Holly.

'Nondisclosures,' said Valentina. 'It can be tempting for staff to take pictures, you know, and sell inside stuff for cash.'

'I don't think that's going to be a problem,' said Holly, who could sense new potential in stress levels.

'Honey, that's what they all say,' said Diane, picking up a cup and the large coffee pot.

Chapter Thirty-Two

The internet was painfully slow compared to LA, but on the whole, Diane was pleased to be at Knockboden. It felt like the right location to host the *Insta-Love Christmas Special* and the beady-eyed portraits could only help in creating a sense of paranoia. There was nothing like onscreen meltdowns, and this was what she hoped for from Jake and Olivia. As she said to the network, 'Sometimes trashy TV is all you need.' For some reason, Diane revelled in watching relationships crumble in conflict.

One by one, the crew padded into the room, well fed and feeling the festive joys, thanks to the decorations. It took a lot for Diane to appreciate a Christmas tree, but Knockboden rustled up a wish inside her for something lovely to be tied up in ribbon.

'Okay, guys,' she said, clapping her hands for attention. 'To state the obvious, reality TV usually isn't written until the footage has been shot and edited, but as our *Christmas Special* is live—'

'We're in the hands of the Insta-gods,' said Preston.

'Let's hope they're in good form on the twenty-third' said Farrah, lying back on an armchair as Valentina applied makeup.

'December twenty-third, streaming at 5 p.m. from Ireland, to reach LA at 9 a.m., New York, 12 p.m., and so forth,' said Diane. 'I need your clocks synced like the smoothest ski run.'

'And speaking of skiing, I'd love a little powder, please, Valentina, when you're ready.' Eric looked at ease in his chocolate-leather trousers. 'Always put your best foot forward, that's my motto.'

'Unless you've been peed on by a canine,' said Diane, sitting on the club fender.

'That's so old, guys,' said Preston, 'change script.'

'Maybe we will,' said Diane. 'Valentina, bring us up to date on last week's episode. This will dictate how much scripting we'll need to do to spice up our grand finale.'

'Sure,' she said, holding a mascara wand like a mini microphone. 'Last week, the public voted for Jake and Olivia, or hashtag Javia, as they're known on Insta, to take the final step to the altar.' Valentina moved away from Farrah, whose eyelids had been wide open in expectation of mascara. 'At first, I'm not gonna lie, I thought hashtag Javia were a little chaotic, but I guess the public voted for them because they like the risk element.'

'Hell, yes,' said Diane, writing notes on her iPad with an Apple pen.

'Hashtag Javia hasn't been without their tensions,'

continued Valentina. 'There was the test where they had to guess each other's vision for living out their retirement—'

'Jake was so off the mark,' said Preston. 'Can't he read women? He thought Olivia wanted to live in a penthouse, when she wants the country.'

'And Twitter is fifty-fifty,' said Valentina, checking her mobile phone. 'For example, @partridgeinapeartree asks, "Can this chaotic couple really marry? Hashtag *Insta-Love*."' Valentina returned to Farrah with the mascara wand.

'But have they got between the sheets?' asked Diane. 'Isn't there even any suggestive footage to start a rumour?'

'Diane, these guys have their eyes on the prize and are prepared to wait for the big night when Jake puts—'

'Thanks Preston, we all have imaginations – we don't need you painting some kind of pornographic picture,' said Diane.

'I was going to say, when Jake puts his arms around his wife, having said I do, then they'll flash their bespoke watches and head for the skies in their dollar-sign sleigh.'

Diane wouldn't admit this to her crew, but the network had made it clear that a wedding failure would boost the ratings and her shares in the show. For the past two years, the weddings had resulted in *I do* from both sides. Three successful weddings would be too predictable.

'Thanks, Valentina,' said Diane, raising her voice to make sure Eric and Farrah could hear. 'Our job between now and the wedding ...' She checked her Rolex Sky Dweller. 'Which is in five days, will be to record some fabulous background commentary from Eric and Farrah, and tuck into tell-all interviews with the dreamboat couple.

'Delighted,' said Eric, slapping the thighs of his leather pants, 'I'm at the ready.'

'Me too,' said Farrah, wincing as Valentina applied mascara to her lower eyelids.

'And as for the confessionals, I'll be in charge of grabbing our Insta-Lovers one at a time for the "off the record" slot,' said Diane, wondering if Bruno Mars' latest Christmas album could bring an atmosphere conducive to kissing by a roaring fire. 'Valentina, I'll need you to keep track of continuity, okay? Wardrobe, makeup, props, etc.'

'You got it. I mean, I got it.'

'Just get it,' snapped Diane. 'And Preston, you've placed cameras in strategic positions?'

'You know it,' he said, with all the confidence of a cat ready for the cream. 'If Jake and Olivia can't resist, I'm going to know about it first.'

Chapter Thirty-Three

Manhattan, New York

'How have you been?' asked Tyrone, keeping his hand around his whiskey and soda.

'It's tough,' said Carl. 'I walked over to Madison Avenue, where she checked out the Barneys and Hermès windows every year without fail, even before meeting me, the guy who loves Christmas windows more than most.'

Tyrone laughed. He wished he could say something to help, but what could he do? The guy was in deep pain, but his attitude was incredible. Always smiling, chatty, asking Tyrone questions. Carl was like a real-life Santa Claus: he just gave, without any expectation. 'Then of course I had to go on to Fifth Avenue and take in Bergdorf's. Sheryl would have gone insane at the mannequins; they've really gone for it this year. One is even blowing bubbles. God, they look so lifelike.'

'Remember when we were walking toward the Rockefeller Center, and we heard 'You Can't Hurry Love'?'

'Hey, yes,' said Carl, lighting up. 'That was crazy. Looking up at the windows to see which apartment the singing was coming from—'

'And at the cars, to see which one was crazy enough to play music so loud.'

'Lo and behold, there he was, live on NBC, singing at the Rockefeller ice rink. God, and wasn't Phil right? It took another three years before I met Sheryl, and then it hit me. I fell hook, line and sinker.' He began to cry and smile all at once. 'I loved her, Ty. I never I thought I'd feel that way, and then boom – she walked in the door wearing that crazy outfit and I don't know how, or why, but she went straight for me.'

Tyrone could only smile, even though he wanted to give in and sob with him. But that wasn't his role. He was the friend who gave strength, kept Carl on top and convinced him to keep going, even when, during the early days, he had wanted to give up.

'And what about you, what's going on in Ireland?'

'What do you mean?'

'Come on, man, I wasn't born yesterday, I know there's someone.'

Shaking his head, Tyrone tried to shrug off the suggestion, but Carl knew him too well. 'She's fifteen years younger than me, okay? It would be crazy.'

'What's crazy? Love is crazy, that's what it's all about.'

'But with the house, the divorce, what to do with Mum ... you know, I think to even try something wouldn't be right.'

'Holly, right?'

'Yes.' Tyrone was surprised.

'You may not realise it, but you've mentioned her name more than once over the past few weeks.' Carl raised his glass to the bartender for refills, and told him to have one himself.

'Did I mention she recently broke off her engagement?'

'Broke off her engagement – okay, so she isn't marrying the guy, whoever he is?'

'Yes, but it shows that she's delicate, right?'

'And come on then, dish it up, there's more, I can tell. Did you make a move?'

'We kissed.' Tyrone felt like a fifteen-year-old. 'We were having dinner and I guess we got lost in the moment.'

'And?' Carl looked at Tyrone the same way he did every time Tyrone screwed up his love life. 'No, wait, don't even answer that, you told her it was—'

'A mistake,' said Tyrone. 'Yes, I did.' He slapped his thigh. 'I apologised immediately and she ran for it.'

'No surprise there.' Carl raised his glass to Tyrone, before taking a large sip. 'You know, buddy, it seems to me this Holly might be the first authentic woman you've ever got to know.'

'Yes, you're right.' Tyrone shook his head. 'She constantly tries to help everyone else but herself ... honestly, she's amazing.' He was surprised at himself for being so open about how much he liked her.

Reaching into his pocket, Carl took out a miniature book. 'I was going to wait and give this to you later, but Sheryl wanted you to have it.'

He passed it over to Tyrone. It was a miniature of *The Night Before Christmas*.

Sheryl had died the night before Christmas Eve. Tyrone thought back to the last conversation they'd had and burst into tears. 'She told me this was her favourite story.' He covered his face with his hands. 'I'm sorry, Carl, I'm meant to be cheering you up, but what you're going through … I wish I could do more.'

Carl smiled and reached over to gently press Tyrone's shoulder. 'She wanted you to have it. She adored you, Tyrone. Who knows, maybe one day you can read it to your kids?'

Tyrone got up from his chair and stepped around the table to hug his oldest friend. 'Thank you,' he replied. 'I don't really know what to say.'

'How about we post up with a stiff Manhattan at the St Regis? Then you can catch a flight to Dublin.'

'I can't just leave – there's still a lot to sort out here.' But he was considering it, telling Holly how he felt about her. Maybe not right away, but soon.

'Okay, well after everything is sorted then. What are you waiting for? It's Christmas – go get her.'

Chapter Thirty-Four

Knockboden, Ireland

Serena descended the stairs and felt a tiny flutter of Christmas anticipation in her belly. She couldn't remember the last time she'd felt that way. It might have been the time she'd longed for a Shetland pony, and her father had dressed up as Santa Claus, coming into the hall with Dumpling tacked up in a felt saddle and a head collar made from red ribbon.

She didn't do breakfast or early mornings, and she preferred to skip morning coffee and dive straight into a pre-lunch tipple. Arriving into the drawing room full of action gave her such a boost. Valentina was applying make-up to Farrah and Eric, while Preston assembled a large, furry-looking thing which might have been a microphone but looked more like a feather duster, and Diane paced the room wearing a headset and holding her mobile phone in front of her.

'Good afternoon,' said Serena, delighted when Eric rose to his feet and nodded his head in elegant respect. 'I trust you all slept and breakfasted well?'

'Like royalty,' said Eric. 'And how about you?'

'I tend not to talk about my night-time experiences,' she replied playfully. 'Unlike your reality stars.'

'Okay, Eric, you're up,' said Diane, nodding briefly at Serena. 'Let's shoot the intro, and I want you to reel in the viewers. Let them hear the nostalgia of Christmas past in your voice.'

'But surely I should be creating a feeling of excitement and expectation? I don't want viewers passing out over their eggnogs.'

'I think you misunderstand me,' said Diane. 'Our Insta-Lovers bring in the young, Farrah is for the stylish and, Eric, you bring a timeless grandeur. Everybody loves a grandpa, am I right?'

'Though sadly I'm not a grandpa,' he said, 'but not to worry.'

'You are not alone,' said Serena. 'My son and heir has so far produced zero offspring, and if he doesn't get a move on, this place will be bequeathed to the urns upon the mantel.'

Excusing herself, Diane left the room to answer her mobile phone and, within seconds, Valentina lay across the drawing-room floor, blowing on her fingernails. 'This polish is infused with crystal quartz – did I tell you?'

'Valentina, you do realise it's 3p.m.?' Preston wondered why Diane had hired her. 'We've got to run through Eric and Farrah's entire script before end of play.'

'It means that I can, like, carry around the energy of rose quartz wherever I go,' she said, as if choosing not to hear him. But the light coming into the drawing room was gorgeous; Preston didn't want to ruin his feeling of calm.

'While we're waiting for Eric and Farrah, could you pop my back?' Valentina stretched herself across the carpet and kept her nails hovering.

'Fine,' he said. Straddling her back, he applied pressure down her spine and moved slowly towards her shoulder blades.

'That feels so good,' she moaned in a way that seemed pretty over the top.

'I feel the same following my siesta,' said Eric, sauntering across the room. 'Apologies, am I disturbing?'

'No, Eric,' said Preston, getting onto his knees. 'Valentina's back was stiff, that's all.'

'Hey, Eric,' said Valentina. 'Your sweater is awesome.'

'That's kind. I've always liked the combination of leather and cashmere. It's a joy to wear heavy textures away from the glare of the Californian sun.'

'Isn't it, though?' agreed Farrah, who looked stunning in her knee-length navy polo neck.

Preston got to his feet just in time as Diane returned, looking irritable.

'Sorry, guys, but while you've been standing around chatting, I've been dealing with Mindeflicks.' Diane looked at Preston, as if to apologise for what she was going to say. 'The network is being a real bitch – they want to see our intros before we go live.'

'Well, I'm ready,' said Preston.

'As am I,' said Eric. He looked amused by Valentina, who was holding her nails up to the window.

'Valentina, what are you doing?' asked Diane.

'It's my rose quartz nail polish,' she said. 'It's, like, so energising.'

'Then use the energy to hand this script to Eric, will you?'

Putting on his thick-rimmed glasses, Eric began to study the sheets.

'Okay, Eric, we'll read through the lines first,' said Diane. 'No need to look at the camera. I just want to get a feel for the scene, then we'll bring in Farrah.'

'Sure,' said Farrah, smoothing down her long hair and then feeling her waist, as if to make sure it was still there.

'In the run up to our *Insta-Love Christmas Special*, the magnificent Knockboden Castle is decked with boughs of holly,' said Eric, his voice smouldering, 'and ticks every box when it comes to the cosy intimacy of a country Christmas.'

Preston raised the tripod to bring his camera to eye level with Eric. The old dog looked damn good on screen.

'Today, I'll be joined by the succulent Farrah Fox.' Eric paused.

'Eric, is there a problem?' said Diane.

'I'm not sure about the word *succulent*. Farrah isn't a *filet du boeuf*, as far as I'm aware.'

'Can we get through this script, please?' said Diane.

'Very well,' said Eric. 'Today, the *succulent* Farrah Fox—'

'Eric, just read normally, can you?'

'Today, the succulent Farrah Fox and I are meeting with Lady Serena Harpur to learn all about the history of this romantic Irish castle.' Eric spoke like a true thespian. 'This is the lady who had the freedom to let her passion cover the bills when times were tough.' He took off his glasses. 'You wrote this, I take it?'

'Yes. And ...?' said Diane.

'Isn't that rather dated? Surely there's a hefty amount of innuendo here?' he said.

'Audiences have a short span of attention. I want the script to shoot from the hip.'

'And my hips are robust,' said Eric, 'but I can't possibly ask Serena *that* question.' He pointed to his sheets.

'Farrah, what about you?' said Diane. 'Can you ask Serena this?'

Eric passed the sheet to Farrah, who sat down on the couch. 'I'm not sure,' she said. 'It's pretty intimate.'

'Serena sold her story to *Penthouse*, for Christ's sakes,' said Diane.

'Yes, but that was thirty years ago. Can't the dust stay where it is?' said Eric.

'Dust? This place is nothing but dust – it's gold dust, and that is what I want you to discuss with Serena as the sexy back story to the show. There is no room for a stale script. Serena sold her photos to *Penthouse* magazine to help pay the bills, and she and her husband had an open marriage. It's an old-fashioned *Insta-Love*. Don't you see? Serena had Insta-Love with many people in this very castle.'

'I'd like to point out that I'm susceptible to ghosts,' said

Eric, 'and I don't like the idea of finding one of Serena's ex-lovers at the foot of my bed.'

'Oh pur-lease,' said Diane. 'You are too much right now, Eric.'

'I am? I haven't heard that for a long time.'

'I need you all to trust my vision,' she said, 'because this adds layers to our hashtag Javia story.'

'How about we all cool down and move the shot to the couch?' said Preston. 'Eric, if you can sit beside Farrah? And Valentina, can you rearrange the cushions?'

Valentina picked up a cushion, dropped it and yelped.

'What now?' asked Diane.

'Take a breath, Valentina, take a breath,' said Preston.

'It's a cat,' she said, taking refuge in Preston's arms as Farrah leaped off the sofa.

Eric, still seated, turned to investigate behind the cushion. 'It's hard to tell,' he said.

'Hard to tell what?' asked Diane.

'It's hard to tell if his chest is moving up and down,' he said.

'You could hold a mirror up to its nose,' suggested Farrah. 'If the mirror fogs up, the cat is breathing. If you don't see any fog on the mirror, this is a good indication that the cat is dead.'

'Thank you, Farrah,' said Diane, rolling her eyes at Preston. 'Eric, I take it the cat's croaked it?'

'The cool room temperature has kept the body in good condition, though rigor mortis has set in.'

'Not Tubbsie?' shrieked Lynette, dropping a plate of

custard creams to the floor. She raced across the room, stood for a moment over the sofa and lifted the cat into her arms. 'He was the gentlest creature I've ever known,' she howled.

'Poor you,' said Eric, putting his arm around her shoulder. 'We're all so very sorry.'

Lynette was crying so much she couldn't get any words out. She nodded at Eric and left the room, cradling Mr Tubbs against her chest.

'Pets can break our hearts,' said Eric, as a gong sounded through the house.

Chapter Thirty-Five

Holly was decorating the dining room. She had gathered snowberries from the woods and put them behind the picture frames and around candlesticks holding the striped candles from Rory's Emporium. She hung embroidery hoop baubles from the chandelier, which gave an instant injection of jollity. Old-fashioned crepe-paper streamers gave pops of colour across the table, and the sideboard looked like a Christmas food hall display. Valentina had been up since first light arranging plates of star-shaped mince pies, gold-foiled plum puddings and chocolate truffles in silky green boxes, strategically placed next to a wooden board with smoked salmon, sourdough bagels and Christmas-tree-shaped crumpets.

'They'll be doing well to get through this lot,' said Lynette, laying the dining table for breakfast. 'I couldn't touch a bite last night, I was that upset about Tubbs.'

'It's sad,' said Valentina, scattering miniature chocolate puddings around the table, while Holly encouraged flames in the fireplace with old leather bellows.

'I just didn't realise you were sounding the gong,' said Holly, 'and holding poor Mr Tubbs in your arms at the same time.'

'You weren't to know,' said Lynette, breathing over a fork before polishing it under her arm. 'It's Serena I'm worried about. I've never seen her so quiet.'

Holly wondered if Tyrone would return before Christmas. Serena said he had a habit of taking an interest in Knockboden and then, the moment he landed in New York, forgetting all about it. Maybe this was one of those times, and Serena would receive a Brown Thomas Christmas hamper rather than her son's company, as she had predicted.

'Morning, guys,' Preston said, looking through a hand-held camera. 'Holly, we didn't see you last night.'

'I was with Serena and her gardener, Edwin, burying Mr Tubbs.'

'I'm so sorry,' he said, and sounded surprisingly genuine.

Holly continued blowing air into the fire with the bellows, even though it was flaming nicely.

'I remember when my mom's cat died, got run over by the mailman.'

'Awful,' said Holly, allowing herself to look at him.

'If there's anything I or the team can do while we're here, all you have to do is ask.' His eyes were piercing, so much so she had to look away.

'Thanks,' she said, returning to the bellows. Maybe she had been too hard on him. 'Was supper okay last night? Lynette brilliantly organised the takeaway from the pub, but it was quite last-minute.'

'It was delicious,' he said. 'Hot stew on a winter's night? What's not to love?'

Holly was about to respond when Diane marched in, looking stressed.

'Any sign of Javia?' she asked, checking her phone and taking pictures of the product on the sideboard.

'They're on their way,' said Preston. 'I just met them upstairs.'

'And footage in motion?'

'Sure is,' he said, 'and all law-abiding so far. Separate rooms, no corridor-creeping. Four days to go until their *Insta-Love* wedding.'

Diane grabbed a box of Christmas Miracle Crunch for the table and placed a couple of gold goblets next to it. 'They were told to be downstairs by 8a.m.'

'Jet lag, I guess,' said Preston.

'Jet lag is irrelevant in reality TV.' Diane checked her phone again. 'And, Lynette, you got the memo that sadly we won't be having your Irish breakfasts for the duration of our stay? Customers skip ads, so we need sponsors' food products in full view while filming.'

During the day, Benoît and François sauntered around Knockboden with armfuls of wood to keep the many log baskets full to the brim, but the arrival of Jake and Olivia put twinning on a whole different level.

'Hey, guys, I'm Olivia,' she said, matching Jake in oversized metallic sunglasses.

'Yo, we're the Insta-Lovers, if you hadn't already guessed,' he said.

'Good to see you, man,' said Preston. 'How was the night?'

'Out cold, dude. I can hardly remember sleeping, I was so tired.' Jake reached out to knuckle-punch Preston hello.

'Same,' said Olivia, whose voice was breathy and gorgeous.

Their teeth were white as snow, making Holly wonder if she should start using baking-powder toothpaste. She needed to stop wearing black all the time. It wasn't as if she was still in mourning for her past life and her broken engagement.

'Got a hangover, have you?' asked Lynette, arriving in with a pot of tea. 'Now, this tea is made from leaves, which is better for the morning after than a tea bag, you know the way.'

'Sure,' said Jake, laughing, 'though Olivia and I can't drink alcohol.'

'Then the tea can only heat you up, can't it?' Lynette always seemed to know what to say. According to Serena, when Lynette's husband ran off with his hairdresser, she had joked that it was her fault for suggesting he got highlights with extra trimmings.

'So what's with the shades then?' Lynette asked as she poured the tea.

'You know Fred Astaire? The dancer, with Ginger?' said Olivia, swishing her silky shoulder-length mane.

'I do,' said Lynette.

'He told Jack Nicholson that shades allow a little more privacy while in public.'

'Ah, right, so when you're famous and you're walking around the village, you won't have the hordes coming after you for a selfie?'

'Exactly,' said Jake. 'But we'd love a selfie with you, Linn, if you'd like?'

'You're very good but I don't do the socials, and my name's Lynette, by the way – that's Lynette, spelled with a Y.'

'Good to know,' said Olivia, with fingers tapping across her mobile phone. 'And, Lynette with a Y ...' She giggled. 'Can you be a sweetheart and let me know when my case arrives? It got lost in transit and the wonderful man at the airport told me it would be here by this afternoon. We gave him the postcode, didn't we, sweet pea?'

Jake was engrossed in his own screen, which was pinging like an Olympic ping-pong rally. 'What? Oh, sure, he said the luggage would be here today, but it's just one bag.'

'It's my wedding dress,' said Olivia, looking up from her phone. 'As in my bespoke original, along with five different outfits to wear between the ad breaks either side of the ceremony.' She squealed, pressing her mobile phone to her chest. 'Hashtag, dreamy, hashtag Javia, that's us, as in J - A from Jake, and V - I - A from me, Olivia.'

'Would you not put your own name first?' asked Lynette. 'O - L - I - A - K - E, hashtag oliake?'

'That sounds more like a form of conjunctivitis,' said Preston.

'I think we're good with hashtag Javia,' said Jake, before Olivia had a chance to say anything, 'but nice try, Lynette with a Y.'

Diane was just finishing a call when she returned to the dining room, clicking at Preston to get ready to film and giving a thumbs up to Jake and Olivia.

'Good to see you again,' she said, putting her phone down and patting their shoulders. 'Feeling good about things, guys? Feeling the *Insta-Love*?'

'You know it,' said Jake, raising his golden goblet and quickly returning it to the table. 'Hold on, baby, don't touch that,' he said to Olivia.

'What's the problem?' asked Diane.

'It's red-hot,' he said.

'That'll be the tea,' said Lynette.

'Why are you drinking boiling hot tea from a metal cup?' asked Diane.

'The contract says we're only to drink out of the goblets,' said Olivia. 'Isn't that right, babe?'

'Totally,' said Jake.

Diane bit her lip, shook her head and took a breath. 'Alright then,' she said, tapping on her phone. 'Here's an additional clause: hot drinks to be drunk in a cup, when not filming.'

'Cool idea,' said Jake. 'Or should I say, hot idea.'

Valentina exchanged the goblets of tea with goblets of orange juice.

'You know, sweetie, we won't even need mirrors when we get married,' said Jake, pouring Christmas Miracle Crunch into a cereal bowl. 'I just look at you, and there I am. Dark eyebrows, that button nose, and those lips, smooth and luscious.'

Olivia giggled. 'Wherever we go, people tell us we look alike,' she said, 'and it's true.'

'It's like we have a connection,' he said. 'Sometimes we look in each other's eyes and know what each other's thinking.'

'Can you save this for the camera, please?' said Diane. 'Preston, are we ready?'

'One minute,' he said, 'I'm just uploading a filter.'

'And you met on Instagram?' said Lynette, hovering around the table to get as much intel as she could for Serena.

'We're in *Insta-Love*,' said Olivia, 'and we're in *Insta-Love* with Ireland too.'

'It's so romantic, I could just die,' said Jake.

'Don't say that word around here,' said Lynette, tasting a Christmas-tree-shaped crumpet. 'The cat here headed off only yesterday.'

'You mean, he died?' asked Olivia. 'I love cats. I want to have a house full of them.'

'Cats? Sweetie, you don't love cats. I thought you couldn't stand cats.'

Olivia smiled lovingly at Jake, patting his shoulder. 'Oh, baby, I was talking about *Cats* the movie. I love kitty cats. I have a huge collection of Hello Kitty dolls in my room at Mom's house.'

Preston had started filming and looked like he was doing

a close-up on Jake's reaction. Holly was surprised by how professional he seemed.

'You know I have an allergy to cats,' he said, taking a sip from his gold flute.

'You can take tablets to get over those allergies, it's not a big deal.' Olivia continued to deliver her lines with a smile, though her eyes were becoming quite large with concern.

Jake stared into his Christmas Miracle Crunch. 'Maybe you're right,' he said, shaking his head. 'You know I'll do anything to be with you, honey, even if it means living in a room full of cats.'

Diane wrinkled her nose at his response and signalled to Preston to wrap up filming the segment.

Olivia smiled up at everyone. 'I'm sorry, we just get so absorbed in each other. It's like there's no one else on earth.'

'We know how to play the game, don't we, Liv? She had signed to an activewear brand before we met, and I've been associated with brands from salad cream to protein shakes.'

'We'd love to use a Montblanc to sign the registry,' said Olivia.

Jake seemed so exhilarated, it looked for a moment like he was going to lean in to kiss her. Diane's eyes lit up, but then he pulled back.

'Jake, not until we're married.'

They found it absolutely hysterical.

'Okay, guys, that's fine, we'll see you for date night.' Diane did not sound enthused.

'Spoken like a queen of socials,' said Jake, punching the air.

Chapter Thirty-Six

Manhattan, New York

The lawyers had been less difficult than expected as Tyrone leaped through the final divorce hoop, but he felt tired all the same. His now ex-wife had sat across the table from him. Previously he would have admired her beauty and tailored style, but this time he saw makeup and excessive jewellery. Something had changed. No matter how good the table in the restaurant or how silky the carpets in his apartment, his city life felt increasingly meaningless. He didn't even get a kick out of scoring new clients. He'd made his money, maybe now was the time to get out.

In duty-free at JFK, Tyrone couldn't resist buying a copy of *Doiley*, which ran the headline 'Geriatric Millennials – Compliment or Insult?' He didn't mind Holly being rude to him – he loved that she wasn't afraid to speak her mind. From a distance, he could see the amount of work she had done at Knockboden – the clearing, the cleaning, the Land

Rover jack beneath the bath … And then there was the kiss. He regretted the way he'd behaved about that. A bottle of Grey Goose and the biggest bag of M&M's could be his peace offering. Flying first class, with the promise of a flat bed and cotton pyjamas, could only add to his optimistic form.

Chapter Thirty-Seven

Knockboden, Ireland

With two days to go before the *Insta-Love* nuptials, Jagger rested his muzzle on a fur hat. 'You like your comforts, don't you, old boy?' said Serena, who was finding the guests irritating. This morning Diane had sent back a perfectly good fried egg, saying it was meant to be poached. Lynette didn't think there was much difference. 'An egg is an egg,' she'd said to Diane, who had replied with, 'And I've had an oeuf,' and walked out of the dining room. Thank goodness Serena had introduced Lynette to *Fawlty Towers*; useful training to deal with these high-maintenance individuals.

'Hey, Serena,' said Preston, breezing through the door and dropping a sack of potatoes onto the floor.

'Hay?' said Serena, remaining seated at the kitchen table with a copy of *The Irish Field*. There was a filly running in the afternoon and she liked to do her homework before placing a call in to the Turpinstown bookies. 'We're in a kitchen, not a stable, therefore the term *hey* seems rather daft.'

'Then, good morning,' he said, correcting himself and bowing his head. That would do, Serena thought, lifting her eyebrow at him. She needed to keep that boy in check.

'Is Holly not with you?' she asked.

'Sorry, Serena, that took longer than I thought.' Holly burst into the kitchen.

'My fault,' said Preston. 'I persuaded her to show me the round tower on the edge of the village. It would make an incredible backdrop for a murder mystery.'

'Speaking of backdrops,' said Holly, 'did you know the delivery of solar-powered Christmas lights has arrived? The twins have dotted them around the branches of the lime tree at the front. It's going to look so romantic for the wedding.'

'It was a neat idea of Diane's,' said Preston. 'Even better if the twins can add mistletoe.'

Holly seemed to be finding him very funny, Serena noted as she looked between the two.

'I'm going to set up in the library and check out the natural light with the cameras,' said Preston.

'Exciting,' said Holly. 'Serena, are you looking forward to your interview?'

Serena pulled a ciggie out from behind her ear. 'As long as it doesn't interfere with this afternoon's racing, it should be fine.'

'Diane's tightening up the script this morning,' said Preston, who seemed to be looking in Holly's direction more than necessary. 'We'll start filming around midday and wrap up for a late lunch.'

'I'll go to the drawing room with you,' said Holly, 'hopefully Lynette has lit the fire.'

'You'd look good on screen, Holly,' said Preston, winking at her. 'If I were producing, I'd add you to the mix.' Holly giggled as they both left the kitchen.

Yes, thought Serena to herself. She definitely needed to keep that boy in check.

Later, in her bedroom, Holly closed the shutters to stave off the cold. Five o'clock and it was almost jet black outside. She turned on a lamp by the mirror and took in her reflection. There was that familiar look in her eyes, the one that said *you know this isn't what we agreed to*. She felt confused about Preston, and guilty for finding him attractive. He'd really saved her bacon at dinner the night before, darting to the Aga, grabbing a tea towel and taking the weight of the iron pan from her. She had almost dropped it. Eight chicken breasts, stuffed with cream cheese, would have landed on the floor and been coated with Jagger's thick black hair. Preston had come to her rescue and dinner had been served. In passing, he'd said it was delicious. Not directly to Holly, but loud enough so that she could hear him as she cleared the plates from the dining-room table.

She had only just righted herself following the kiss fiasco with Tyrone; the last thing she wanted was another complication. She needed *Delay-Love*, not *Insta-Love*: she had vowed to give romance a wide berth. But then again, had she ever stuck to anything? This was her own private matter. What if she were to make a little effort with her appearance? She wasn't breaking anyone's trust. A little bronzer, perhaps mascara. Nothing dramatic, just a small nod to the old days, a dalliance with how she used to feel when striding down Molton Street on her way to a temping job. Turning heads.

But as was typical, just as Holly was beginning to feel good about herself, up flashed a WhatsApp message from Giles on her mobile phone. She put down the mascara wand to read the message. Leaving Giles unread would make her feel even worse. He said he was still missing her, but aside from that, he wanted to know if she'd like him to forward some post to her new address. Mariah was the most discreet person, so Holly wasn't at all surprised that Giles hadn't a clue as to where in the world she was. Could she be tempted to send him her address? No. It was over: that was that. She turned the mobile phone face down on the table and carried on with her makeup.

Chapter Thirty-Eight

In the kitchen, a Christmas playlist blasted out from Alexa as Holly added slender slices of courgette to a hot pan of rosemary oil. She felt brightened by her makeup, and her tweezed eyebrows. Condensation streamed down the windows as the cooking heated up the room.

'This place is turning into one of those fancy restaurants,' yelled Lynette from the back kitchen.

'That would be nice,' Holly shouted in response. She decided to add crushed garlic, and thyme if she could find it. Rummaging through a box of vegetables on the floor, she heard Lynette screech. Quick to respond, Holly stood up and walloped her head on an open cupboard door.

'Oh no,' she cried, cupping her hand over her left eye. She felt an immediate swelling and a kind of numbness beneath her hand.

'Don't worry, I'm fine,' said Lynette, coming into the kitchen. 'The lid came flying off the fabric conditioner, fast as you like.'

Holly knelt on the floor, feeling dizzy.

'God almighty, Holly, what are you doing down there?'

'I don't know,' she said. 'I'm afraid to move my hand.'

'What happened?' Lynette crouched down next to her.

'Hey, something smells good in here.' Preston's voice. That was all she needed. How embarrassing.

'I'm fine,' Holly whispered to Lynette. 'But can you ask him to go?'

'Preston, thank God,' said Lynette. 'We've got a poorly girl here.'

'Lynette, I'm fine.'

'You poor sweetheart,' said Preston. She could feel his hand on her back. 'Is it bad?'

'I don't think so,' she said. 'No blood, as far as I can tell.'

'How about we get you off the floor and onto the chair?' he said. 'And Lynette, sweetie, can you find some ice?'

'Leave it to me,' said Lynette.

Holly kept both her eyes closed, partly because she was mortified and didn't want to see the expression on his face. She heard a chair being pulled out from the kitchen table, and then felt his hands around her waist, lifting her gently up from the floor.

'Frozen peas,' said Lynette. 'That's all I can come up with for now.'

'Good thinking,' he said. 'And pass me a towel?' Holly felt like she was a patient in *Grey's Anatomy*, with Patrick Dempsey requesting implements from his assistant. Preston slid his hand over Holly's and replaced it with the bag of peas wrapped in a tea towel.

206

'Lynette, could you run to Valentina and ask for a tube of arnica? The sooner we can get it on, the better.'

'Will do.' And Lynette was gone in a second, leaving the kitchen silent except for the low spluttering sound coming from the Aga.

'This will help the swelling,' he said, almost in a whisper.

'Oh God, the courgettes,' said Holly, opening one eye to find Preston looking straight at her.

'It's all okay,' he said. 'Everything's going to be fine.'

Chapter Thirty-Nine

Jagger and Daiquiri were snoozing by the stove when Tyrone entered the hall at Knockboden The dogs leapt up and began barking in ecstasy as they circled his feet. The place looked incredible. Beyond his imagination even. He had to hand it to Holly: it even smelled different, and it wasn't just the spices in the hall or the pine from the trees. The air of chaos that had plagued the house had been lifted. Warmth came from the fireplaces and white fairy lights were twinkling on the Christmas trees. Tyrone almost felt like he had jumped into his own version of *It's a Wonderful Life*.

Tyrone pushed open the kitchen door and felt the wind rush out from his sails. A good-looking guy was standing close to Holly.

'Sorry, I'm ... I didn't realise—'

'Tyrone? No, it's fine,' she said, moving out of the man's way to look at him with one eye.

'What's happened? Holly, are you okay?'

'She's fine,' said the guy, who seemed weirdly territorial around her.

'I banged my head on the cupboard, and peas to the rescue.' Holly's voice seemed unusually high-pitched.

'Preston Minde,' said the guy, reaching out his hand. 'And you are ...?'

'This is my house. Tyrone Harpur.'

'Right, okay,' said Preston, picking up a wooden spoon to shuffle courgettes around the pan. 'Holly's doing just fine. I'll keep an eye on the stove.'

'Thanks, Preston,' said Holly, smiling up at him.

Tyrone couldn't believe how jealous he felt, like some kind of teenager. God, how did he manage to drive himself so crazy, time after time? He was like a professional in misunderstanding women.

'Okay, then,' he said, putting the vodka and chocolates on the table. 'Holly, I'm glad you're okay. I got you these.' He kept the magazine rolled up under his arm, feeling that the geriatric joke wouldn't quite land in front of Preston.

'That's kind,' she said. 'How did it go?'

'As expected,' he said. 'But I'm going to hit the hay. No point in fighting the jet lag.'

'Sleep well,' said Preston. 'Good to meet you.'

Tyrone did not like the tone in Preston's voice. In response, he pulled what he knew was his worst fake smile.

Chapter Forty

'Jake Lyford and Olivia Stack, known to their fans as hashtag Javia, have won the public vote,' said Eric, with his feet propped up on a coffee table. 'And as they prepare their marriage vows, the time is coming for their final step.'

Serena stood at the drawing-room door, watching the solo rehearsal.

'My apologies,' he said, getting to his feet and putting his iPad on the table. 'I didn't see you there.'

'No need to stir,' said Serena, noting a pair of cowboy boots by the fireplace. 'You're much shorter in your stockinged feet, aren't you?'

'I've always liked a good heel,' he said, returning to his chair.

The lawn had been lightly thawed by the midday sun, creating an attractive well of grass at its centre. The views from the drawing-room window never failed to warm her heart, much like the whiskey in the mahogany chest. Opening the lid, she found a pair of Waterford tumblers and a bottle sufficient for two generous measures.

'My husband always kept a bottle in here for emergencies,' she said. 'I've maintained the tradition.'

'Are we in an emergency?' Eric asked, walking towards her to fetch and carry the bottle and glasses to the table.

'Depends on whether you'd think it very naughty if I lit a ciggy?'

'I think it's okay to break the rules every now and then, don't you?'

'The doctors want me to cease smoking,' she said, as Eric took a lighter from his pocket and flicked it into a flame.

'And you're refusing to quit?' he asked.

'I've agreed to inhale every third puff.'

'Whereas my good lady doctor suggested I give up drinking.'

'And?'

'We agreed that I wouldn't drink at lunchtime,' said Eric, checking his watch. 'Whoops, slight boo-boo – it's a quarter to one.' He had a way of looking at her which made her feel joyful.

'Now, how about you tell me why on earth you're working on a TV series about teenagers not bonking before they marry? The youth are archaic, are they not?'

Eric laughed. 'To be on Irish turf, I'm anybody's. I couldn't resist the offer of a flight to Ireland, all expenses paid.'

'Don't you like LA?'

'Sure I do. I'm there for the lifestyle. Not that I drive around in a Bentley.'

'Who drives their own Bentley? If you have a Bentley, you must have driver.'

'True,' he said. 'Then let's say I chose LA because of casting and restaurants. I like to eat well, and if I work, I eat.'

'We all make our way, in whatever way we can,' she said. 'I've always felt bohemian, even though my parents couldn't stand it.'

'And the *Penthouse* shoot, how was that? Ground-breaking for an Irish woman to do something like that in those days.'

'Desmond had put what money was left from his inheritance into stocks a year before he died.' Serena looked at the tarnished clock on the mantelpiece. 'He lost it all within a couple of months. Can you believe it?'

'That's tough,' said Eric.

'But he was one of the few Irishmen to receive the full honours of a British knighthood, because he also held British citizenship.'

'Which explains why you are a lady, though I suspect you always were,' said Eric.

'His knighthood was largely in recognition of his work in raising thousands of pounds for the causes of culture and charity across Ireland, north and south.' Serena reached for her necklace. 'He gave me this the day we married.'

Eric got to his feet and peered over her. 'An anchor,' he said. 'A sign of safety, I believe.'

Serena pressed the pendant to her chest. 'I feel as if we must have met before, you and I.'

'No,' he said, 'because I'd know if we had, I can tell you. I'm like an elephant when it comes to remembering people.' Eric took a pair of glasses from his pocket and put them on for about six seconds, and took them off again. 'Tell me, Serena, were you always aware of your beauty?'

'Oh yes,' she said, without having to even think about it. 'From the word go.' She was about to tell Eric about her time as a deb when Diane came into the room like a small hurricane.

'Sorry to interrupt. I'm scanning for shoot locations.'

'Fine,' said Serena. 'I would offer you whiskey but I'm out of glasses – and whiskey, for that matter.'

'No thanks,' said Diane, glaring at Eric. 'I do like you by the fender, Serena. The armchair suits you.'

'It was my mother's favourite,' said Serena.

'A story in itself,' said Diane. 'Perhaps you could –'

'She died in this very chair.'

'Oh, I'm sorry.'

'No need, she'd had enough by then. Nodded off just after breakfast. We really had all necessary visits complete by afternoon tea.'

Diane held out her fingers like pistols and pointed them to the ceiling. 'Hold that thought, Serena. Let's get the camera rolling, if I can find out where the hell Preston is.'

'Put another log on the fire and refresh my glass,' said Serena, resting into the cushions, 'and I'll gladly sit here for the rest of the day.'

Chapter Forty-One

'It feels so Christmassy,' said Olivia, filming the popcorn garlands on the hall tree. 'It's just all so gorgeous, and *so* original.'

'How can you view the tree with sunglasses?' said Serena, coming from the drawing room. Before Olivia could answer, she added, 'That was a statement, not a question,' and then made a beeline for her study.

'Any sign of your dress?' asked Holly, stepping in to smooth over Serena's impatience.

'They've promised it for this morning.' Olivia hovered over her gold-tipped boots to film her toes tapping the floorboards.

'Wow, you're very calm,' said Holly, trying to work out if Olivia's eyelashes were real.

'I trust in the universe,' she said, 'and I've prayed to Saint Anthony, just for backup, so I'm all good.'

Holly was thinking that maybe she should take up trusting in the universe.

'I'm going to do a slow dress reveal on Insta Live.' Olivia held up an imaginary dress. 'First the hem, and then I'll work my way gradually up as far as the midriff, with a final reveal on my wedding day.' She gave a squeal of delight. 'Come in for a selfie, Holly.'

'I don't really think—'

'Come on, my fans will love you. I'll call you my Christmas Holly!'

Olivia pressed her cheek next to Holly's and began clicking her tongue.

'Olivia, what's that noise you're making?'

'It's what I do when I'm having my picture taken.' She put her mobile phone on the floor and stood opposite Holly. 'Press the tip of your tongue to the roof of your mouth, and smile at the same time.' Holly did this and could hear dolphin-like sounds in her ears. 'It totally works, and makes your smile so *extra*.'

Tyrone walked downstairs looking very amused. 'I didn't realise marine life was part of Christmas tradition?'

'You should try it, Tyrone,' said Olivia, picking up her mobile phone. 'Can I take a picture of you with Holly?'

'If you like,' he said.

'That's it,' said Olivia, directing Tyrone and Holly to stand in front of the Christmas tree.

'Hold on, are those lights flashing again?' asked Holly.

Tyrone put his arm around her. 'You'll have to teach me how to stop the lights switching programmes,' he said. 'You seem to be the only one around here who knows how to do it.'

'It's easy,' said Holly, as Olivia encouraged them to make dolphin sounds and smile.

Tyrone looked at her. 'If you don't watch out, you'll become indispensable around here.'

'Perish the thought,' she said, before returning to her dolphin imitation.

'Gorgeous,' said Olivia, turning to Preston as he arrived downstairs with the camera on his shoulder. 'How about I teach you my trick on how to have a gorgeous camera smile?'

'If you want to sound like a dolphin, now's your chance,' said Tyrone.

But Preston didn't seem to hear them as he pointed his camera to the ceiling, where water trickled through the rose.

'Oh Christ,' said Tyrone, standing in the hall with his arms folded.

'OMG,' said Valentina, coming from the drawing room with her makeup bag. 'What's going on?'

'Someone has obviously taken a bath in the old dressing room.' Serena stood outside her study, almost expressionless. 'Why should I be surprised – it only takes an idiot to pull the plug from a bathtub meant to be out of use.'

Holly and Lynette placed towels on the hall floor as if they were setting up an indoor picnic, while everyone else stood in a circle looking up to the rose in the ceiling.

'Massage, anyone?' asked Lynette, wiggling her fingers in the air. 'Good for stress relief?'

'What about Edwin and those French twins? Can't they sort it out?' asked Serena.

'Must you?' said Tyrone, as Preston continued to film the ceiling.

'Keep rolling, Preston, this can be a nice backdrop to the Irish castle love story,' said Diane.

'Has a pipe burst?' asked Eric, standing next to Serena.

'It's the contents of the bath, nothing more,' said Serena 'The water will stop in due course.' And she was right: the water gradually reduced to drops. 'It's hardly surprising, when I'm forced to sticky-tape over structural problems.'

'Don't you get involved in these *structural problems*, Tyrone?' asked Diane, like she knew she was stirring things up.

Holly looked at Tyrone, wondering how he was going to react. 'Preston,' said Holly, 'maybe it's better not to film for the moment.'

'It's no big deal,' said Diane, signalling to Preston to keep the camera rolling. 'It might not even make the cut, but it's good background.'

'And here we all are,' said Tyrone, 'watching the water seeping out from the plasterwork.'

'Hey, Tyrone, settle down, man?' said Preston, putting down the camera.

Holly was about to say something when Tyrone turned on his heel and walked out to the front hall.

'Where are you going?' Serena yelled after him, but there was no reply.

'Is there something we can help?' asked Benoît and François, holding up a walkie-talkie each. 'Lynette called about a flood – you need a boat?' They smiled like angels.

Valentina stepped forward, seemingly mesmerised. 'You two, you're actual twins?'

Chapter Forty-Two

The vision for Jake and Olivia's date night was minimalistic at first, focusing on candles and glasses to allow the Insta-Lovers' glamour and beauty to light up the dining room. However, when Diane realised Jake and Olivia would be separated by ten feet of carved cherrywood as they dined at each end of the table, she changed tack. In addition to the food provided by the holiday sponsors of the *Insta-Love Christmas Special*, Valentina filled the table with extravagant bling brought in from last-minute sponsors, including an ink-blue linen tablecloth with silver stars and handmade Christmas crackers containing pure leather wallets, silver cufflinks and enamel bangles. A pair of twenty-four-carat gold-plated pine cones, which doubled up as salt and pepper shakers, adorned both place settings, along with a twenty-foot garland of leaves and pine cones painted in frosted silver. The results were stunning.

'You're all miked up?' asked Diane, accompanying Olivia to the dining room.

'I am, thank you. Preston has been brilliant.'

'Great, and you can think of me as a shadow,' said Diane. 'I find it can be helpful to prompt a few conversations, you know? How about asking Jake if he's proposed to anyone before, unless you've asked him that already?'

'No, I actually haven't,' she said. 'I guess I would be interested to know.'

'Then try it out,' said Diane.

'I'm feeling a little nervous,' said Olivia. 'Can I get some fresh air before I sit down?'

'Sure, take your time,' said Diane, happy to have the opportunity to put some unsettling questions into Jake's mind.

The lighting in the drawing room was low and sexy. After their date, Diane had every intention of getting the Insta-Lovers in here alone – alone except for the cameras, that was.

'Looking sharp, Jake,' said Diane, noticing his authentic bow tie. 'You tied that yourself?'

'I took a course on YouTube,' he said, looking confident in his velvet dinner jacket paired with metallic gold trousers. 'I want to make every effort to impress my future wife.'

'Of course you do.' This show had better be third-time lucky, so she could cash in her shares.

'Check in before you get going with those vows,' said

Diane. 'I'd love you to get quite intense in the dining room, really show your commitment to what you're doing. I think the viewers will like it.'

'You're the boss,' said Jake, making an 'a' sign with his fingers. 'What's good for the ratings is good for hashtag Javia, right?'

Serena stood outside the front door, her breath clouding out in front of her. If that was a shooting star she'd just seen, she'd make a wish, but it was more likely to be a satellite. Modern technology was such a bore.

'I'm sorry,' said the female half of the online couple, 'I didn't realise you were here.'

'I'm here for one of my alfresco smokes,' said Serena, lighting a ciggy. 'I'm not meant to smoke inside, despite this place being my home.'

The girl smiled. She seemed sweet, though her coat, reminiscent of a pink bin liner, was a mistake.

'Remind me of your name?'

'Olivia.'

'You are terribly pretty.'

'Thank you.' She beamed another very white smile and placed her hand on her heart.

'Why are your clothes so tight? It looks like you're wearing a wetsuit.'

'Jake and I feel tight clothes connect us to ourselves.'

'Fair enough, but aren't you chilly?'

'Not at all.' She laughed. 'We're wearing slimline thermals.'

'What?'

'They're by a vegan label called Fauxfurlines,' said Olivia, making a kissing sound with her lips. 'Hashtag collaboration.'

'Furry underwear?' said Serena.

'Once we're Insta-Married, they're sponsoring us, and Jakey and I will be on billboards in NYC and LA.'

'And in return, they give you free furry undies?'

'Sure, and our followers will go through the roof.'

Serena's mind began to race. Perhaps sponsorship and this collaboration business could work for her? She could get a dog-food brand to sponsor Jagger and Daiquiri, and what about a gin brand?

'Could you line up some connections? I can still pose and I'm certainly not shy.'

'You don't think the sequins are too much?' asked Farrah, standing in front of the camera.

'You're gorgeous, Farrah, honey, the camera loves you,' said Preston.

'Yes, a delight,' said Eric reassuringly. 'You give sequins class.'

'And we're rolling, Preston, and ... action,' said Diane.

'*Insta-Love* is a Mindeflicks original,' said Farrah, pushing out that energy, 'and Mindeflicks is a subscription streaming service and production company founded by Charles W. Minde.'

Diana gave the 'cut' signal to Preston. 'Good, Farrah, let's continue and get this in the can before we film dinner.'

'Valentina, my nose,' said Farrah, pointing to her face. 'Powder, sweetie, powder.'

Valentina could move it when she wanted to, and duly fluffed the makeup brush around the nose designed by the finest surgeon in Beverly Hills.

'And action,' said Diane.

'At home, you've been following our Insta-Lovers as they've endured weeks of tests to prove how willing they are to wait and only love for real once they say I do.' Farrah did a little dance when she said 'for real'.

'Don't dance, Farrah,' said Diane. 'If I wanted a dance, I would have called on Beyoncé.'

'Shall I continue?' asked Farrah, who, to be fair, took direction well.

'Please,' said Diane, 'and I want you to raise the stakes and use that breathy voice of yours to build drama on what's coming.'

'You got it, Diane,' said Farrah.

'Jake Lyford and Olivia Stack, known as hashtag Javia, have been voted this year's favourite *Insta-Love* couple, by you, the gorgeous public.'

'Cut,' said Diane. 'Now to you, Eric. Bring the emotion home.'

'In a remote Irish castle, our *Insta-Love* finalists must journey through the romantic corridors of mistletoe and festive lights,' said Eric, 'monitored by cameras in unspecified locations. There is no hiding from love on *Insta-Love.'*

'That's right,' said Farrah. 'Will they give in to the temptation of Christmas passion, or will they say "I do" and win the prize money of a hundred thousand dollars and lucrative sponsorship deals, including a beach house and an apartment in Houston, Texas?' Farrah turned dramatically to her co-host. 'Eric, what do you think?'

Eric did a little jog on the spot to gear himself up until the camera turned to him.

'Let's get our Insta-Lovers to the church on time, and find out if they have rung the church bells or resisted the melody,' said Eric, punching the air in his designer velour tracksuit. 'Will hashtag Javia ditch, or will these Insta-Lovers hitch? Stay tuned, live at this Irish castle, 12 noon, Eastern Time.'

'And cut,' said Diane. 'Let's film dinner and see just how crazy in love these guys really are.'

Chapter Forty-Three

Church candles brought an angelic feeling to the dining room of Knockboden, but the same could not be said about the sponsors' food. Ted's Turkey Joints and Snowball Potatoes by Julie Dorell, judging by the smell, were going to be inedible. At best, the texture of the turkey could be described as cardboard, and the potatoes felt more like hard cricket balls than snowballs.

Diane directed proceedings from the fireplace, using a pen as if she were conducting the Insta-Lovers on their TV dinner date.

'Welcome, hashtag Javia,' she said, her voice tight. 'Jake and Olivia, once your dinner plates are in front of you, we'll start filming.'

'Sure,' said Olivia, sweeping lip gloss across her mouth and calling to Jake seated at the other end of the table. 'Can you hear me down there, sweetie?'

'I can read your lips,' said Jake, pulling either side of his bow tie. 'I've got twenty-twenty vision for you, baby, and that's a good line, I'm going to use it. Okay with you, Diane?'

'Of course, but make sure you don't eat the food,' she said. 'Just play with it – you can eat dinner later. We want the mike to be clear, so sounds of munching on air are not an option. Get it?'

'You bet,' said Jake.

'And action.'

'Jake, sweetie, can you hear me all the way over there?' asked Olivia, sweeping white polished nails through her hair.

'Thank God for my eyesight, because no matter where I am in this huge Irish castle, I can see you through my twenty-twenty vision, sweetheart.'

'Ted's Turkey Joints are so good,' said Olivia. 'I'm, like, ready to lick my fingers they're so good.'

'And the Snowball Potatoes by Julie Dorell?' said Jake. 'Wow, they're, like, out of this sweet world.'

'And cut,' said Diane. 'Guys, can we play the subtlety card, please? You've got to space out the sponsor compliments – viewers don't want us cramming ads down their throats.

'But I'm starving,' said Jake. 'Can't I put a mouthful of Ted's Turkey down my own throat?'

'You can eat afterwards,' said Diane flatly. 'Let's go again, and this time pop a Winterbottom's cork.'

'Can't we have booze? I could really do with just one drink,' suggested Olivia.

'Read the contract,' said Diane. 'No booze.' She raised her pen in Preston's direction. 'And action.'

Jake stood up and grandly took a bottle of Winterbottom's Non-Alcoholic Prosecco from the ice bucket on the table.

The foil and wire had been removed for filming ease. Slipping his rose-gold aviator sunglasses down from his forehead, he placed his palm over the cork and twisted the bottle until it popped.

'Another skill I learned on YouTube.' Jake walked to Olivia's end of the table and poured Prosecco into her golden goblet. 'This Winterbottom's Prosecco is so good.'

Diane signalled with a thumbs up to Preston and then twirled her fingers at Olivia.

'Thanks, sweetie,' said Olivia, 'and before we toast, can I ask you something?'

'Uh huh,' he said, taking a sip of Prosecco and returning to his seat.

'You know about your relationships before we met?'

'I do,' said Jake, gazing down at the turkey leg, now cold, on his plate.

'Did you ever propose to anyone before me?'

Jake took a sip of Prosecco and shook his head. 'That's such a weird question,' he said, laughing. 'I mean, I proposed to my mom when I was, like, six years old.'

'You know what I mean, honey bunny. You haven't actually proposed to anyone else, have you?'

'And cut,' said Diane. 'Well done, you hit that nicely, thanks, and you can tuck in. Preston, let's go.'

'I know what Diane's playing at,' said Jake. He had taken a mouthful of turkey at least four minutes ago and was still chewing.

'What's that, babe?'

'She wants to put a wedge between us.'

'I'm sure she doesn't,' said Olivia, politely attempting to eat the hard-as-rock potato with a knife and fork.

'Diane asked *me* to ask *you* about your mom coming to live with us in the future.'

'There's no way that's ever happening,' said Olivia. 'You have no idea what a fireball my mom is. She'd be on your case the whole time and totally wouldn't go for the tattoo on your back.'

'Right?' said Jake, who looked relieved.

'You'd have to keep your shirt on the whole time, honey,' she said. 'We couldn't do any Insta Lives unless you were totally covered up.'

'That's no way to live, is it, sweetie?'

Olivia took a sip of Prosecco and nodded frantically. 'We are so on it, babe, our heads are so focused. Let's stay alert and get to the altar.'

'A strong woman is such a vibe,' he said, patting his heart.

'It feels like a crazy fairytale,' said Olivia. 'How about your vows? Have you written them yet?'

'I have just one line,' said Jake. 'Cheers to for ever, to freedom, to the two of us.'

'Of course, honey bee,' she said, squeezing her lips together and blowing kisses to him.

Valentina sauntered into the room. 'Diane has asked if you two would like to curl up in the drawing room? You can have it all to yourselves?'

'That's sweet,' said Olivia, 'but we both have a crazy

amount of posts to make, so I'll be going straight to my room.'

'But please do thank Diane from us,' said Jake, 'and pass on the message that Olivia and I are hashtag HappyToWaitUntilOurWeddingNight.

'One more thing,' said Olivia. 'Could I possibly have a hot-water bottle tonight? I was a little cold last night.'

'Sure,' said Valentina, closely watching the expression on Jake's face.

Chapter Forty-Four

'I'd say you'd find more bum coverage on a *Love Island* bikini,' said Lynette, holding up a pair of skimpy knickers rumoured to belong to Farrah Fox. The Aga was covered in underwear, from boxer shorts to lacy thongs. Holly's eyes were drawn to the Marvel-themed boxer shorts and she found herself wondering if they belonged to Preston or Tyrone, then decided that the blue-check pair looked more like Tyrone's style.

'Lynette, how about we send the next load of washing to Turpinstown?' said Holly, pairing socks together. 'This can't have been part of the agreement.'

'It's Christmas week, Holly. There's no way we'd get it back in time.'

'Then how about we just offer to do one more wash of essentials?'

'You mean smalls?' said Lynette. 'That's what my granny always called them, and I tell you, she wouldn't believe how small the smalls are these days. Sure, you could floss your teeth with one of them silk thongs.'

Holly and Lynette were howling with laughter when Valentina arrived, holding her iPad like a page-boy carrying a ring to a groom at the altar.

'Hey, girls. That's a wrap on date-night filming. How are we here?'

'We're fine,' said Holly, slightly gritting her teeth. Valentina was okay, but the crew had a habit of arriving in the kitchen unannounced.

Valentina circled the kitchen table and eventually said, 'Silk milk.'

'Sorry, what?' Holly pulled on an apron to seem busy and hurry this visitation from Valentina along.

'Hot and frothy milk,' she said, 'for Preston's morning coffee. Can you make sure that's available for breakfast tomorrow morning?'

'Yes, of course. Hot milk for breakfast. Easily done,' said Holly.

'Preston's on a call with his dad right now,' Valentina continued. 'You know he used to be an actor?'

'I didn't,' said Holly, opening the Aga and lifting out a tray of roast potatoes. 'Lynette, did you?'

'No notion,' she said.

'In his defence, just because an actor isn't right for a role, it doesn't mean he isn't talented.'

'He's definitely got the confidence,' said Holly.

'Yes, but losing out on a blockbuster gig is always a setback. There are plenty of victims like that in Hollywood circles, and for some it's a major blemish on a résumé.' Valentina smiled. 'But not Preston. He's got his looks, and you know what, he works for his dad, so it's no biggie.'

Valentina had been resting her pert backside against the kitchen table but then, to Holly's relief, made her way towards the door. 'I'm glad we had this talk, you know?' she said.

'What talk, Valentina?' asked Holly. She was not feeling very patient.

'Letting you know that Preston and I, well … you know?'

'Oh, okay,' said Holly. 'That's cool.'

'Yes, though not on location, but in LA, away from the camera lights, you know?'

'Fine,' said Holly. 'I'm off men, Valentina. You have nothing to worry about.'

'I wasn't, like, worried, Holly. I just thought it was fair to let you know.'

'I'll consider myself told then.'

'I did mention that we'll need a cake for tomorrow night, didn't I?'

'Cake?'

'Didn't we tell you? It's Preston's birthday.'

'I don't think I'll have time to—'

'Chocolate, please,' she said, 'that's his favourite, and sparklers, Preston loves sparklers.'

'What? No, I don't have sparklers, but—'

'I'll leave it with you, okay, sweetie?' said Valentina, in a tone of perfect condescension.

Relief wasn't a strong enough word to describe Holly's

sentiments when Valentina left the room. She felt a breeze and wondered what next, only to find the hens beneath the kitchen table.

'You two, who left the door open?' she said, pulling out a chair. Pooping before their exit, the birds moved across the kitchen like red, feathery dinosaurs.

'Gross, gross, gross,' said Holly. In the absence of any kitchen paper, she grabbed a tea towel and swept the poop up from the floor.

'Just as well the health and safety bloke hasn't been to call,' said Lynette, plunging a spoon into a bowl of lemon curd and taking a very large mouthful. 'I knew there was chemistry between you two.'

Holly was going to deny it but had a moment to think as Lynette took another spoonful of lemon curd.

'Fine,' she said.

'Ha!'

'But, it doesn't mean there's anything going on.'

'Who says?' Lynette's eyes lit up.

'I say, and anyway, I'm here to work, this my job.'

'Maybe *Insta-Love* is contagious,' said Lynette. 'Just as well we didn't skimp on the mistletoe, then, isn't it.'

Chapter Forty-Five

The chosen backdrop for the *Insta-Love Confession Booth* was Serena's study. The room was crammed with books piled on top of books, upon which balanced silver-framed photos and statuettes of horses. Diane was tempted to include a drinks trolley in the corner of the room, laden with ancient bottles of weird concoctions, but keeping Winterbottom's Non-Alcoholic Prosecco in mind, she thought better of it.

Diane wanted to have the upper hand, commanding Olivia's responses as best she could. She sat like a tennis umpire on a high stool, while Olivia sat in a green leather armchair which reeked of dogs.

'Are you wearing waterproof mascara?' asked Valentina, powdering Olivia's nose before sweeping her hair back with smoothing tongs.

'No need,' she said. 'I won't be crying.'

That's what she thought. Diane had every intention of drawing emotion out of her like a string of vegetarian sausages from Craig's in West Hollywood.

'Obviously the viewers will only see you, Olivia, and hear

your voice in this segment, so don't worry if my questions seem random.'

'Does this room seem warmer than the others?' asked Olivia, adjusting the collar of her jacket.

'Not really,' said Diane. 'It's as close to the Ice Age as everywhere else in this house.' She nodded at Preston to proceed with filming. 'Olivia Stack, one half of hashtag Javia, here we are in a grand old Irish castle, where you are due to say "I do" to Jake Lyford at the altar. How do you feel about becoming someone's *wife*?'

Olivia looked impressive, almost professional. 'I've always been a fan of Beyoncé,' she said, pausing for a breath. 'And I'm pretty sure she told Oprah that the best advice she'd received was to "make sure you have your own life, before coming someone's wife".'

'Nice,' said Diane.

'And I've done that,' said Olivia. 'I have my life, I have thousands of followers across my socials and now I'm ready for my journey with Jake. He's my lifer.'

Diane wasn't getting the reaction she wanted. 'You don't feel nervous at all?' she asked, trying a different angle.

'Sure I do, but not enough to tempt me to duck out. I signed up for this and I'm ready. My head is with him. I'm ready for hashtag Javia to become official on a marriage registry.'

'What about your wedding dress? There are rumours it was designed by Vera Wang.'

'As all the best politicians say, I can neither confirm nor deny the rumour,' said Olivia, sitting forward with enthusiasm, 'but I can tell you that it's gorgeous. There are silk buttons the whole way up the back, the most exquisite lace across the neck—'

'But isn't it missing?' Diane put on her deepest look of concern, and it worked. Olivia immediately looked anxious.

'The airport authorities swore they'd deliver yesterday morning, but there is still no sign of it.'

'That's *very* stressful,' said Diane. 'How do you feel about it?'

'I'm pissed,' said Olivia. 'I'm getting married in two days' time and I haven't yet been able to do my countdown reveal of the fabric.'

Diane nodded her head. 'Would you like a glass of water, sweetie? You look like you're getting upset.'

'No, thanks, I'm just going to have to hope and pray,' she said, filled with vulnerability, until she put in another request. 'I'm concerned that the yellowing marble around the fireplace is clashing with the green chair. Can we re-shoot?'

Diane had failed to squeeze as much as a tear out of Olivia. She was tempted to bring in Eric to handle Jake's confessional, but the risk of him rambling off down memory lane was too high. Her new tactic was to move the confessional location to the billiard room, where Jake could take action shots as he responded to her questions.

'You're a good-looking guy,' said Diane, matter-of-fact, 'despite your Christmas sweater.'

'You don't like it?' he said, pushing out his chest to show off the green and red sweater with a gold bow across the front. 'It's fun, and that's what I'm all about.' With a grin, he aimed his cue at the target ball.

'You seem confident.'

'I've got to back myself,' he said, pocketing the ball, 'and I'm not afraid to go after my emotions.'

'Do you want kids?'

'I'm still quite young,' he said, chalking the tip of his cue. 'I want to travel the world, pursue a huge career in representing brands and please myself.'

'You're set on a life without kids, then?'

'I wouldn't say that. I come from a big family. I'm always around my cousins and I'm used to that, but for now, it's all about *numero uno mio*.'

'And what about the L word?' asked Diane. 'If you're going to marry Olivia, then you love her, right?'

Diane knew she was on to something here. She had come across this kind of spineless hesitation from her interviewees in the past.

'Love? That's a big word to me,' he said, rubbing the stubble forming on his chin. 'Sometimes I'm worried it's too good to be true, but I'm convinced that all roads lead to Olivia. That's where my head is at.'

Damn, Jake was insanely slushy.

'And do you think Olivia's commitment to you is genuine?' There was nothing like drumming up a little paranoia.

'What I want is someone who always chooses me,' he said. 'Someone who accepts me for who I am. Liv and me, we can just chat about the smallest, most random things. That's how I know we're right together.' He beamed a smile and slipped his sunglasses back on. 'That's how I know she's my Insta-Lover and my future wife.'

With a foot between them, Jake and Olivia climbed the stairs. The day had been long, with date night and then Diane raking up tricky questions to get a reaction. But they'd watched all the previous shows; they knew how this worked.

Jake paused on the landing next to a portrait of a handsome couple, standing beneath an oak tree.

'That was intense,' said Olivia. 'You know, Diane suggested I ask you about a pre-nup over dinner, but it didn't feel right.'

Jake looked genuinely interested. 'That's a good question. You know, I haven't really thought about it. I mean, obviously we'd share the prize money.'

'Right,' said Olivia, nodding her head, 'and the sponsorship deals.'

'As long as the wedding happens,' he said.

'You know, I think I'm going to go to bed and start again tomorrow.'

Jake reached his hand out towards her. 'My heart is racing,' he said. 'Can we go somewhere? Somewhere without cameras?'

'It's too risky,' Olivia whispered. 'With so many cobwebs, I can hardly tell where the cameras are, and the thought of losing all the prize money, the sponsorships ... we can't, honey.'

'It's our wedding in two days' time.'

'Do you really think we can pull this off?'

'Of course we can.'

Chapter Forty-Six

It could have been the gin, poured by Eric's heavy hand before the late dinner, or the red wine, but judging by the way Farrah leaned into Tyrone at the table, they were all getting pretty smashed. Holly had taken a shortcut by ordering a lemon tart from the Turpinstown Arms, which no one even commented on, and now she felt like letting her hair down. She could sense Preston looking at her across the table, and noticed Valentina glaring at her.

'I don't know how you do it,' said Farrah, slurring into Tyrone's ear. 'So handsome, with two wives and living between here and New York.'

'Temporarily,' he said, looking up at Holly. He really wanted to get out of there; Holly knew it. Even when it seemed like he had accepted her role at Knockboden, it was as if he resented her presence at the table, or being with the crew. He seemed to have it in for Preston too, giving them both filthy looks when they were in conversation.

'Tyrone, is the fire still going in the drawing room?' said Serena, tipping her cigarette ash onto Eric's side plate.

'I don't know. Is it, Holly?' Tyrone asked as she was telling Preston about her last job in London.

'I think so,' she said, returning immediately to Preston.

'There's something about Knockboden that generates the most extraordinary energy,' said Serena. 'Which reminds me, where are the Insta-Lovebirds?'

'Instragramming,' said Preston. 'They'll be at it all night.'

Valentina seemed to be the only person to find his joke funny. 'It's your birthday tomorrow, Pres; how are you feeling?'

'Lucky as usual,' he said, glancing at Holly.

'I'll check the fire in the drawing room,' said Holly, 'and if Diane's in there, I'll leave her to it.'

'No, no, Holly, you've done enough,' said Farrah. 'You know it was my jog,' she said, pointing her finger against her forehead and cackling with laughter. 'Sorry, I mean, *job*, it was my job at my grandparents' farm to put wood on the fire.'

'Is that so?' said Tyrone, refilling his glass.

'You all stay here,' said Farrah, wobbling to her feet. 'I'll call you when I've got the home fires burning.'

Preston stood up just in time to catch Farrah's elbow and steady her. 'Farrah, how about I keep you company?' he said, winking at Holly.

'Stay here, Pres,' said Valentina. 'I'm sure Holly can accompany Farrah, can't you, sweetie?'

'No, Preston, you should stay with Holly,' Farrah insisted. 'Youngsters stick together – isn't that right, Tyrone?'

He wasn't going to answer that. Farrah was a fabulous

woman, sexy even, but she'd had more than one too many.

'What about me?' said Valentina, taking a mouthful of stilton. 'What age *category* do I fit into?'

Farrah ignored her. 'Everyone, come on, why can't we have *Insta-Love* off camera?'

'I'm going to make some coffee,' said Tyrone, getting up from the table.

'Then, Serena and Eric, why don't you come with me to check the fire? We can leave Preston and Holly here.'

'I am off to bed,' said Serena. 'My beauty sleep is calling.'

'Good thinking,' said Eric. 'Not that you need as much as an ounce of beauty sleep. My pillow is also calling me, in my own room, of course.'

'It's okay, guys, I think Farrah could do with some quiet time in the drawing room,' said Preston.

'What's that, sweetie?' Farrah linked arms with him and reached over her chair to have another swig of wine.

'Come on, Farrah,' said Preston, 'let's go for a wander. It'll do you good.'

'Promise, no Mr Bossy Boots,' she said, wagging her finger.

'I promise.'

'And Valentina, do you think you could bring this upstairs and give the button a stitch?' asked Eric, taking off his tweed jacket. 'You know how I like to close the top button when I'm standing on camera, it makes for a much cleaner silhouette.'

Valentina did not look impressed as she took the jacket and, giving Preston a look of longing, she left the room.

'If there's going to be an exodus, I'm definitely making some coffee,' said Tyrone.

'I've always had a thing for older women,' said Preston softly, as they crossed the hall. The drawing room was delightfully empty, except for the gorgeous Christmas tree.

Farrah didn't seem to notice and kept on walking. 'Isn't this room the best?' she said, tilting her head back to look at the scalloped ceiling.

There was no sign of Diane. Closing the door, Preston guided Farrah to the couch next to the fireplace.

'How about we lie back on the couch and you can talk me through the plasterwork?' he said.

'Don't you mean *sofa*?' Farrah closed her eyes as she sat down, melting into the cushions. 'God, it's deep, isn't it?'

'It is,' said Preston, looking over to the door to make sure the coast was completely clear.

'You were a beauty in your time, weren't you?' he said. 'Men must have panted after you,' he whispered into her ear. 'What would you say if I put my hand down your blouse?'

No response.

Preston decided she was hot, for an older lady. Older than a cougar, younger than Mrs Robinson, until she began to snore.

'I figured as much,' he said. 'You're so past your sell-by date, aren't you honey? Those fake tits don't do anything for you either. What a waste of your royalties.'

Chapter Forty-Seven

The next morning, an open box of paracetamol sat on the drawing-room coffee table beside a box of of Margy's Mint Candy Cane. The candy tasted like toothpaste, but the crew ate them all the same. Anything to distract from their hangovers.

'That was right in the eye,' said Farrah through tight lips as Valentina applied hair spray. 'This is not what I'm used to.'

'My role as a makeup artist seems to get overshadowed by an abundance of demands.' Valentina directed her little rant towards Preston, who didn't seem to notice. 'Anyone would think I was Diane's P.A. the way she treats me.'

Diane was busy scribbling on her iPad and wouldn't have reacted even if she had heard. She and Preston were well practised at faint nods when it came to Valentina's minor complaints.

'Come on now, ladies,' said Eric, rubbing his hands together. 'Teamwork, isn't that what it's all about?'

What was he wearing? Farrah was very fond of Eric, but she had her reputation for elegant dress to maintain. At the Oscars, Page Six had likened her style to Kate Middleton.

'Eric, I'm not sure your leopard-print pants are going to work with my dress,' she said, adjusting her elasticated belt.

'I'm not expecting you to wear them,' he said.

'Funny,' she said. 'I'm talking about when I'm standing next to you. You know I'm wearing Chanel?'

'Is it real?' asked Valentina.

'Yes, Valentina, it is.' Farrah was taking no prisoners this morning. 'Coco would never have put one of her models in the same space as a man wearing leopard-print pants.'

Serena settled into the armchair and Farrah, looking out of sorts, sat on the fender as the well-seasoned wood put up thick, red flames.

'We'll keep this unscripted, okay?' said Diane, holding the clapper board. 'Preston, are you happy with the light?'

'Sure,' he said. 'I'd say both ladies look perfect.'

'How about me?' aske Valentina. 'Do you like my mistletoe earrings?'

'Sure, sweetie,' said Preston. 'Though I prefer life-size mistletoe for obvious reasons.

Farrah shot a look at Preston.

Serena could hardly bear the games between the young. Valentina clearly wanted to slip into Preston's bed, but he was dangling her by the tail, the same way Mr Tubbs used to play with mice, God rest him.

'Serena, I'll need to touch up your makeup before your interview,' said Valentina, buckling a belt of brushes around her waist like Clint Eastwood in a western

'No thank you,' she said. 'I'm satisfied with my lipstick.'

'Valentina's makeup is an essential,' said Diane.

'You think I need makeup because I am old?'

'Not at all,' said Preston, winking at Valentina. 'It helps to pick up the light, that's all.'

'Fear not, Serena, I gather ageism is in decline,' said Eric. 'Warren Beatty and Shirley MacLaine are still working, and they're well into their eighties.'

'I can't imagine Shirley allows anyone else to apply her rouge,' said Serena.

'She does,' said Eric. 'She told me over lunch a few weeks ago.'

Serena raised her eyes at him. 'Shall I fetch you a bucket, in case you want to throw out some more names?'

'If you like,' he said, tapping the heels of his cowboy boots together like Dorothy from *The Wizard of Oz*. 'Perhaps I could take you out to lunch and I can tell you more Hollywood tales?'

'You are kind, but I'll be able to take myself out to lunch once Knockboden lands on the international stage, thanks to this filming. Can someone bring me a vodka and soda water?'

Diane checked her watch.

'It's my house, isn't it?' said Serena firmly. 'I can't bear judgement. What's the matter with a cocktail at 11.30 a.m.?'

'Nothing at all,' said Eric. 'How about I make a drink, while you ladies get started?'

'Lovely,' said Serena.

'And if I move slowly, it could be closer to midday, in which case I can join you,' he said, turning to Diane. 'In keeping with my vow not to drink until lunchtime, you see?'

'My father didn't believe that girls should be educated,' said Serena, savouring the last of her vodka.

'You are kidding me?' Farrah gasped.

'I had a series of dotty governess, mostly employed for being pretty, rather than their teaching skills,' Serena replied, crunching into another piece of shortbread. 'These really are terribly good – are you sure you won't?'

'Thank you, no,' said Farrah, 'but I do want to hear more about your upbringing. I'm fascinated – no, I'm actually insanely jealous. How did a woman who wasn't educated turn into such a force?'

'A force? Is that what I am?' Serena felt thrilled by the description.

'I think so,' said Farrah. 'I'm just wondering how those sexist traditions lasted for so long?'

'They aren't completely extinct,' said Serena, feeling dumpy next to the Californian beauty, whose boobs looked so firm they might have been packed with mincemeat.

'You were expected to marry well, I guess?' Farrah asked.

'By the time I reached the marrying age, money was too tight for my parents to keep to their principles. I wanted to be an air hostess, and to my surprise, they said go ahead.'

'You were an air hostess?'

Serena enjoyed Farrah's reaction. 'Almost. Desmond said my figure would have been a dangerous distraction to the pilot on duty.'

'Desmond?'

'My late husband. He was a breath of fresh air – my true bohemian and the reason I didn't have to take to the skies. A shame, really. In those days all you needed were looks and the ability to mix a nice gin and tonic. Now the poor loves have to carry rubbish sacks and charge people for cups of tea. An outrage, don't you think?'

'And you made the right decision?' Farrah looked serious. 'Choosing Desmond over a career which could have taken you all over the world?'

'I did,' said Serena.

'You loved him?'

'Loved him? I worshipped him. Broke my heart saying goodbye.'

'You left him?' Farrah leaned so far forward, it looked like she might come flying off the fender at any moment.

'No,' said Serena, 'he left me, sadly.'

'Another woman?'

Serena pulled a ciggy from behind her ear. 'That depends on whether you believe that God is a woman or a man.'

Chapter Forty-Eight

Holly had woken up in a foul humour and had managed to avoid everyone so far by tidying up cupboards in the back kitchen. No amount of mindfulness podcasts, deep breathing or Coco Pops could shift her mood. Last night, she had expected Preston to join her in the kitchen for a little flirtation as she cleared up. Instead, she'd had Tyrone as her galley mate, monosyllabic and stacking plates. Their hands touched once or twice, and though she felt a frisson, after his knockback there was no way she was going to do anything other than ignore it. Then he disappeared with the dogs for a late-night walk around the house without so much as a 'thank you for dinner, let alone the mountains of work you do – besides the fact that you haven't been paid, even though you've been here for nearly three sodding months'.

The pattern continued when she found she was expected to lay on a three-course dinner for Preston's birthday, and the cooking was starting to tip her over the edge. Was this all the past decade had taught her? How not to burn a chicken or make lumpy mashed potatoes? So far, her life seemed unbelievably hard work.

Too impatient to wait for a thaw, Holly drove Serena's Mercedes carefully along the icy roads to Turpinstown. The snow on the car bonnet didn't budge as she inched around the corners and her hands felt so cold she thought they might stick to the steering wheel. Christmas pop songs bellowed from speakers around the town square of Turpinstown, where an enormous tree covered in Ho, ho, ho letters stood next to a wooden waffle hut surrounded by six-foot-tall snowmen and polar bears.

In a bid to cheer herself up, Holly went into the village shop to buy a hot chocolate. There was a sign behind the counter for freshly made Rocky Road, which was an appropriate description of her situation in life.

'Just one hot chocolate, then?' asked the lady behind the till.

'Yes, please, and a slice of Rocky Road.' Then Holly remembered she needed tights for the wedding. She had a black skirt, which she could wear beneath her least scruffy top. 'Do you sell tights by any chance?'

'Tights?' asked the woman.

'Yes, black tights, or even sherry coloured?'

'Ah, tights,' repeated the woman. 'I wasn't sure what you meant, but I'll tell you this and I'll tell you no more—'

'Yes?' Holly was wondering what on earth she was going to say.

'The only fabric we have here are dishcloths, but we've got a special deal on the selection boxes – three for five euros.'

Holly shook her head. 'Thanks, but I don't think so.'

'How about chocolate snowballs?' The woman's sales pitch continued. 'Six for two euros.'

Holly followed the woman's eyes to a bucket of foil-wrapped chocolates. They looked suspiciously like the chocolate eyeballs you'd find on sale during Halloween.

It was a relief to get back to the car. Holly turned on the radio, and the universe belted an emotional snowball as 'A Holly Jolly Christmas' blasted from the car speakers. She rested her head on the wheel and accidentally sounded the horn. Within moments, a banging started on the car window and there was Tyrone.

'Holly, are you okay?'

She wiped her eyes, turned off the radio and put down the window.

'Is this yours?' He held up a paper cup. 'It was sitting on the car roof.'

Holly nodded her head. 'I'm so stupid, I can't even remember hot chocolate.'

Tyrone looked worried. 'Can I hop in?'

'Thanks,' she said, taking the cup of hot chocolate from him as he got into the passenger seat. 'You must think I'm bats.'

'No, but I suspect you may have bitten off more than you can chew, though I've never liked that expression.'

'Me neither, except you couldn't be more right.'

'Holly, what's really the matter?'

'I've been asked to cook a "celebratory dinner" for Preston, and I guess it's a big deal because his dad owns Mindeflicks.'

'But that's ridiculous.'

Holly began to cry again.

'Not you,' he said, 'just the situation, it's ridiculous.'

Tyrone took a clean handkerchief out of his coat pocket and passed it to her.

'A song came on the radio and it reminded me of being with Mum and my brother, Gabe – and before you ask, he's Gabriel.' Holly laughed and felt a lot better. 'Mum had been so excited about the wedding – I mean, totally obsessed. From the moment we set the date –'

'Was it meant to be this year?'

'Christmas Eve,' she said, cringing. 'And Mum literally booked a wedding planner and began drafting canapé menus and booking a choir. You can only imagine the guest list. She's nuts about Christmas and because my dad has always paid for everything, she goes completely overboard.'

'And then she had to cancel it all.'

Talking with Tyrone reminded Holly of her visits to the hairdresser when she was in London. She'd try being silent in the chair, giving nothing away as the scissors trimmed and tamed, but then the questions would come. 'You're from Ireland? Oh, I love Ireland, my nan's family come from there.' Feeling cornered, Holly would tell the hairdresser far too much. Her mum's obsession with Christmas. Her dad, living with his makeup-artist girlfriend. Her brother, who'd had the right idea travelling to Australia on his gap year, and who was still there, six years later. She'd recall her mum's put-downs, and how she'd been made to feel more and more disorganised and, bam, she had to get out. It was a sequence she'd become accustomed to, but it was exhausting. Holly would talk about her father too: how everything went back to him, how as the silence between them grew, the greater her discomfort became. How her childhood felt like an unfinished crossword puzzle.

'Sorry,' she said to Tyrone, 'I don't know why I'm always off-loading my troubles on you.'

Before he could respond, there was another bang on the window and they both jumped. A couple of kids had thrown snowballs at the car and were doing star jumps in the carpark, daring Tyrone to chase after them. He put down the window, suggested they 'sod off' and turned back to Holly.

'Well, as we're old friends, let me know how I can help with this famous birthday dinner.'

The supermarket on the main street heaved with trolleys, one cramming into the other as staff, overheating in Santa hats, attempted to maintain a semblance of order.

'It could take us hours to get through this lot,' said Tyrone, standing in the doorway. 'How about we do an online shop? If we order now, it could be with us after lunch.'

In the car, they devised the menu, had a giggle and complained about the revolting sponsor food. What age was Preston? Who cared, and thank God for Betty Crocker icing. They were going to take every possible shortcut.

'Hey, look,' said Holly, 'it's the twins.' Standing outside a café, François and Benoît looked chic in slouchy checked tweed coats, each with a girl on his arm. 'Those girls both look like their Christmases have come at once.'

Chapter Forty-Nine

The reminiscing had unsettled Serena; she knew it. This was an old feeling, not unlike when Desmond had died. She looked at her reflection in the mirror, her hollow cheeks and sunken eyes. Where had she gone to? Whatever about reality TV, she knew her own reality was a pill she'd have to swallow sooner rather than later. This house rental was no more than a sticking plaster. The entire income from the shoot would have to go into the snivelling hands of that Ken Gates. A thought flashed up about another sale, perhaps jewellery. But these days, what would her pearls fetch? And even then, the proceeds would enable her to limp on for no more than a month or two. And there were wages for Holly, Edwin and Lynette, too. They were loyal beyond reason, she knew that.

There was a knock on the door, and Tyrone's head appeared.

'I'm sorry to bother you in your bedroom, but I thought you might like this before dinner.' He put a glass of brandy on the dressing table in front of her. 'They want to film in the dining room, so it may be quite a performance.'

'It's fine,' she said, picking up her silver hairbrush and then putting it down again.

'Mum, is there something bothering you?'

She couldn't bear it when he hovered. 'Why should there be *something* bothering me?'

'I don't know, maybe you're feeling guilty?'

'Guilty, why? And can you sit, please, you're making me dizzy.'

'When the hall was flooding, Diane asked you if I helped you financially.' Tyrone sat down on the corner armchair.

'To which I nodded in reply.'

'No, Mum, you said, and let me quote you on this, "I am expected to run this place single handed."'

'Which I have done.'

He made sure not to raise his voice; he didn't want a row. 'You know, the water leaking through the ceiling was quite fitting, because that is exactly what you've been doing with my money.'

'Tyrone—'

'Rather than fixing the problem properly, what happens? Edwin flashes a piece of Gorilla Tape – one swish and it holds.'

'It held for some time,' she said.

'You know, Mum, I want to help, really I do, but this whole charade has got to stop. How about we leave it and get through the next two days, then we can hit the reset button once Hollywood hits the road?'

Serena looked at both their reflections in the mirror. 'I quite like having them here,' she said. 'I'm considering asking Diane if she'd like to run some workshops in the spring.' It did sound like a good idea once she'd said it out loud. 'She can bring budding talent here to learn from experienced actors.'

Tyrone got back on his feet and stepped away from the dressing table. 'They wouldn't have to look far, would they? You are the greatest actor of them all.'

'What are you talking about?'

'I wasn't going to say anything until after Christmas, but I received an email from a guy named Gates.'

'Oh?'

'He didn't beat around the bush. Gave me the choice of a figure to pay or a lawsuit. I asked one of my team in New York to look into the company and by all accounts it appears to be a slimy operation fronted by a representative who attempts to be civilised.'

'The man's a fool.'

'But something tells me the people behind him may be less civilised.'

Serena took a sip of brandy and began brushing her hair. What else was she to do?

'Mum, what were you thinking?' He sounded upset and she hated herself for it.

'What choice did I have?'

He shook his head. 'I don't want to get into this now. I want to attempt to enjoy the madness going on in the house.'

'Then off you go,' she said.

Tyrone walked towards the door. 'And Mum? Just to let you know, I've paid Ken Gates. You can forget about it.'

'I'm so sorry, darling,' she said, trying to cover her tears. 'I'm a hideous person.'

'Hey, Mum, it's okay.' Tyrone came to her side in an instant, gently taking hold of her forearm. 'It's been tough, and confusing. I get it, really I do.'

'Are you going to put me in a home? You know, at dinner last night, I gazed up at the murals on the dining-room ceiling. Your father said they cost half as much as building the house itself. I do wonder if it was worth it.'

Tyrone looked at her. She was tired and worn out. He gave her a long-awaited hug, and she hugged him back. 'Mum, I'm not going to put you in a home, I promise.'

Serena pulled a tissue from a box surrounded by cream lace. 'I never liked either of your wives, if that's of any help,' she said, smiling a little. 'You've been unlucky, that's all.'

Chapter Fifty

There were eight speeds on the light control box for the Christmas tree, seven of which would give even the calmest person the jitters. Holly crouched beneath the tree and pressed the button several times, until the lights stopped flashing.

Next to the stove in the hall, she saw Olivia sitting alone on an armchair.

'I don't know what it is about today,' said Holly. 'There's something in the air.'

Olivia stared at her phone.

'Are you okay?'

'I'm not sure.'

Mirroring her, Holly sat on the chair opposite, beneath the staircase on the right.

'This talk of social currency,' said Olivia, putting her mobile phone down on the floor. 'The likes, engagements, my followers … They say it's meant to feel like "having it all", but I just don't know if I feel that way.'

'I've only had a tiny insight, compared to you,' said Holly, 'but Instagram almost drove me crazy. I had to do a complete cold turkey.'

'I used to spend hours scrolling and chatting to guys online, and then I'd meet them. Some even ghosted me – it was like the most depressing thing. Doomscrolling.'

'I can remember when dating felt like a second job,' said Holly. 'Swiping through a hundred people to find someone who was even slightly interested.'

'And I can't tell you how many times I've deleted apps and socials from my phone.'

'Same,' said Holly.

'By the time I met Jake, I'm sure I had decision fatigue – and it might seem like a fancy term, but it was real as hell.' She looked like she was going to pick up her phone again, but then sat back in her chair. 'I spent more and more time posting about my perfect life. It was literally soul destroying, but it's still the easiest way to meet people. And then the disappointment of really liking someone online but then, in reality, realising the chemistry isn't there.'

'Yes,' said Holly. 'It's the worst.'

'I took a break for a year from posting, and it was so good for me … made me feel more present, and the weird thing is, within about three days of being back online, Jake slipped into my DMs and struck up a conversation, commenting on a post about my favourite pudding. Turned out we are both ice-cream fanatics.'

'And you clicked when you met on the show?'

Olivia took a moment to answer, as if she wasn't sure what to say, but then seemed to rev up an extraordinary positivity. 'We did, just like that, and we literally clicked instantly. The *Insta-Love* is real, Holly. It's not just a reality show gimmick.'

'Don't you find it exhausting, though? Having to pose with your every move?'

'No, not really. My mom always said to make hay while the sun shines, while opportunity knocks, you know the drill. Especially at this time of year, when lots of brands are dabbling. Jake appeared in a cinnamon candy commercial last week, and now he's promoting hair trimmers as a stocking-filler for dads. It's not like we can retire on it, but it's cake and we're eating it.'

Despite Olivia's enthusiasm, Holly couldn't quite believe her online life was as good as she was making it out to be.

'Yes, I've learned to be way more straight-talking now,' Olivia continued. 'Not just with relationships, or in business, but literally every aspect. I mostly do what I want.'

'That sounds good.'

'You could do it too, you know? Did you see my post with you and Tyrone? You guys make the cutest couple. The comments were incredible – I meant to tell you.'

'Can I see?'

Olivia picked up her mobile phone and walked over to Holly. And there it was: the photo of Tyrone with his arm around her. They seemed a little startled to be in front of the camera, but they looked good together – their height, their smiles.

'That's so weird to see,' said Holly.

'Why?'

'Because we aren't a couple.'

'Really? I totally thought you were.'

Holly had a quick scroll through the comments: 'Cute couple … Lord and Lady of the Irish Castle … Irish eyes are made for smiling … #CastleLove'.

Chapter Fifty-One

'It's like a winter edition of *Top of the Pops* out there,' said Lynette, pulling meat from the Ted's Turkey Joints and putting it into the dogs' food bowls. 'The twins have music playing from their mobile phones while sweeping out the coach house for the wedding.'

'It might be the safest place for them,' said Holly, lifting a dish out of the fridge. 'Valentina looked like she wanted to unwrap both of them on the spot when they met.'

'She's a right goer, she is,' said Lynette, 'but I think her heart's in the right place.'

'Whose heart?' asked Tyrone as he came into the kitchen. Even with greasy-looking hair and smudged eyeliner, Holly looked gorgeous. He was finding it easier to admit this to himself, now they were friends.

'We were just talking about Valentina and her crushes,' said Lynette. 'She probably fancies you too, Tyrone.'

'I'm off dating,' he said, 'it's my early New Year's resolution.'

'And I'm off the biscuits, but we'll see how long that lasts.'

Tyrone tried to keep a straight face as Holly began cutting the string from a chicken. 'Do you think this will be enough for six, if I joint the chicken? Valentina's a vegetarian, so I bought a Linda McCartney burger for her.'

'We can do FHB,' said Tyrone.

'What's that?'

'Family Hold Back,' he said, 'obviously I wouldn't expect Mum to, but I could.'

'So can I,' said Holly. 'Not that I'm family, obviously.' But her mild embarrassment was disrupted when the string around the chicken twanged back and sprayed chicken juice over her face.

'That is about the most disgusting thing I have ever experienced.'

'I can rival you with this,' said Tyrone, heaving a black sack out of the bin to distract Holly from her mild embarrassment. 'What is in here? It completely stinks of fish.'

'I think your mum's still eating smoked mackerel, even though poor old Mr Tubbs is no more,' said Holly. 'Still, she seems to be holding up with having a house full.'

'And even more of a miracle, the fuse board is holding up. And how about you?'

'As long as the Aga can muster enough heat for me to cook dinner, I think we'll be okay, but as I've told Serena a million times, I'm not a chef, by any stretch.'

'What's that?' said Serena, arriving with Jagger and Daiquiri.

'I was just saying—'

Reaching into the bread bin, Serena pulled out a crust. Dipping it into the butter dish, she threw it up in the air, and it fell into Jagger's mouth.

'Nice catch,' said Tyrone.

He pulled out his mobile phone, checking to see if another reply had arrived on Facebook from Gabriel 'Gabe' O'Leary. There had been only three profiles, and only one in Sydney. He knew it was stepping out of line, but maybe this was the one thing he could do to help Holly. Even though she swore she wanted to have Christmas apart from her family, the thought of her being alone really bothered him. She clearly had been close to her mum, and he knew her brother was returning home to Ireland for the wedding that wasn't actually going to happen. This could be the opportunity she needed to reignite that closeness. Gabe had responded to confirm that he was in Ireland now, sounding begrudging at having booked a flight for a wedding which had been 'postponed by my sis #indecisive as usual'. Tyrone had suggested he and his mum might like to visit Knockboden as a surprise and left it at that.

Chapter Fifty-Two

'That blasted tree is flashing again,' said Serena, descending the stairs and as always thinking of the deportment she'd learned from Nanny. If only she knew the impact she'd had on my life, she thought to herself. 'Holly?' She'd have to sound the gong if Holly didn't appear.

Reaching the foot of the stairs, she noticed Olivia. 'What's the matter?' she asked. 'Don't tell me, it's either fiancé problems, or you're sitting there for a better connection with the internet.'

Olivia shook her head, half laughing, half crying. 'It's my dress.'

'Sadly, there's no denying it's an unfortunate choice.' Serena attempted to be sympathetic but what did the girl expect? She was wearing a hideous black meringue adorned with battery-operated reindeer lights.

'My wedding dress,' explained Olivia. 'The airport claims it's been delivered but it hasn't arrived.'

Serena had a lightbulb moment. 'Then I have a idea,' she

said. 'Find Holly and ask her to bring you to my room.'

Olivia's eyes brightened. 'Really?'

'I may very well have a solution.'

The smell of fried onions had been absorbed into Holly's jumper and she apologised for it the moment she and Olivia stepped into Serena's bedroom.

'What took you so long?' Serena lay across her four-poster bed, swathed in mustard-yellow velvet.

'That's a very high bed,' said Olivia.

Serena did an almost perfect Pilates roll-up. 'There's something comforting about sleeping at a good height. I've never met anyone who doesn't sleep better in a four-poster.' The bedroom was panelled in oak, and each of the three windows provided an entirely different view. 'Take a look at my bathtub, if you wish,' she said, 'and I'll pull out the box from beneath my bed.'

Holly and Olivia followed Serena's hand, which pointed towards a door painted in roses. Inside, they found a huge, copper bathtub in which a small child could easily swim. 'Do you think it actually works?' asked Olivia. 'Do you think Serena would let me do an Insta Live in there?'

'Only with your clothes on,' she bellowed. 'I have sharp hearing.'

The girls returned to the bedroom to find Serena sitting on the floor with a large navy box in front of her.

'I squirrelled this away in case it got thrown onto a skip,' she said.

'As if we would,' said Holly, winking at her boss.

'What you are about to see is Dior.'

Olivia clapped her hands and let out a yelp of happiness. 'I love discovery boxes,' she said. 'Please can I film this?'

'Most certainly not,' said Serena. 'The contents are deeply private. However, should you wish to marry in this piece of art, that's a whole different matter.'

'You honestly think I could wear your Dior?'

'Yes, but naturally you would put me in touch with your agent and we would come to an arrangement.' Serena smiled at Holly. 'You see, I've learned a thing or two already from our Hollywood guests.'

'Clearly,' said Holly, carefully lifting one side of the box while Olivia raised the other. 'One, two and three,' said Holly. The lid came off and a moth flew out.

'Cheeky,' said Serena, rummaging her hands through yellowing tissue paper and lifting out the top of a dress made of heavy satin. 'But it used to be white, I don't understand it.'

'The colour looks a little off,' said Olivia, 'and I'm not sure about the neckline.'

'It was very de rigueur in its day, may I tell you.' Serena looked put out.

'I'm sure it was,' said Holly, 'and of course you looked beautiful in it.'

'Naturally.' It was one of Serena's favourite words. 'But for you, Olivia, I think it is not to be.'

'I sketched my wedding dress when I was eighteen years old,' said Olivia, 'and when Charles Bishop Altertate agreed to create my design, hand-stitched, in Parisian silks, it was my dream come true.'

'How do you think Charles will react if you aren't wearing his dress on TV for the ceremony?' asked Holly.

'I think he'll turn to carbs and never invite me to fashion week ever again.'

Chapter Fifty-Three

The chicken was in the bottom oven, keeping warm until it was needed, and Preston's birthday cake, which may have been slightly raw in the centre, at least looked glamorous, thanks to Betty Crocker's icing and the gold spray which had arrived with the online shopping.

'It's looking very organised in here,' said Tyrone as he entered the kitchen. He turned to look at Holly. 'That jumper suits you.'

'This? I found it in a cupboard; I was freezing.' She was starting to blush. 'It isn't yours, is it?'

'No, it belonged to my late father.' Tyrone laughed, and after a second, so did Holly. 'And he'd be happy for you to wear it, I'm sure of that. How about a drink?'

'Almost,' she said. 'Could you find seven side plates for the starter?'

'Consider it done,' said Tyrone, immersing his head in the large dresser. 'Does it matter if they're chipped?'

'The candlelight can hide any imperfections,' she said.

'Spoken like a big-house professional,' he said, carrying the side plates to the Aga. 'These haven't been used for I don't know how long, and wait ...' he said, holding up a plate. 'Yes, it looks like this one was last used for poached egg circa nineteen-ninety.'

'Hilarious,' said Holly, absorbing Tyrone's good mood. She opened the Aga door and gently pressed her fingers on one of the ramekins filled with cheese soufflés. They were looking pretty good.

'I've been wondering about you lately, Holly. About your being here.'

She wondered if the soufflés were ready to come out. Another couple of minutes wouldn't do them any harm. 'Sorry, go on, Tyrone, you were saying?'

'I was thinking about how we're both here, you know, at the same time.'

Holly then decided to plate up the soufflés after all, before Valentina arrived, tapping her watch.

'It could be really cool,' said Tyrone. 'I mean it is great ... really very ... well, you know, hanging out with—'

Holly looked up at Tyrone. 'Me too. I couldn't have coped without you lately. You've been a real help.'

'You're welcome,' he said, a little surprised. 'Though apart from grumbling and mixing drinks, I'm not sure I've done a whole lot. Sweet of you to say.'

Holly put on some oven gloves and opened the Aga again, lifting out the tray of immaculately risen soufflés.

'Wow, move over Nigella,' he said, grabbing the plates warming on the Aga and laying them out on the table.

'They don't look too bad, do they?' she said.

The ramekins were boiling hot. Reading her mind, Tyrone wrapped a napkin around the first one. Holly held the ramekin and ran a knife around the edge of the first soufflé.

She looked at Tyrone. 'How do you feel about returning to New York?'

'Well, I like routine so I think it will be good to get back to exercising, make some work decisions and maybe free up some more time.' He passed a plate to her and she put it on top of the ramekin. 'One thing my ex-wives had in common was they both said I worked too hard. I guess I'm a majority shareholder so maybe I should sit back a little. I don't know.'

'Here goes nothing,' said Holly, flipping the ramekin upside down. She noticed how clean his fingernails were; she really had to stop finding him so attractive. 'Et voilà.' She removed the dish to reveal a thick crust of cooked soufflé resting on top of a congealed mixture pooling around it. Her hands began to shake. 'Oh no,' she whispered, high-pitched and short of breath.

Tyrone put his hand on her shoulder. 'Hold on, Holly,' he said. 'It may just be that one. Try another.'

Quickly, Holly ran the knife around the next ramekin and, placing the side plate on top, she flipped it over to produce an identical result.

'Holly,' she heard him say, as she put down the knife. Pressing her hands onto her eyes, she tried to contain tears and panic, but both came.

'I'm such an idiot, I'm a bloody hopeless fool.'

'It's not your fault,' he said, 'the Aga must be low.'

'No, it's not the Aga,' she said, the back of her throat slightly choking. 'I should have poured boiling water into the bloody roasting dish. Of course I should have. But I poured in cold water. It didn't have a hope.'

Tyrone lifted up the third and fourth ramekin, attempting to help in some way, but it was pointless.

'I told Serena I was a miserable cook,' she said, flinging the napkin onto the floor. 'Just look at it. It's a complete disaster.'

'Firstly, cooking was not what you signed up for, Holly. And how you've put up with us all for this long is beyond me.'

Holly nodded in agreement, but was more interested in solving the culinary crisis.

'But I'm very glad you're here,' he said, grabbing the paper towel. 'Now, my father always said three things have to go wrong to make a disaster.'

The kitchen door opened slowly, and Holly braced herself for either Serena or Valentina to arrive and belt out wails of disapproval. Instead, Lynette curtseyed in the doorway, wearing a black dress and white apron.

'You like my outfit?' she said. 'Diane wants to film a section of tonight's dinner as background for the wedding and so Valentina asked me to make an effort.' Lynette did a twirl. 'I borrowed this waitress outfit from my mate who works in the Turpinstown Inn. It's a bit tight, but—' Lynette read Holly's face, suddenly shutting up very quickly. 'Or maybe I should have dressed for a funeral?' she said, prompting Tyrone to take off his jacket.

271

'Not necessarily,' he said. 'Lynette, can you start making some toast?'

'Toast I can do, governor.'

'And Holly, can you find six egg cups?'

Holly wanted to cry again, but seeing Tyrone's reassuring face, she decided to trust him.

Chapter Fifty-Four

The dining-room table was like a scene from *Dynasty*. Farrah's hair had so much volume, Valentina must have used half a can of hair spray. The shoulder pads in Diane's blazer, along with her lightning-gold earrings, came rocketing in from the 1980s.

'Can we move the candlesticks to the left?' asked Valentina, wearing a belt of makeup brushes. 'I'm worried the flame might cause a shine on Farrah's forehead.'

'Candlelight is flattering, though, isn't it?' said Preston, circling the table with his camera.

'We want to give this scene an appearance of opulence,' said Diane, 'as if the Harpurs of Knockboden dine like this every night.'

'Wouldn't that be lovely?' said Serena, taking a cigarette from behind her ear and passing it to Eric. 'We're officially breaking the indoor ciggy rule.'

'Not before I tuck into this creation,' he said, as Holly put a plate of slender toasted bread, sitting alongside an egg cup and silver spoon, in front of him.

'The silver spoon was my idea,' Lynette whispered to Eric. 'Adds a touch of class, don't you think?'

Dipping toast into his egg cup, Eric took a mouthful and closed his eyes. 'It's been an age since I've eaten soldiers,' he said, clasping his hands together.

'And Holly, this cheese dip is outrageously good,' said Farrah. 'How much cream is in here? Actually no, don't tell me. Ignorance is bliss.'

'It is rather different,' said Serena. 'I told you she was an excellent cook, didn't I?'

Holly looked at Tyrone, sitting at the head of the table, and smiled a thank you.

The candles from the Turpinstown Euro Store were burning so quickly, wax was already beginning to drip down the candelabra.

'That candle makes a rather good analogy for Hollywood,' said Eric, retrieving a piece of wax, which he shaped into a tiny ball. 'Melting at speed. Hollywood, as *we* once knew it, is over.'

'The same can be said for most aspects of life,' said Serena, enjoying the red wine. Holly had offered to fill her water glass, but she might as well have been offering antifreeze.

'Farrah, are you wearing your earpiece?' asked Diane. 'I may want to feed you some questions once the camera's rolling.'

'We thought we'd discuss life after your marriage,' said

Farrah, making eyes at Serena. 'A relaxed chat, which Preston will capture on camera.'

'Can't a lady relax over her supper?' asked Eric. 'Be an angel, won't you, Farrah? You're wearing white after all, which is of course becoming to a lady of a certain age.'

'Lay off, Eric,' said Diane. 'You don't need to butter her up. Let's eat dinner and get on with the scene.'

'Speaking of dinner,' said Valentina, with a hefty amount of cleavage on show, 'can I have a side of kale with whatever this is?'

'You have a vegetarian burger with potatoes,' said Holly, who had been totally put off cooking.

'This potato is heavenly,' said Farrah, speaking with her mouth full. 'What do you put in this? It's just *incredible*.'

'Herbs,' said Valentina, reaching across the table to brush Farrah's nose.

'How do you know?'

'Your mouth,' said Valentina. 'There's parsley or something stuck between your front teeth.'

'Lots of onions,' said Holly, to distract from Farrah as she dealt with the parsley. 'Cream, obviously, and plenty of—'

'You're not going to say garlic, are you?' said Farrah.

'Oh God,' said Holly, feeling faint.

'Holly?' said Valentina. 'It was, like, on the contract? I mean, Farrah's face literally blows up like a balloon, doesn't it?'

'Only if it's cooked,' said Farrah, taking another mouthful. 'Remember the time in DC, when we were going to the White House?'

'Wait,' shouted Holly.

'And you ate the mousse?' said Valentina.

'Let's not discuss the mousse again,' said Diane. 'Preston, because it's *your* birthday, I'm going to work the camera.'

'Hold on, Farrah. I'm so sorry, but I added garlic to the potatoes,' said Holly.

'But you didn't cook it beforehand, did you?' Farrah looked really well and seemed very cool about it. Valentina must have exaggerated her allergy.

'Are we good to go?' asked Diane.

'Isn't it somebody's birthday?' said Valentina, much more interested in batting her eyelids at Preston.

'You know, I think that wine has gone straight to my head,' said Farrah, putting her knife and fork together. 'But go on, Eric, twist my arm and pour me another glass.'

Tyrone never mentioned the garlic, though he must have noticed how alarmed Holly had been. He helped Lynette to clear plates from the table as Holly, keeping her chin up, lit a red candle and placed it on the birthday cake. The shimmering gold icing looked impressive.

'*Happy birthday to you,*' sang Valentina, putting the lemon cake in front of Preston. '*Happy birthday to you / Happy birthday dear Pres-ton / Happy birthday to you.*'

'Isn't this just darling?' said Farrah, slipping into work mode, clapping her hands together with joy and playing the game.

'Blow out the goddamn candle, already,' said Diane,

holding the camera on her shoulder. Extinguishing the flame, Preston plunged a knife into the centre of the cake and cut the tiniest sliver.

'I'm coming in for a close-up with you, Preston and Serena,' said Diane, hovering on the other side of the table.

As Preston posed for the camera, Farrah got out of her chair and wiggled her way onto his lap. She proceeded to drop his slice of lemon cake into her mouth, just like Julius Caesar might have fed grapes to himself, except she missed. Gold icing, along with the cake's partially cooked centre, drizzled down the front of her white blouse.

'Damn it,' said Farrah, getting to her feet.

'Somebody get a cloth,' ordered Valentina. Swiping a tea towel from Lynette's shoulder, she began patting the front of Farrah's blouse.

'No need to fuss,' said Serena. 'Eric, shall we go and sit on the sofa?'

'What's going on?' said Farrah, looking down.

'We'll have you cleaned up in no time,' said Valentina.

'Wait, is there chocolate in the lemon tart?' asked Farrah.

'No,' said Holly, relieved to be definite about one thing at least. 'Definitely no chocolate.'

'If it isn't chocolate,' said Valentina, 'then what is it? And what is that gross smell?'

'Oh Christ,' said Holly, grabbing the tea towel from Valentina's hand but quickly realised it was the same one she'd used to pick up the hen poop.

'You know what, Valentina?' said Diane, with a sense of urgency in her voice. 'Can you forget the blouse and apply some powder to Farrah's forehead?' Holly looked at Farrah, and then at Tyrone. She froze.

'Did somebody put more wood on the fire or something?' said Farrah, feeling her cheeks. 'My face is feeling hot and I can feel a sort of tingling sensation on my lips, and actually, my whole mouth.'

Diane put down the camera and, rushing to Farrah, she held her face in her hands. 'How's your breathing?'

'It's fine,' she said.

'Stomach cramps?' she asked.

'Maybe, just a little.'

'It's okay,' said Preston. 'I've got a certificate in emergency first aid.'

'I've never heard of a garlic allergy,' said Serena.

'It's rare, but it's real,' he said. 'We're going to need anti-histamines.'

'My ex had allergies,' said Lynette. 'I've got some in the cabinet at home.'

'I'll drive you,' said Tyrone, squeezing Holly's elbow as he passed by. 'I won't be long.'

'I've got to get the hell out of here,' said Farrah, and kicking off her heels, she raced out of the door and up the staircase.

Chapter Fifty-Five

Holly used the 'sniffer snuffer-outer', as Serena loved to call it, extinguishing all but one candle on the dining-room table. Then she sat for a moment at the head of the table, studying the print over the mantelpiece. Birds of paradise, perching gracefully with long tail feathers, sharply contrasting to her own situation. She was a headless chicken, teetering on the roof's edge of a great big house. Serena had trusted her, and now she'd blown it.

'How you doing, Holly?' Preston walked into the dining room. 'Mind if I join?'

'Is there any news on how she is?'

'Farrah? I think she'll be okay. I joined Valentina and Diane at the bathroom door for all of thirty seconds, and when we heard her getting sick, we judged it best to leave her to it.'

'Which bathroom? Oh God, there's only one that isn't—'

'It's okay, she's a smart lady. Farrah locked herself in the bathroom that has the heating.'

'I keep thinking about a girl I used to work with,' said Holly, pushing her wine glass towards him for a refill. 'She always carried an EpiPen with her, just in case, because without it—' Hot, exhausted tears filled Holly's eyes. Another fine mess, she thought to herself. The tangle which seemed to follow her around was raising its head once more.

'Hey, sweetheart,' said Preston, his voice gentle. 'No harm has been done.' Through blurry eyes, she watched him sit back in his chair, completely at ease. 'Farrah's well known for enjoying a little *drama*,' he said. 'You have to remember that before she presented television, she was an actress. Farrah enjoys an audience, that's all. She'll be completely fine by the morning, you'll see.'

'But I'm such an idiot, Preston. I could have killed her.' She picked up a napkin and blew her nose, thinking it was the sort of thing Tyrone would really disapprove of.

'You're no idiot,' he said, staring at her mouth. 'You're gorgeous.'

Holly shook her head, and couldn't help but smile.

'I don't think your garlic-smothered potato is going to make it onto the list of ways to kill people anytime soon.'

She tried to think of something clever to say, but instead she sneezed, and leaning forward, she brought her hands to her face.

'You'll need this,' said Tyrone, taking a white handkerchief out of his pocket as he strode into the room. He passed it to her.

'Back already?' said Preston.

'Obviously,' he said. 'Lynette's just been up to Farrah

and it seems it was a fool's errand as *Ms Fox* is apparently steeping in the bath, having got over her allergic reaction.'

'Thank God,' said Holly, blowing her nose. Folding up the handkerchief, she tried to hand it back to Tyrone.

'No, you keep it,' he said.

'You're looking tired, big guy,' said Preston. Tyrone glared at him, maybe because of the ironic 'big guy' comment, or maybe because … Holly wasn't sure, but either way, they made for an uncomfortable threesome.

'Are you're sure you're okay, Holly?'

'Sure,' she said, 'and I'll put the dogs out before I go up to bed.'

'No need to worry,' said Preston, putting his arm across the back of Holly's chair. 'She's in good hands.'

'I wasn't *worrying*,' said Tyrone, and leaving the room, he closed the door behind him.

'How long do you think that candle can burn for?' said Preston, taking a sip from Holly's wine glass.

Chapter Fifty-Six

Preston scraped the frost off the glass of his bedroom window and looked over the red sky shadowing the hills as the early morning sun rose. His father would have quoted 'shepherd's warning', if he'd been there. But this morning, as Preston turned to the bed, the sky felt like a good omen. Blonde hair spilled out over his duvet, and as much as this sight gave him pleasure, it also felt like a victory. It had been a good night, a surprising night. Farrah was an experienced lover. She'd asked him if he wanted to get naked, and he hadn't hesitated.

His striped pyjama bottoms were on the floor. He put them on, pulled a sweatshirt over his head and picked up his iPad before leaving the room. Part of his morning routine was to check the reality TV surveillance cameras during the night, and the corner chair at the end of the corridor had the strongest internet coverage. He signed into the camera software and pressed Download.

Preston walked along the corridor and sat down on the chair. He felt his face flushing as he watched the footage. What if he accidentally pressed the upload button, he thought, smiling to himself. Plenty of people had done that in the past. It could easily happen, especially if the person was sleepy – dedicated to their job, but sleepy all the same. A hashtag, especially when automatically programmed into the iPad, could slip in too. It was a common mistake. Unfortunate, but common.

Returning to his bedroom, he enjoyed the cold air breezing through his pyjamas. Serendipity had landed on his shoulders; he was feeling lucky.

'Preston?'

He turned to see Tyrone standing on the landing, wearing a coat, his hair ruffled.

'Did you have a pleasant night?' Preston asked.

'Jagger has gone missing,' he said. 'Did you see him before you went to bed?'

'Let me think.' Preston deliberately took his time. 'Holly and I ... last night, it's all a little hazy to be honest.'

Tyrone shot him an irritated look.

'If you don't mind, I'm kind of freezing my ass off out here,' said Preston and, turning around, he walked back into his bedroom.

'How about we stay like this all day?' he whispered, spooning into Farrah.

'I was hoping you'd return with a coffee,' she said.

'Wouldn't you prefer a more natural stimulant?' Preston ran his hands around the curves of her ass.

Farrah pushed herself up in the bed, holding the duvet around her chest.

'Do you remember what you said to me in the drawing room the other night?' she asked.

'Which other night?'

'After dinner, when I'd had too much to drink.'

'What did I say exactly?'

'You thought I wasn't listening, but I sure as hell heard every word.' It was Farrah's turn to be in control and this gave her tiny shockwaves of excitement.

'I don't know what you're talking about,' said Preston, pulling back the sheets and climbing on top of her.

'You offended me,' she said, and masterfully flipping him onto his back, she mounted her toy boy. 'You are an arrogant snake who thinks he can take advantage of a woman in her prime and get away with it.' Farrah stared down at him. 'I'm here for compensation, and I expect a good time.'

Farrah Fox was feeling on top of the world.

Chapter Fifty-Seven

Holly had a hangover, a really awful hangover; she deserved every inch of the headache. Pushing her hands deep into the pockets of her Puffa jacket, she walked down the avenue, calling for Jagger. He'd been gone for more than forty minutes, though time seemed to be moving fast and slow all at once.

'Jagger, come here, boy.' Suddenly he came bounding towards her and she felt utter relief at the sight of him, his pink tongue hanging out of his mouth. 'You're soaking,' she said, hugging his cold, sodden neck. 'Bloody lucky for me you came back,' she said. 'Though lucky for you too, because we all love you so much.' She glanced up to see Tyrone walking towards them. He looked furious.

'There you are,' he said. 'In fact, there you both are.' He put out his hand to help Holly to her feet.

'Why are you looking at me like that?' she said, standing opposite him.

'Like what?'

'I'm not sure. It's hard to tell if you're cross with me, pleased to see me, or completely indifferent.'

'I thought you had put the dogs out last night and forgotten to bring Jagger back inside.' His voice eased up a little and he sounded less cross. 'I only found Daiquiri this morning when I walked in.'

'No, of course not,' she said, looking down at Jagger, who had parked himself between them. 'I woke up far too early.' Holly rubbed her head. 'In fact I've hardly slept. Daiquiri didn't want to walk but Jagger of course did, and he ran off after something and I've searching for at least forty minutes.'

'Fine.'

'And now he's back, safe and sound.'

'I just—'

'Look, Tyrone, I don't know what you thought was going to happen last night—'

'I wasn't *thinking* anything,' he said, as they walked towards the back door, 'if you're referring to Preston.'

'The only thing I got comfortable with last night was a wine bottle, to get over the shock of having almost poisoned Farrah.'

Holly felt an incredible urgency to eat. The aroma of bacon coming from the kitchen arrived just in time as her hangover reached its peak.

'Morning, you two, in the mood for a scramble?' asked Lynette, holding up three eggs in each hand.

'Definitely,' said Holly.

'Tyrone?'

'Not right now, thanks, Lynette. Any sign of my mother?'

'Eric came in earlier, asking the same question,' said Diane, unfolding a newspaper at the table. '"Relief as Moore jumper returned safely." What sort of headline is that?'

'*The Turpinstown News*,' said Tyrone, filling the kettle at the sink. 'Cutting-edge journalism.'

'It's not one bit funny, neither,' said Lynette. 'That yellow jumper meant the world to that man. He's the county surgeon, and he wears a lucky yellow jumper when performing his trickiest operations.'

'What's a jumper?' asked Valentina.

'It's a sweater,' replied Diane, passing the paper across the table to her. 'Lynette, a coffee refill, please?'

'On the table,' said Lynette, 'right next to you.'

'So it is,' said Diane. 'Valentina, could you?'

Valentina moved in to lift the coffee pot and knocked over the remains of Diane's coffee.

'What the fucking hell?' Diane held her phone out in front of her.

'Don't panic,' said Lynette. 'This tea towel is clean – absolutely no hen poo on this one.'

'OMG,' said Valentina, looking over Diane's shoulder.

'Farrah is actually a meme. She is trending,' said Diane, bringing her hand to her mouth as she watched the footage.

'Can I take a look?' Holly stood next to Valentina as they watched over Diane's shoulder. There was a woman on her knees and groaning intermittently over a toilet bowl next to beautiful a roll-top bath. She was presumably throwing up, judging by the sounds she made. Holly noticed the long scar down the woman's back as she turned her head to wipe her mouth with a towel. It was Farrah Fox, no doubt.

'How did it get online?' asked Holly, stepping back from Diane.

'I don't know.' Diane paced the kitchen like a boxed mare. 'I need to think.'

'What's going on?' Tyrone looked exhausted.

'Did you put the camera system in the bathroom?' asked Holly. 'Is that even legal?'

'The footage is tagged "@FarrahFox",' said Diane, 'and it trails back to your fuck-up, Holly. Serena promised to build catering in as part of the fee, and what do we get? A drop-out-of-life dumb-ass who can't read a goddamn allergy list.'

'Diane, take it easy,' said Tyrone. 'Let's talk it through.' He tapped into expressions from his marriage counselling. 'The facts can depend on many things.'

'I'm so sorry.' Holly looked to him for reassurance. 'I had no idea,' she said. 'I swear, none of it.'

'I don't give a rat's ass,' said Diane. 'This is all your fault.'

Tyrone watched Holly dissolve in front of him and he wondered if he should reach out to comfort her, but then he thought of her with Preston.

'What's that about a rat's ass?' asked Farrah, looking sensational in a woollen dress with a thick leather belt.

Diane rubbed the back of her neck. Turning away from Farrah, she put her head down, like she was trying to work out the best way to drop the bombshell.

'Has something happened?' Farrah asked.

'How about I make your favourite coffee with silk milk?' Valentina offered Farrah a chair.

'I don't want to sit, do I, Diane? I mean, by the look of you all, something's going on.'

'You crock of shit,' roared Diane. They all turned to see Preston standing at the door with a grin on his face.

'A little internet sensation to start the day. Nothing quite like it,' he said.

'You did this, you fucking Christmas grinch.' Diane picked up the first thing to hand and hurled a box of Karl's Festive Fancies at him.

'I accidentally pressed a button when I was dutifully checking the night's camera activity, that's all.'

'You are a piece of work,' spat Diane.

'I get it,' Farrah said. 'Preston's been sharing bedroom secrets. Honestly, Diane, don't worry about it. I wanted to shake things up, that's all.' Farrah's eyes almost twinkled, oblivious to what was really going on. 'It's been so long since I've had an allergic reaction, it actually reminded me of what the fuck I'm doing on this planet. I'm here for a good time, and Preston was happy to entertain.'

Tyrone had never felt such relief. He almost wanted to hug Farrah in gratitude for being so bloody ... well, honest.

'Honey, there's something you need to see,' said Diane, passing the iPad to Farrah.

'Don't you dare land this on me, Diane,' said Preston, attempting to defend himself.

She looked like she might actually punch him.

'I know your game, Diane,' said Preston. 'You think roping in the oldies to present the show is going to boost your demographic. But it's a joke, the ratings are melting faster than a snowman in a sauna. What do you say to that?'

'Preston,' said Farrah, in tears, 'you filmed me throwing my guts up and put it online?'

'See?' he said, ignoring Farrah. 'No denials coming from Diane.' He turned to Farrah. 'No, *Farrah*, I didn't film you. I mean, you think I'd *want to film you*? What do you take me for?'

'Goddam you!' Lurching forward, Farrah grabbed a pan of scrambled eggs and hurled it at him.

'I always said that lad would end up with egg on his face,' said Lynette. 'Which reminds me, some lad in a van arrived the other day with a delivery.'

'What kind of box?' asked Valentina immediately.

Everyone turned to look at Lynette, including Farrah, who managed to stop crying to hear the news.

'He was eating a breakfast roll, which is why I remembered.'

'And …?' prompted Valentina, who had sent out at least ten scouting emails for a last-minute wedding-dress sponsor.

'I'll take a look. I think it's somewhere in the back kitchen. I hope to goodness that Daiquiri hasn't got all territorial again and cocked his leg.'

Chapter Fifty-Eight

Leftover sausages from breakfast rested on the sideboard as Diane and Valentina frantically tapped into every piece of technology they could find. Laptops, iPads and iPhones now covered the table.

'Far-rah out dude!' ran the headline on *Entertainment Roundabout*. 'Can't the hacks come up with something better?' asked Diane. 'I mean, does she look like someone who takes drugs?'

'How about: "Too Farrah for TV presenter during bender in Irish Castle"?' Valentina shook her head in disbelief.

'She'll have to make a statement,' said Diane, 'or the network will sue for negative association.'

'It's gone totally viral.' Valentina couldn't disguise the excitement in her voice. 'Farrah is like a hot potato.'

'What's that about the humble potato?' Eric arrived in the kitchen, carrying a bottle of vodka like a candle.

'You haven't heard, have you?' said Diane.

Putting the bottle on the kitchen worktop, he checked his

watch. 'It's 11a.m. Is there anything more pressing on the agenda than my making a Bloody Mary for the lady of the house?'

'Christ, Eric, can't you be serious? Something big has happened.'

'What sort of big?' he asked, taking a carton of tomato juice out of the fridge. Opening the seal, he made a face. 'I can't bear processed tomato juice, but I suppose a dash of Tabasco will help matters.'

Diane had to muster every ounce of restraint to stop herself from losing it. Eric's charisma was getting old. All he thought about was mixing drinks and coming up with his next line to flatter whichever female was in front of him.

'How can I explain this simply?' She turned to Valentina.

'It's a film of Farrah,' Valentina told Eric. 'Preston said he *accidentally* posted it online.' Valentina's rising intonation hovered higher with every sentence. 'Twitter has gone, like, crazy, accusing Farrah of being a drug addict, or attention-seeking with her skinny body and the scar.'

'That about sums it up,' said Diane.

'And what's the problem?' he asked, pouring vodka into a couple of tumblers, followed by tomato juice.

'Mindeflicks will go crazy, that's what. They are obsessed with their clean-as-a-whistle reputation,' said Diane.

'Preston is literally leaving the second the wedding has been streamed,' said Valentina. 'I'm so over him.'

'Doesn't his father own the company?' asked Eric.

'At this point, it's irrelevant,' said Diane. 'We're all screwed and, as far as I'm concerned, that little weasel can leave with his tail between his legs, and may that pipsqueak of a dog pee on him one more time.'

'It is very bad luck to have such a guy on board, isn't it?' said Eric.

'Bad luck? Luck had nothing to do with it,' said Valentina. 'Preston, posting the film online, it was, like, so intentional.'

'The garlic, I mean,' said Eric, squinting his eyes as he read the label on the Tabasco. 'There isn't a bad bone in Holly's body. Poor love must be feeling dreadful about it all.'

'Feeling *dreadful*, as you put it, Eric, isn't going to clean up the mess,' said Diane, holding a phone to each ear.

'I can't find the best-before date on this,' he said, shaking a few drops into both glasses. 'Don't suppose Serena will mind, though, as long as it brings a little spice.'

Maybe Preston had been right about Eric and Farrah. They were old cannon fodder. She'd made a blunder in casting and *Insta-Love* was going to plummet.

Chapter Fifty-Nine

'If I see that Preston, I'll take out the shotgun,' said Serena, sipping on her Bloody Mary.

'Mum, you don't have a gun.'

'That's beside the point. Now, I want to see Holly.'

'I don't know where she is.'

'What do you mean you don't know where she is?'

'I have no idea. Farrah fled in tears in one direction and Holly in the other.'

'Holly was crying?'

'Of course she was crying, Diane laid into her.'

'Didn't you defend her? It wasn't her fault,' said Serena.

'Whose fault was it then?'

'Preston, that's who. Why can't you man up for once, Tyrone? That girl has poured her heart and soul into Knockboden and she'll be leaving with nothing. A reference from me won't be worth a damn.'

He didn't want a lecture; at this point he didn't know what he wanted. All Tyrone knew was that Holly had got into his head, under his skin. There were a hundred reasons why they weren't right together. He was set in his ways; Knockboden was a weight around his neck. Holly had to travel, to let off steam. If he told her how he felt, she'd end up feeling trapped; she'd resent him. No matter what his heart said, he had to do what was right for her.

'Why can't you take ownership of what's happening in front of you, Tyrone? I'm sure that's what went wrong with both your marriages. You refuse to face up to what's happening.'

'And what is happening? You tell me. A film of Farrah is currently moving at the speed of light across the internet, which according to Diane puts *Insta-Love* in the bad books with Mindeflicks, and so the wedding is looking like a downer before the organ has even hit a note.'

Serena straightened her back. 'How can something fall apart with this speed?'

'What, as opposed to a slow crumble, like Knockboden?'

She took an envelope from beneath her arm and handed it to him. 'It is an apt time for me to present this to you.'

'What is it?' Was she really going to give up on Knockboden? It was so odd, because a part of him loved his mother's determination to keep on going.

'The signature you've been wanting for years.'

He slipped his finger across the top of the envelope and pulled out several sheets of folded paper.

'Take the place and sell it, along with any stick of furniture that is worth something.' There was no more bravado.

'Don't be ridiculous.' Tyrone felt like the bad guy, like he had forced her into it. Why?

'This is what you wanted, isn't it? You've been moaning about having to give me money for years. Well, now you can have it all. Take Knockboden.' Serena put on her practical voice, but he could hear her heart breaking. 'Tear her down. I honestly don't care any more.'

Tyrone held his mother's hands in his. 'You don't mean it, Mum.'

'I tried damn hard to get this place working, but the gods don't want me to succeed.'

He shook his head and tried to reassure her. 'I think we need to digest what's happened, and then we can decide together.'

'My mind is made up, Tyrone. And don't worry, I'll give Holly her notice, so you don't have to. She isn't thriving, Tyrone. That girl is running from nothing to nothing.'

'I think you've got this wrong. Holly told me herself being here is the first time she's felt job satisfaction.' Tyrone shook his head. 'This is moving way too fast – you just want to shut everything down?'

'I don't need to, Tyrone. The universe is taking care of it for me.'

Chapter Sixty

Holly opened the drinks cabinet, upturned a crystal tumbler and peered at the bottles. All except for the vodka, gin and whiskey, the rims were sticky and neglected. Unscrewing the lid from the vodka bottle, she poured an inch. *Never mix your drinks*, said her father's voice in her head. Defiantly, she added gin, whiskey and flat ginger ale. Down in one. Then she poured another inch of vodka, tightening the lid to deter her from returning for more. There was a bottle of dusty Martini, almost full, at the back of the cabinet. She pulled out the green bottle and held it up to the light. It was her mother's favourite Christmas Day drink.

'Booze?' asked Farrah, peeping her head around the library door.

The women sat cross-legged in front of the fireplace, staring at a charred log surviving on burning embers.

'Cheers,' said Farrah, sipping a vodka martini. 'You know, I can't even feel the alcohol? I think I'm numb. I just can't believe he'd sell me out like that.'

For a woman in her fifties, she was incredible. Her skin was glowing, her body was strong and the look on her face made it clear that she was going to take the next chapter of her life and make it fabulous.

'I feel ridiculous to have thought I even liked him,' said Holly, leaning forward to throw a log on the fire. 'He seemed so innocent and well-meaning.'

'Oh, he's well-meaning in some ways.' Farrah was grinning. 'You know I slept with him last night?'

'What?' This confirmed what Holly had suspected: her radar had fused. That was it. She had no sense of direction when it came to men, none at all.

'It was just sex,' said Farrah. 'I wanted to prove that I was still seductive, that I've still got it.'

'Farrah, you're a classic beauty. You don't need him to prove anything.'

'Oh, I know, but those little games have always kept me on my toes.' Farrah's face crinkled as she laughed. 'I've always been like this. I'm really quite daring deep down.'

'And your scar? Do you mind my asking?'

'I was diagnosed with scoliosis when I was fifteen,' she said, 'but I didn't let it put me off my dream. I moved to LA to become an actress and, at that time, I had a thirty-two-degree curve in my spine, can you believe it?' Farrah pulled up the back of her jumper and turned to show Holly.

'Gosh, was it painful?'

'Sure, especially when I was waitressing. That didn't suit my back at all, but it did force me to deal with it.'

Holly admired Farrah even more than before. She would

make the most amazing spokesperson for scoliosis. 'And this was before you got into TV?' Holly had to draw inspiration from this. She had to find something meaningful to do.

'At thirty, I was old by Hollywood standards, but I said, "To hell with it." I moved back east to my parents, had the op and stayed there to recover.'

'And then?' Farrah had the makings of her own movie.

'I started my career from scratch, aged thirty-one and three-quarters, and from then I stopped counting the years and focused on what I wanted.'

Jagger curled up next to Farrah, his silky black head resting on her feet.

'This guy knows how to take life easy, doesn't he?'

'You're amazing.' Holly was feeling more than inadequate.

'Amazing? *You* might think so,' said Farrah, looking so glamorous with her curls tucked into her oversized polo-neck. 'But until now, I've always hidden behind it – you know, privately – using my scoliosis as the reason for my late start, as my excuse for not making it.'

'But you're on TV; you host shows,' said Holly.

'Yes, and once upon a time, in the nineties, I was hot property, but look at me now. Eric and I grasp at any work that's thrown at us. Let's face it, Holly, I'm online – and at the end of the line. The footage Preston *accidentally* uploaded has only speeded up the inevitable ending of my career.' She reached down and stroked Jagger's ears as she spoke. 'All my life I've been looking for perfection.' Her eyes filled with tears. 'I'm proud of my scar,' she said. 'I was brave and I got through it. What's there to be ashamed of?'

Holly put her arms around Farrah and hugged her.

'It's just crazy that it's taken a trip to Ireland and a garlic reaction to fix myself.'

'Oh, the garlic,' said Holly, putting her hands to her face. 'I'm so sorry, Farrah. I just mess everything up.'

'No, honey, that's not true at all.' Farrah took Holly's hands from her face and held them firmly. 'You have shaken me out of some twisted reality I'd landed myself in.'

'Really?'

'Yes, and Holly, you've got your whole life ahead. It's time to start living it, because, believe you me, it won't wait around forever.'

Chapter Sixty-One

Holly made her way up Grafton Street, the kind of place she would usually avoid at this time of year. And yet now she found herself being swept along the busy Dublin street, marvelling at the incandescence of hundreds of thousands of LED lights sparkling overhead: golden stars and snowmen, gingerbread houses and flocks of geese, all magically crafted by the power of luminescence. The air smelled of marshmallows and hot chocolate and cinnamon waffles. There were happy faces everywhere, most people laden with shopping but content to carry the extra weight, jostling back and forth along the street. Music rang out from carol singers and guitar strummers every dozen metres. A semi-circle of shoppers paused around a mother and daughter, dressed in matching Christmas jumpers, singing 'Rockin' Around the Christmas Tree' with gusto beside Weir & Sons. A woolly-hatted couple sang along as they marched past arm in arm. A father was rounding up his children near the Brown Thomas window display, the little ones screeching with excitement as they held up their star balloons. A pair of young men beamed with pleasure as they shouldered what appeared to be a canoe, wrapped in red paper, down the centre of the street. It was packed with people, but it was also full of love and hope and positivity. Holly looked up at the lights again and, to her surprise, she realised she was smiling.

Holly may have been a little drunk when she'd called her father to arrange the visit. His girlfriend, who answered the phone, sounded relieved by the suggestion. It had been five years since they'd met, and it wasn't as if Holly missed her father – that wasn't the point of her visit. Something about Farrah's story had made Holly want to meet him face to face and get some answers. She was feeling so muddled in her life, she figured she may as well dive into the deep end.

On her way towards Merrion Row, Holly walked behind a chatty and well-tailored family. A flurry of snow began and the scene turned into what could have been worthy of a Christmas ad, as the family climbed the steps to the Stephen's Green Club, hugging each other by the entrance. Holly thought how amazing that a family could get along like that. But maybe they weren't even related. They could all be friends of mixed generations, so fond of each other they gathered like a family.

Giles would have a family like that one day. He'd have Christmas all mapped out, an itinerary to make sure everyone was thought of and all needs met. He'd have personalised ornaments on the tree, and there would be an occasional grand gesture, perhaps another ring for his wife, or a necklace or a car. That was his style. But it wasn't for Holly.

She looked up at the Stephen's Green Club one more time. It had been clever of Tyrone to send his mother there. That had been just before their kiss. Their brief kiss, for which he'd apologised. Holly wished she could empty the contents of her head into a skip, in the same way they had emptied the clutter from Knockboden.

A pretty Christmas wreath hung on the door of the Fitzwilliam Square town house. Holly pressed the intercom button and thought of Lynette, who would have been impressed by the well-polished brass door knocker.

'Is that you, lovie?' came an energetic voice from the speaker. 'Come in, it's open.'

The hallway looked like a high-end florist's. Ivy was draped around paintings, and poinsettias splashed colour across a slender glass side table, with pots of snowy-white lilies, long stemmed red roses and white orchids.

Holly lightly touched the loops of cranberry garlands as she walked along the corridor. Her father was sitting sideways on a chair at the kitchen table, trying to pull a brown shoe on to his foot. He looked as if he was locked into a bent position.

'You're here early,' he said, without looking up at her.

Holly checked her mobile phone. 'Gretta said to be here at 9a.m.'

'Your mother was always late.' His thinning hair skimmed his forehead and his cheeks were red with broken veins.

'I'm not late,' Holly said. 'It's 9a.m. exactly.'

He looked up at her briefly. Holly had to steel herself not to walk out, reminding herself that her visit was fact finding, nothing more.

'There you are, Holly,' said Gretta, breezing into the kitchen. She wore an emerald-green tracksuit, and her hair was pulled back into a smooth ponytail. 'Give us a squeeze then.' Gretta stood back to look at her. 'Gorgeous as always,' she said. 'We were so glad to hear from you, weren't we, Peter?'

'That's an original, you know?' he said, ignoring Gretta's comment and pointing to a bamboo sculpture. 'Cost a bloody a fortune. Can't see the point of it myself.'

'Your dad and I have different tastes,' said Gretta, bending down to tie his shoelace. 'But that doesn't stop us, does it?'

He looked at Holly, and nodded at an empty chair across from him.

Holly sat down.

'You got sheepskin beneath you, girl?' asked Gretta, hoisting herself back up.

'Thanks,' said Holly. 'The chair feels lovely.'

'How about a quick coffee? We have ten minutes before the choir practice and Sydney's going to drive us,' said Gretta. 'Since I don't drive, and your dad's been out of sorts, Sydney's been ferrying us all over town, hasn't he, Pete?'

'It doesn't matter,' he said. 'I can't even get my shoes on.'

'Rubbish,' said Gretta. 'They're expecting you, and Holly's come to hear you sing, isn't that right?'

She looked up at Holly with hopeful eyes. Despite the home comforts, life did not look easy for Gretta.

'She's got things to do,' said Peter.

'Once I'm back at my desk by midday,' said Holly, hoping they wouldn't ask about her job, 'I can join you.'

'Brilliant, and Sydney will drive you back – you're based in Wicklow, aren't you?' asked Gretta, as if trying to open up a conversation between Holly and her dad. 'I'll leave you to it then. I'm going to pop upstairs and do my hair.'

Holly could already feel the strain of being in her father's company.

'She never does things by halves,' he said, when Gretta left the room. 'I was in a bad place when I met her,' he added. 'Drinking too much.'

'Do you still drink?'

'Not a drop.'

'What do you do then?'

'Strange question.'

Holly shrugged her shoulders.

'I read the FT after breakfast,' he said, briefly making eye contact. 'Keeps me up on stocks and other rubbish.'

'Good for you,' she said, knowing her tone was bitter. She tried not to sound like that but it seemed impossible.

'You alright for money?' he asked.

'I'm fine, Dad,' she said quickly. 'I work.'

'Of course,' he said, pressing his thumbs together. 'And your mother, how is she?'

'I haven't seen her for a while.' It was so weird. He didn't know anything about Holly's engagement, her broken engagement or, in her mother's eyes, the postponement. How could a father have such little interest in his daughter?

'You see the extension?' he said, pointing to the terrace through the glass doors. 'It took Gretta's people a long time to get planning, but like a dog with a bone she persisted.'

'Very smart,' said Holly. She wondered if he'd heard the sarcasm in her voice and swore to herself this would be the last time she'd see him. The feeling of rejection was as raw as ever.

The silence seemed long, but may have only been a couple of minutes.

'I didn't want to leave you, or your brother.'

'Then why did you?' The question left her lips without her having to even think. It was the question she had wanted to ask him since she was six years old.

'We were never in love,' he said, matter of fact. 'We married too young, and it was a rush. We had no options in those days; your mother's family were concerned about people. About what they'd say.'

'And what were *the people* going to say? Was it about you being so young or about you're not being in love with her?' Holly felt punchy. She was going to say whatever came to mind.

306

'She was pregnant with your brother, and we got engaged. It was those times, Holly. Your mother's family were religious; there was no way out.'

Holly had known about her mum's family and the religion, but she'd never thought about the marriage or the timing of it. 'Then why did you have me?'

He shook his head. 'I don't know, Holly.' He said it quietly.

'You don't know?' Holly got to her feet. Not abruptly. She was calm, composed and over him. 'What am I meant to say to that? What would *anyone* say to that?'

'But I'm glad we did, Holly.' He pushed himself up out of the chair, leaning both hands on the table. 'Having you only made my leaving twice as difficult.'

Was that meant to have been a compliment?

'I'd like to write you a cheque.'

'I don't want a cheque.'

'It's a wedding present, nothing more.'

She felt really upset. 'How do you know about my wedding? And by the way there isn't even a wedding. I'm not getting married.' Holly caught her breath. 'I'm not ever getting married.'

She wasn't sure if he registered what she had said; he seemed to barely react.

'Gretta's done so many courses in psychology, I can't keep up. She says your mother's obsession with Christmas is her way of trying to make up for my leaving on Christmas Eve. My timing, I know ...' Holly's father rubbed his forehead. 'I just think she's still trying to create better memories for you and for Gabe – he told me about your wedding. Who do you think was paying for the marquee? I gather your mother even ordered a hot air balloon, painted to look like a giant snowflake.' Peter laughed, but Holly did not.

She was no better than her father. Holly hadn't had the courage to tell her mother that the wedding was off, just as he hid behind his cheque book and lame jokes. Holly jumped when Gretta came swinging around the corner, wearing a long coat and with gold fluff across the toes of her boots. 'Come on, you two,' she said. 'Get your coat on, Pete, they say it's going to snow after lunch.

'I can't join you,' said Holly. 'I'm sorry, but I've just remembered something and I've got to get back to—'

'What job is that?' he asked. Holly looked at Gretta.

'It's out of town,' she said, realising her father wasn't well, 'towards Wicklow.'

'Then come with us,' said Gretta. 'Stay for ten minutes to hear your dad sing and Sydney will drive you back. Can't he, Pete? You and me can take a taxi home again, and Sydney can drive Holly?'

'Fine,' he said.

'Take this with you,' said Gretta, snapping an amaryllis flower from the arrangement in the hall as they left the house. 'Amaryllis is a symbol of strength,' she whispered to Holly, 'and you're strong. That's why you're here.'

Chapter Sixty-Two

The cathedral pews were empty, except for Holly and Gretta, who had talked non-stop on the drive from the house. All Holly could think about was her father's explanation. It seemed straightforward. He'd never really loved her mum; she had been pregnant and they had a shotgun wedding. But he'd still left them. That was the hard part. She'd checked her phone: another batch of WhatsApp messages had arrived from Lynette and Valentina, both asking Holly where she was and when she'd be back. They seemed to think she had gone shopping for more Christmas decorations. Holly's mum had also messaged to say how lovely it was to have Gabe home. Holly didn't feel any less guilty for holding back the truth about her wedding.

'You can't believe your dad's singing, can you?' said Gretta. 'He's the oldest, obviously, but they've been so good to him.' She put a piece of gum in her mouth and chatted on as the choir warmed up their voices. 'It's the dopamine, you see? The singing, it releases the feel-good vibes and lowers the heart rate. Just what your dad needs.'

Holly nodded. She wanted to leave but had promised to stay for the first part of the performance.

'They'll be dressed in white gowns on Christmas Eve,' said Gretta. 'Because this is a rehearsal, it doesn't look as Christmassy, but close your eyes and listen. You'll get goose bumps, I swear to you.'

There was a rustle of papers as twenty choristers stood in a crescent, raising their music sheets in front of them. The conductor waved her hands and Holly closed her eyes.

And the choir began to softly sing 'Have Yourself a Merry Little Christmas', the sound building as they moved through each heartfelt lyric.

Holly closed her eyes and felt hot, fighting tears running down her face. She wanted desperately to hate her father, for leaving them, for leaving it so late to explain.

Opening her eyes, there was her dad was standing in the aisle, looking straight at her.

'I am very sorry,' he said, sitting down beside her in the pew. 'I'm sorry for everything. Can you forgive me?'

Holly smiled, wiped the tears with her sleeve and nodded her head. This, she had not expected.

Chapter Sixty-Three

Diane had to push the negativity about Farrah to one side and win what was in front of her. She sat by the fire in the drawing room, viewing last night's confessionals on her iPad.

'Okay, Olivia, this is your last night before you get ditched or hitched on *Insta-Love*. How are you feeling?'

'I feel kind of sick to my stomach about how real this experience is.'

Diane smiled. She was totally not going through with this.

'Can you explain why you love Jake and why you think he's somebody that you want to marry?'

Olivia paused. 'I think … I don't know, can we skip that question for a moment? Actually, I know the answer. He's my role model, my best friend.'

'And what about physically … you must be excited?'

'Super-excited,' she said, sweetly blushing and turning away.

'Do you worry about not being compatible in the bedroom department?'

'Not really. People in the old days did it all the time. I guess that's the whole point of this experiment. Connecting on a deep mental level, our online connection.'

Olivia looked pale onscreen. Diane shot a message to Valentina to up the concealer and bronzer during makeup.

Eric had done a nice job with Jake.

'So, Jake, what's going on in your head right now?' he'd asked.

'There is massive chemistry between us,' said Jake, dressed in a robe with Winterbottom's Prosecco across the chest pockets. 'For me, marriage is teamwork and I think this will propel us to new heights. I have everything planned out: our travels, our five- and ten-year social media strategy. It's going to be awesome.'

'I never could resist the love of a good woman,' said Eric, nodding his head, 'but do you have a fear of commitment? Or is there someone else who may be a better fit?'

Jake looked around. 'I doubt it. My eyes are on Olivia.'

Mindeflicks could rest easy. These guys were not going to go through with it; the public were about to be shocked and the altar scene was going to go viral. Bingo.

Diane looked up at the door, hearing a gravelly cough.

'Hello?' The house was a little creepy at times, though it could just be the stress of following Preston's last outrageous move. His father would laugh it off, but the second Preston had fulfilled the camera work, she was going to kick his sorry ass to the curb. There was the cough again. 'Is there someone there?' she asked.

A man stood in the doorway wearing a bright orange woolly hat and a heavy tweed overcoat.

'You couldn't skin a cat in that weather,' he said, resting his hand on the architrave while he kicked off his shoes. 'Can I see the lady of the house? I'm Father Flynn.'

God, he was like something out of *The Quiet Man*.

'Father,' she said, jumping up from sofa. 'Sorry, I'm slow off the mark. I've only had two coffees so far; I'm better on my third.'

He walked into the drawing room and put his woolly hat on the drinks cabinet. Diane reached out to shake his hand, which he clasped with both his hands. It felt like a kind of blessing, a quiet moment with the quiet priest. God, she loved Ireland. She felt almost moved.

'I might have a nip of whiskey to get me settled,' he said, releasing her hands.

'Whiskey,' said Diane. 'Of course. Let me find someone and I'll organise. You like it on the rocks?'

'A drop of well water,' he said. 'That's the girl.'

'I'm Diane Striker, the producer of *Insta-Love*, by the way.'

'Isn't that lovely,' he said, bowing his head. 'I wrote a play once.' She could see his mind whirling. 'Will I ask my housekeeper to bring it?'

'You're very kind,' said Diane. 'Maybe we'll focus on the wedding for today.' She smiled to herself. Perhaps she would have to resort to working on freelance plays. The negative coverage on Farrah had shaken her judgement massively.

'Grand,' he said, eyeballing the armchair by the fire. 'I'll have a sit-down and then you can let me know the order of service.'

'I'll give this call sheet to you to look over,' said Diane. 'The most vital detail is that the marriage has got to happen at precisely 15.12 Irish time, so that we can sync in across the time-zones.'

'Right you are.'

'So we have four hours, or perhaps three.'

'That's grand,' he said.

Chapter Sixty-Four

#Javia were filming one last Insta Live by the Christmas tree, both still dressed in matching reindeer pyjamas.

'There goes the tree again,' said Holly, hunkering down to press the control box.

'Thanks, Holly, feeling the love,' said Jake. 'Feeling the love.'

And Holly was feeling pretty good. She hadn't realised that it was an apology from her father that she wanted, or had so badly needed. Those words in the cathedral had made all the difference.

She turned the handle to Serena's study door. It felt like a kind of déjà vu from her early days at Knockboden.

'Push harder,' said Serena, from the other side. 'That door has always been a nuisance.'

Holly arrived carrying the amaryllis in a slender vase and placed it on Serena's desk.

'Is this a show of appreciation, Holly, or are you buttering me up for a favour?'

'Neither,' she said, sitting on the fender. 'I brought this back from my dad's house.'

'You've been to see your father?' Serena lit a ciggie and threw the match into the waste paper bin. 'You see, you can't teach an old dog new tricks.'

Holly nodded her head in agreement. 'And I don't think Dad and I will ever be very close, but somehow I feel better having seen him.'

'I think your approach is admirable,' said Serena, looking distracted. 'While you're there, throw a log on the fire, would you, darling? Edwin said the wood was damper than usual.'

Holly placed the log on the fire and, picking up the bellows, she pushed the nozzle underneath and blasted air into the smouldering wood.

'I do love an open fire,' said Serena as bright orange flames danced up behind the logs. 'Not everything worth having has to come at the push of a button, wouldn't you agree?'

'Elbow exercise complete.' Holly put the bellows back onto the wood basket.

'Which just about sums up what I'm about to say to you, Holly, and this has nothing to do with Farrah's unfortunate run-in with the garlic.'

'Oh God, what are you going to say?'

'I'm very reluctantly handing you your notice.' Serena stood up from her desk and, stepping over Daiquiri, she walked to the fender and sat next to Holly.

'Wow,' said Holly. 'I seem to be on some kind of odd trajectory, except that I'm not sure in which direction.'

'But you must have plans, Holly?'

'Plans? I've never made plans.'

'Maybe it's three hundred and sixty degrees,' said Serena, throwing her ciggie into the fire. 'My generation didn't make plans either. We didn't need to. We became debs, we married, we did as we were told … apart from me, naturally.'

'But what about your B&B business?' Holly was trying not to panic about where she was going to go. 'And I know the TV project has been close to mayhem at times, but couldn't that be something to pursue in terms of renting out the house?'

'I want to hand Knockboden to Tyrone,' she said, throwing her ciggie into the fire.

'Did he ask you to?'

'He has asked me for nothing.'

Holly gave out to herself for jumping to conclusions about Tyrone.

'I can never pay him back for the sort of mother I've been, but this is a gesture and, more than anything, I've had enough, Holly. I'm ready to throw in the towel.'

The fire began to crackle, filling the air with sound, which was just as well, because Holly felt speechless until Diane came bursting through the door. 'Is Farrah here?' She looked very excited.

'She must be in her room,' said Holly, standing up.

'Out with it, Diane, what's happened?' asked Serena.

'That goddamn post Preston made. I've just had a call from, get this, the producer of *Silver Stars*.' Diane looked incredibly excited. 'You've heard of the show, right?'

'I have,' said Holly, turning to Serena. 'It's like a sort of *Strictly Come Dancing*, except without the dancing part.'

'If they aren't dancing, then what are they doing?'

'They're themselves,' said Diane, 'legends, aged seventy and older, who've done it all and seen it all. They want me to produce the US series, and Farrah to front the show.'

'And she thought her career was shot,' said Serena.

'It's gone so the opposite of how I thought it would,' said Diane, 'and they've got a celebrity list as hot as my ass.'

'Oh, I love good news,' said Serena.

'There's an NDA on this one, so I can't give you names,' said Diane, 'but—'

'NDA – is that some sort of drug?' asked Serena.

'Nondisclosure agreement,' said Holly.

'This is big,' said Diane. 'It's so huge and just to give you an idea of those involved, we've got a Grammy-winning music producer, a duchess, a legendary singer from a rock band and a sexy 007 – and that's just for starters.'

Chapter Sixty-Five

A white Range Rover, with blacked out windows and #Insta-Love embossed across the bonnet, sat on a silver tray in the back kitchen. It was a work of cake art, created by the trending chef Cagney Wenson. His most recent cake had been so lifelike, the father of the bride had attempted to search up Google on the iPad, only for his finger to slide across the sheer, black icing. Diane had earmarked the Range Rover cake as the centrepiece next to which the newlyweds would be interviewed, and the show wrap-up was going to feature Insta-Mr & Mrs slicing a knife across the bonnet.

The lighting equipment had been quietly set up in the coach house by Preston, who had received news of Farrah's fabulous new position on *Silver Stars* with a smidgen of good grace. 'Suck on that,' Diane had told him. How could she resist?

She sat in front of the monitor, wearing her wardrobe-staple skinny jeans and leather jacket. 'Run the interview with Charles Bishop Altertate,' she said to the studio in LA.

'My dresses are light-hearted with a fun energy to them, rather than feeling too serious,' said Charles, his French accent bringing elegance to the show. 'My outfits are environmentally conscious and can be reworn,' he said. 'Separates and suiting have a longer shelf life, and with Carrickmacross lace, which also featured in the dress of Princess Kate, I say ooh la la to that.'

Florists carried in tubs of hellebores, cyclamen and ornamental cabbage to create a Secret Winter Garden vibe. François and Benoît, who had been advised to steer clear of the Turpinstown Inn due to being caught up in a love triangle featuring the hairdresser's daughter, the estate agent's niece and the undertaker's sister, brushed down the walls.

'Diane, have you seen Father Flynn?' asked Valentina, inspecting the flowers. She wore a pale pink dress with a plunging neckline, especially for Benoît and François. She couldn't decide which one she'd set her sights on, so she figured she go for dual focus. 'No one has seen him. The parish housekeeper, Babs, said he arrived this morning.'

Oh Lord above, thought Diane. Had she really left him in the drawing room? She'd been so distracted by Farrah, she'd opened the drinks cabinet and suggested he help himself. 'Have you looked in the drawing room?' she asked, holding her hands over her face and peeping through split fingers.

'It's a nice day for a white wedding,' said Tyrone, walking into the kitchen. Holly was leaning out of the window and the air coming in was freezing. 'Billy Idol, 1983,' he said, but still no response.

She turned and looked at him with icing on her nose. 'You know you said it takes three things for a situation to be classified as a disaster?'

'Oh God, what's happened?' asked Tyrone

'I think two out of three things have happened, so we are close to disaster.'

Holly looked so shocked, he didn't know if she was going to cry or scream. Jagger and Daiquiri stood either side of Tyrone as if it was just a normal day. He followed Holly's eyes and looked down at the dogs. 'Why are their muzzles covered in white icing?'

'The Range Rover,' she said. They walked to the back kitchen and there it was: a car without a bonnet.

'Ah,' said Tyrone. 'That can certainly fit into a weighty category of hurdles to get over.'

'I think it's going to take more than a spatula to paper over this,' said Holly.

He wanted nothing more than to take her into his arms. She was trying so hard to stay calm, but his reaching out to her wasn't going to help.

'And the second thing?' he asked, trying to keep things as light as possible.

The four-poster bed in Serena's room had never looked more gorgeous. The afternoon light against the mustard-yellow velvet was a picture in itself.

'Your thoughts?' asked Serena, standing by the bed with a ciggy.

'Let me get that for you,' said Eric, pressing on his lighter.

Tyrone took a closer look. 'Out cold,' he said.

'How full was the bottle to start out with?' asked Serena.

'I have no idea, but it's three-quarters empty now, or a quarter full, depending on the way you look at it,' said Holly.

'Hey, guys,' called Valentina from the corridor. 'Has anyone seen the father? Diane left him in the drawing room.'

'We're in here,' shouted Serena, and they all stepped back to present their findings to Valentina.

'Is he dead?' she whispered.

'He's drunk as a Christmas skunk, and for some reason he gravitated to my bedroom,' said Serena. Turning to Eric, she added, 'I can assure you, he has *never* been in this room before.'

'Who's going to tell Diane?' asked Valentina, looking at her mobile phone. 'The wedding starts in twenty minutes.'

Chapter Sixty-Six

The iPad read 14.58. Diane paced beneath an arch of fairy lights, answering call after call from the Mindeflicks LA studio. The back story to Jake and Olivia's online connection for *Insta-Love* was currently streaming, with sponsors' ads running intermittently. All they needed was Father Flynn, and the Insta-Lovers, due to arrive in four and a half minutes, according to her iPad. The live stream was at 15.12.

'Edwin, any sign of Father Flynn? Valentina sent a message to say they were on it.'

'Your guess is as good as mine,' he said. 'My Babs says he's often late for these dos.'

'Late for a wedding? That's a bride's job, not the priest's.' Diane's breath felt short, but she just had to remember that her next gig was lined up with *Silver Stars*. She was happy as hell about it. 'Farrah and Eric?' she asked, as Valentina arrived with a look of panic on her face.

'On their way.'

'And the band?' asked Diane.

Valentina directed Diane to the sight of Benoît and François sitting on stools with banjos. 'I may as well tell you, we're having an extraordinary time.' Valentina grinned at the twins and then turned back to Diane. 'The band who were originally booked to play live for the wedding got snowed in.'

'The White Doves got snowed in? Valentina, are you kidding me?'

'I'm serious. They're from this place called Donegal, and they are, like, totally snowed in.'

'The golden French wonders here are going to play as Olivia walks up the aisle?' Diane and Valentina looked around the coach house. 'Okay, not the aisle, but up the cobblestones then?'

Valentina signalled to the twins and they began to play traditional bluegrass. '*It's grand to have someone to love you,*' they sang in harmony, their French accents sounding romantic, upbeat and light-hearted. '*She's the queen of all your treasures / Your castle is a happy home,*' sang the twins, both plucking well-chosen chords on their banjo.

'This is insane,' said Diane, 'and I LOVE it.'

'Valentina, where the hell is the Father Flynn? Olivia is literally arriving in four minutes, the ads are running, and the network thinks it's a go,' said Diane, with her headset on.

'Tyrone is sorting it. He'll be here.'

'You know, Valentina, I think for the first time in my life,

I really don't know.' Diane felt frozen on the spot. If she called the network, they'd have to switch to a re-run and the sponsors would go ballistic. She'd get it in the neck. Why hadn't she realised it was all heading in one direction? Preston's cock-up with Farrah's footage should have been symbolic enough for her to pull the whole thing. Even more gutting was that she'd thought Olivia wouldn't go through with the wedding. She had changed her tune now. She wanted them to marry – who gives a flying fuck about the ratings? Christmas had got to her, Serena had got to her, and she felt like she wanted to cut through the bullshit. Diane was pretty sure hashtag Javia was hashtag Insta-history.

'Sorry, excuse me,' came a voice. 'So sorry again, we're in quite a rush.' He, or she, was wearing a dog collar, a full-length black dress and a patent leather handbag, similar to one the Queen might have carried. Tyrone followed.

'Pleasure to see you,' said the person with the dog collar.

'Diane, I'd like to introduce to Harold Scott, a friend of Harry and Freddie Rose over at Farley Hall.'

'You know your lines?' asked Diane, who felt pure relief to see a dog collar on location.

'How fabulous, Harold, darling,' said Serena, rocketing up and giving him a big kiss. 'The last time we met we were going to exchange dressmakers. Where have you been?'

'Babysitting our grandchildren, mostly,' he said, 'but, gosh, it's good to be back in Ireland. We haven't been over since Bellamore was due to be sold.'

'Ah yes, the era when the big houses were in jeopardy,' said Serena. 'And in came the young, and look at the job they're all doing.'

'Concerts and hot tubs, bell tents and distilleries. And what about this place? Going to release it to the son, are we?'

'All in hand,' said Serena, looking at Tyrone, who was more at ease then she'd ever seen him. She might even call him happy. That was a word she hadn't thought she would ever associate with him.

Diane waved her hand over her head. 'We've got a hundred and twenty seconds to go,' she said. 'Harold, do you have any idea what you're doing?'

'I'm quite used to this funny business,' he said. 'I've watched these shows before with my wife, and I believe the question is, would you like to ditch or hitch?'

'You got it. Positions, lights?'

Jake, dressed in a white suit and matching bow tie, moved from foot to foot like a boxer about to go into the ring. 'I'm ready, guys. Preston's got me all miked up.'

'All we need is the bride,' said Diane, noticing Preston leaning against the brick wall, looking very sulky. 'We have one hundred seconds.'

Everyone turned around.

Chapter Sixty-Seven

'And roll the intro,' said Diane, as they watched a monitor with reindeer hearts pulling a sleigh across the screen, with bells instead of tin cans hanging from the bumper.

THE INSTA-LOVE CHRISTMAS SPECIAL

'Okay, Farrah and Eric, let's keep it snappy and fresh,' said Diane. 'Preston, you ready?'

'Yes,' he said. To his credit, Preston could put on his professional boots when called for.

'And action,' said Diane, throwing her hand in the air.

'Happy Christmas, guys, and welcome to the *Insta-Love Christmas Special*, wherever you are in the world,' said Farrah, looking sensational in a white trouser suit.

'We're here at a stunning castle in Ireland,' said Eric, 'where hashtag Javia have been settling their nerves before they meet at the altar.'

'Over the past eight weeks, we've all climbed into the hearts of hashtag Javia, but it hasn't been without its drama,' said Farrah. 'Let's take a look at the Insta-Lovers'' engagement ups and downs since they met just eight weeks ago.'

'And switch,' said Diane. 'Okay, we have forty-five seconds.'

Holly watched the monitor. Jake brushing his teeth and shaking his head; shots of them drawing a list of pros and cons as to their compatibility. Olivia in tears during a meeting with a fortune-teller.

'That's rather bleak,' said Holly.

'And we're back,' said Diane. 'Go, Farrah.'

'With tartan-covered benches and twinkling white garden lights, the coach house is a setting that lends itself to intimacy,' said Farrah, standing at the altar. 'In just eighty seconds, the stunning Father Harold will ask our Insta-Lovers if they'll ditch or hitch.' Farrah turned to smile at Harold, who gave a little wave to the camera. 'Don't go far, we'll be back in sixty seconds.'

'And hit the sponsors' messages,' said Diane to the network into her iPhone. 'Good work, guys. Now, please can someone assure me Olivia is about to arrive?'

In the yard, Olivia stood alone. This wasn't how they had planned things. She had wished for snow, and this part was coming true, but the other part she hadn't wished for turned out to be what she really wanted.

'Are you okay?' asked Holly, walking towards Olivia with the torch on her phone switched on. 'There's literally sixty seconds to go, but, Liv, you don't have to decide this now. Who cares about the show – it won't be the end of the world – but you walking into something you aren't sure about? That's not okay.'

'I love him,' said Olivia. 'I know it's real between us. I knew it from the second we met, from the moment we—'

'For Christ's sake,' roared Diane. 'Get your ass in here, Olivia.'

She checked her mobile phone. Their Instagram page was going crazy, the numbers literally flying up before her eyes, hashtags lining up, one after the other.

#JavaForever #WhiteWedding #InstaLove #InstaLace #InstaWeddingLove

'*I'm dreaming of snowflakes and champagne,*' sang Benoît and François, leading the audience, '*golden bubbles and girls in white dresses.*' As the second verse commenced, Olivia walked into the coach house, the diamonds on her veil sparkling. The twins played harmoniously on their banjos as Olivia walked with her head down, holding a magnificent bouquet of Irish dried flowers from the acclaimed Amelia's Garden. The walk towards the altar seemed twice as long as it had in their practice yesterday. But there stood Jake. He looked glorious in white, his dark hair slicked back, his face perfectly moisturised.

Holly, wearing a velvet fitted jacket, long skirt and runners, raced in and quickly stopped behind a chair when she saw Jake and Olivia standing at the altar.

'We are gathered here today,' said Father Harold, grandly, 'to bring together this man and this woman in holy matrimony.'

Holly felt more butterflies.

'Babe, you look so beautiful,' Jake mouthed to Olivia.

'Dearly beloved,' said Harold, having applied a fresh layer of lip gloss. 'We are gathered here today to bring hashtag Olivia and hashtag Jake—'

'There's not need to say the goddamn hashtags,' Diane said into Harold's earpiece.

'Hashtag Jake ...' Harold repeated, 'to find out if you want to get hitched or ditched following your *Insta-Love* journey.' Harold held the microphone as if he were the lead singer of a pop band. 'Jake Hunter Lyford, do you take this gorgeous woman to be your lawfully wedded wife? In other words, do you want to hitch this glorious creature, or ditch her?'

'Are you kidding me?' asked Jake. 'I'm hitching with this baby until I take my last breath.'

Diane signalled to Harold to move it along. Olivia looked increasingly upset.

'And you, Olivia Ann Stack, do you take this fine-looking man, though perhaps a touch heavy on the tan, to be your lawfully wedded husband? In other words, Olivia, would you like to hitch or ditch today, at this beautiful Irish castle?'

'Few could get away with that style,' said Serena. 'I do like a man in a dress, it's very avant garde.' The congregation quietly giggled and Harold tapped his microphone for attention.

'Do you?' he asked seriously.

'I'm so sorry, Jakey, but you've got to ditch me. I'm no good for you.'

Serena let out a sigh of immense disappointment.

'Liv, sweetie, what's going on?'

'I can't marry you. I'm so sorry.' And she ran back down the aisle.

'Wait!' Jake took the microphone from Harold. 'Olivia, this isn't a movie, this is real life, and you owe me an explanation.'

She stopped, but didn't turn around.

'The mikes,' asked Diane to Valentina. 'Check her mike, is it working? Are we still streaming live?'

Valentina gave a thumbs up. Olivia's sniffing was coming through to the feed.

'I can't, Jakey, we're on different pages.'

'What pages? We're on the same page. Hashtag Javia, hashtag *Insta-Love* for ever. We even have the same Instagram page.'

'I can't work with your five-year plan.'

'If it's too intense, we can make it longer. We can travel for twice as long. We can do anything, honey. Don't you see? We are masters of our own destiny.'

'That's just it,' said Olivia, turning around. 'I've dreamed of this moment since we met.' She turned around, unable to speak through the tears.

'Why, baby?' Jake asked, walking towards her, away from the altar. Then he realised.

Olivia nodded and fell into his arms.

'Oh, Livvy, screw the five-year plan.' He hugged her and, removing her veil, he kissed her head. 'I want you, baby, I want your baby, I want our baby.'

Farrah put her hand over her mouth and laughed and cried at the same time.

'Divine inspiration,' said Lynette, crossing herself.

'A Christmas baby, how lovely,' said Father Harold.

Diane looked shocked. She had not expected this.

'But where's the footage?' Farrah gently took the microphone from Jake. 'How did it happen?'

'I'm eight and a half weeks pregnant,' she said. She looked at Diane and then glanced around the coach house. 'I know it was against the rules, and I'm sorry, but when we met in person at the auditions, the chemistry between us was wild and I guess we got wrapped up in each other.'

'That's one way of putting it,' said Lynette, elbowing Holly.

'I swear we didn't as much as touch each other during the show, did we, Jakey?'

'As much as I wanted to, we never did, I swear, but, Liv, I can't see my future with anyone but you.' He took her hand.

Diane thought her blood pressure was going to burst. Mindeflicks was going insane with the sheer unpredictability of what was happening, and yet they wanted more.

'I want to be with you, and our hashtag *Insta-Love* Baby,' Jake said. And when Olivia answered, 'I want that too,' he jumped into the air, giving a victory yell.

'Then, if we're all agreed,' said Father Harold, taking back the microphone, 'I now pronounce you husband and wife.'

Clapping and whooping erupted from the audience.

Chapter Sixty-Eight

'The vicar wears Prada' read the *Daily Mail*, while online, #InstaBaby #DivineIntervention #IrishCastleWedding #InstaIrish cruised up the social media superhighway. Mindeflicks was utterly delighted as an avalanche of baby-product sponsors competed to jump on board.

'I've been very lucky in my life,' said Eric, sitting by the drawing-room fire. 'I've been blessed by television and met lots of like-minded people. It didn't always turn out as I'd hoped, but overall, it did, and I am extremely grateful.'

'You're a wonderful person, Eric,' said Serena, 'and this gin and tonic was worth waiting for.'

With Eric, thoughts spilled from her lips. It was the first time in her life she'd been able to do this. With Desmond, she'd had to watch out for his small sensitivities, curbing certain opinions, and with her son, they were such opposites, she constantly had to rework her thoughts before she spoke. Perhaps that was why she had lied to Tyrone. She'd been afraid to admit she was hopeless with money, that she couldn't resist taking chances, taking risks.

'I've made so many stupid mistakes. I'm a bloody fool for thinking I could do it alone.'

'I think you're being too hard on yourself,' said Eric. 'Time makes us all bolder.'

'You know, I looked in the mirror this morning, and I saw an old woman who looked remarkably like me.'

'Who was she?' he said, trying to humour her.

'It was the first time I'd ever seen myself as old.'

'You're not old, Serena, you're experienced.'

'I like that.' She laughed. 'You know I do, but Eric, can I be faithful to one person? Can I be faithful to you?'

'I'd like it if you could try,' he said. He got to his feet and offered her his hand. Together they danced as Eric hummed 'Snowflakes and Champagne'. Their timing was immaculate, like debutante professionals.

'Why do I feel like I can tell you anything?' she whispered to him.

'Because we're soulmates,' he said, pausing to look in her eyes. 'You know, I've never regretted not marrying or having a family, but I do wish I'd found you sooner.' Gently, he kissed her ring finger. 'You will let me spoil you a little, won't you?' he said. 'We can be like mussels on a rock in the ocean, for as long as time allows.'

'I've always preferred oysters,' she said, pressing her face against his cheek.

'Oysters, then. Maybe even oysters with pearls.'

Chapter Sixty-Nine

Christmas Eve, Knockboden

The frost was so heavy, it took Tyrone three attempts to pull the front door open. On the steps stood a well-dressed man with sprinkles of snow on his shoulders and a striped, white-ribboned box in his hands.

'I presume this is a wedding gift for Jake and Olivia? I'm afraid you're too late. They've already gone on their honeymoon.'

The man looked confused. He turned to point his key at the shiny Volvo, making double-sure it was locked.

'Though how you found the location, I'm not sure? The address wasn't publicised on the live broadcast.'

'I'm here to see Holly O'Leary,' he said. 'I'm an old friend.'

'Holly? Ah, okay,' said Tyrone. 'I have no clue where she is, though halfway down a bottle of champagne with my mother is always a possibility.'

'Sorry?'

'The house has been a den of celebration since the wedding.'

To say the man looked forlorn was an understatement.

Tyrone turned to see Jagger and Daiquiri walking next to Holly as she carried a tray of coffee into the drawing room.

'You're in luck,' said Tyrone. 'Why don't you come in?'

'I don't think so,' he said, holding the box as if it were a hot casserole.

'Holly?' Tyrone called. 'There's somebody at the door for you.'

'Coming,' she yelled back. 'God, I've got a thumping head—'

She stopped speaking the moment she caught sight of him.

'Holly?' asked Tyrone. 'Are you okay?'

'Giles,' she said.

'You're Giles?' asked Tyrone.

He nodded and seemed to shrink away from the door, very unsure of himself.

'I'll leave you to it,' Tyrone said, calling the dogs and walking down the front steps towards the yard.

'I wasn't sure whether to come, and I'm sorry, because I asked Mariah over and over for your address until she finally told me.'

Holly nodded. Mariah had called last night, apologising profusely for having told Giles, but saying she did think they had to lay the ghost of Christmas past to rest. He looked very tired. 'It's okay, Giles, really. I don't mind. It's good to see you.' And she meant it. His face had never looked kinder. 'Won't you come in? It's freezing out there.'

'No, I couldn't possibly.' And he handed the gift to her. 'I wanted you to have this.'

336

Holly looked at him, wondering if this was the way it was meant to be: Giles arriving in his polished car, sweeping her off her feet, or at least re-proposing to her and whisking her away.

'I was going to give it to you over lunch – at least, the lunch when you returned the ring.'

Holly ran her fingers over the lid of the box. 'I'm the worst person.'

'No, you aren't. In fact, you've actually given me the push I needed.'

'What do you mean?'

'I'm moving to Dubai.'

'What?'

'Stem-cell research. It's a new venture, massively funded, and I'm really excited about it. For the first time in so long, I'm going back to the lab and leaving the boardroom behind.'

'That's so good,' said Holly, feeling an odd well in her stomach. A sort of empty feeling. Maybe she had been storing Giles in the back of her mind as a kind of safety net? The person who would always take her back. But maybe that was what he was here to do?

She opened the box to find a circular pendant with H engraved on it and a delicate gold chain. 'Giles, it's so pretty.'

'I thought we could add the initials of our children as time went by.'

'You had it all figured out—'

'Until I didn't,' he said, even laughing a little.

'I'm so sorry,' she said, reaching out for his hands. 'Truly, I am.'

Chapter Seventy

In the front hall, Edwin piled the crew's luggage into the wheelbarrow and chuckled as the Christmas lights began flashing again.

'I swear those lights are trying to tell us something,' he said to Holly, as she slipped beneath the tree for what seemed like the one hundredth time.

'How are you feeling, Holly?' he asked. 'It's sad to see this lot go, even if it is Christmas Eve, with my Babs waiting at home with mince pies.'

'Diane and Farrah have both given me open invitations to stay with them in Los Angeles, and Valentina even gave me a waterproof mascara as an *Insta-Love* souvenir.' Holly was starting to feel very emotional as they all prepared to leave, but it was her goodbye to Serena that she dreaded.

'Here comes another one,' said Edwin. 'I can fit one more bag onto the barrow, Diane.'

'Thanks,' she said, bounding down the stairs and landing a rucksack into Edwin's arms. 'And Holly, one hundred million streams so far,' she said. 'Mindeflicks says this is by far the most-watched season of *Insta-Love*.'

'That's amazing,' said Holly. 'It was such a gorgeous sight, seeing Jake and Olivia driving away in their open-top Jaguar.'

'That's *Insta-Love* for you,' said Valentina, filming herself as she descended the stairs. 'You can bet we'll be seeing their baby every step of the way on their socials.'

'But, guys, you know the best part of this whole thing?' said Farrah. 'It's those two.' They all looked to the front door, where Serena and Eric stood arm in arm next to Tyrone.

'You would say that,' said Valentina. 'You're, like, such a romantic.'

'And what about you and your French twins?' asked Diane.

'We're going to meet in Paris after Christmas,' said Valentina, making a heart-shape symbol with her hands. 'Their grandma has a chateau in Normandy, and they *both* want to take me there.'

'Brilliant,' said Farrah. 'Good for you.'

'Whereas Farrah's going to be too busy for romance,' said Diane. 'As soon as the New Year bell tolls, it's going to be go, go, go with *Silver Stars*.'

Farrah's immediate thought was that she'd have time to diet over Christmas. But then she remembered her resolutions. No more diets, no more putting herself through hell. Healthy living was her mantra. 'What about Preston?' Farrah couldn't help feeling a little grateful to him for reinstating her confidence, even if he had meant to do the opposite by posting the footage online.

'He's returning to daddy with his tail between his legs,' said Diane, 'particularly as Daiquiri began sniffing his boots with interest before he stepped into the taxi.'

'I'm, like, so over him,' said Valentina. 'I couldn't care if a pack of wolves peed all over him.'

Holly scooped up Daiquiri into her arms and giggled as he licked her face.

'You know, guys, if you had told me a week ago this was how things would turn out,' said Diane, pulling on a gold knit woolly hat, 'I would have said you were dreaming. It's been a plot twist beyond my imagination.'

Frost glittered on the trees and hedging as the *Insta-Love* Range Rover drove down the avenue. The entire experience of having the crew to stay had felt surreal but, as Holly reasoned with herself, isn't 'surreal' the whole point of reality TV? From the front steps of Knockboden, she looked out over the white fields and tried to think positively. She was heading into a new year, a new phase. To go travelling was the answer and once she was far enough away, she would tell her mum that the wedding had been called off. At least her brother being home from Australia for Christmas was the perfect antidote and certainly gave Holly some breathing space. Once her mum had digested the news, Holly would visit and maybe they could begin again.

'There you are, Holly,' said Serena, looking beautiful in a long dark coat and a soft grey felted wool beret. 'Aren't you freezing? Where's your coat?'

'I'm wearing at least six layers beneath this jumper,' said Holly. 'All of your training on beating the cold has paid off.'

Serena smiled and stuffed her hands into her pockets. 'First things first,' she said. 'I have transferred a robust sum into your bank account – at least, I had Tyrone's secretary do it.'

Holly was about to object, as she couldn't bear the thought of Tyrone paying her wages.

'And before you say anything, you have been paid with the proceeds of the *Insta-Love* monies, as we originally agreed, though I admit it has taken longer than expected.'

'Thank you.' Holly wasn't sure what Serena's idea of *robust* meant, but it would surely buy a plane ticket and keep her afloat for a few weeks while looking for a new job.

Serena took her hands out of her pockets. 'I'd like you to have this,' she said, handing a flat velvet box to Holly.

'But I haven't got you anything,' said Holly. 'I feel terrible.'

'Open it,' ordered Serena.

Holly opened the box to find an opal pendant, with a gold necklace.

'My mother gave it to me for my eighteenth birthday,' said Serena, 'and I'd like you to have it.'

'I can't possibly.'

'Please do,' she said. 'I like the thought of it keeping you safe on your travels.'

Holly held the necklace in her hands. She couldn't speak.

'It's quite alright not to know where you're going, Holly,' said Serena, with added strength in her voice. 'You don't have to have all the answers.'

Serena put out her arms and gave Holly a hug that they both wished could go on and on. The mutual comfort they had brought to each other was immeasurable.

'But you do have to be sensible, Holly.' Serena stepped back, sniffed sharply and patted her eyes. 'If I haven't heard of a sensible plan by January the thirtieth, Eric and I will send a search party and bring you to stay with us in Hollywood. Got it?'

Serena knew how to make goodbyes easy. Her phrase 'Got it?' was one she'd learned from her mother: it somehow distracted from the emotion and demanded attention instead.

'So, they came good after all,' said Tyrone, putting his arm around his mother as Lynette called out several email addresses to Holly, making sure they kept in contact. 'And the cake never got eaten, at least not by humans.'

'What's that?' asked Serena.

'It's nothing,' said Tyrone, thinking of the dogs' muzzles covered in white icing. 'Just one of the many extraordinary moments of wedding build-up.'

He watched Edwin carry Holly's rucksack to his car. He had spent the past hours wondering where she would go. Maybe to her family, but knowing Holly, she'd choose to go to the station, buy a ticket and take her chances. She seemed hell-bent on going it alone.

Serena followed Tyrone's gaze as Holly knelt on the steps, hugging the dogs. 'They're going to miss her,' she said.

'What?'

'Jagger and Daiquiri – they love that girl.'

He nodded his head.

'I wasn't born yesterday, Tyrone. I know chemistry when I see it.'

Tyrone attempted to fob off his mother, but she wasn't having it. 'What's holding you back? I can see it in your eyes. That handsome face of yours starts to shine when you're around her.'

'She wants to leave.'

'You're really going to let her?' Serena stepped in front of him and held her son's face tenderly. 'This kind of energy, Tyrone, it's to be treasured. It's the universe's way of telling you there's something more. I had it with your father.'

'And Eric?'

'We have a companionship,' she said, kissing him on both cheeks.

Eric held the passenger door of his VW Golf open, brushing the snow off the wing mirror.

'Your carriage awaits, m'lady,' said Eric, pulling up the collar of his leather jacket. He looked like someone who was looking forward to Los Angeles sunshine.

'Before I go,' said Serena, giving Tyrone a hug, 'I suppose I'd better mention that I'm proud of you.'

'That is high praise,' he said as they walked to the car.

'But, darling, what if Holly wants you to call her back?' Serena wasn't giving up easily. 'Some women don't have the confidence to say what it is they desire, and honestly I feel that's the only way any of us can have what we deserve.'

Tyrone gave Eric a handshake and, turning around, he saw Holly standing at the front steps. 'Shall I call her over?' he asked his mother.

'Please don't, we'd only cry and neither of us wants that,' said Serena, stepping into the car.

Eric revved the engine and beeped the horn. 'It's never too late, remember,' said Serena through the car window.'Look at me: Hollywood here I come.' And like a bride hurling her bouquet, she threw doggie treats out of the car window as Jagger and Daiquiri barked their heads off. 'I'll be back, my darlings. Be good for Tyrone.'

As they drove away, Edwin offered his handkerchief to Lynette, who blew her nose so loudly Jagger darted between Tyrone's legs.

Chapter Seventy-One

Holly and Tyrone stood on the Turpinstown bridge watching a train disappear into the tunnel. It was an old-fashioned scene, with patches of freezing fog drifting around silhouettes of people standing on the platform seeking one more glimpse of the person they'd brought to the station.

'You know where you're going?' asked Tyrone, as he lifted the rucksack onto Holly's back.

'Beyond a ticket to Dublin and a taxi to the airport hotel, I have no idea,' she said, catching sight of a very grey cloud. 'I'm thinking of being like the girl in the movie who arrives to the airport and asks for a one-way ticket to somewhere beginning with ...'

'What letter?' he asked.

'I can't even decide on a letter.'

They smiled at each other and looked away.

'I might au pair for a while, or find a nice yacht to work on, who knows?' Neither of them had mentioned Giles, who had left earlier.

'Going with the flow,' said Tyrone, instinctively turning up the collar of her coat. He felt the softness of her hair brushing against his hands.

'You know me,' she said. 'I'm your classic millennial.'

'And it's been quite the master class. You might be shocked to hear it, Holly, but I think you have somehow altered my way of thinking.'

'It takes more than that to shock me,' she said, stepping back. 'I may even have learned from you.'

'Okay, I'll admit that is a shocking admission – but a two-way street. I like it.'

Holly walked backwards as they parted.

'You'd better go,' he said, the words crushing against what he wanted.

He cast around for a clever line to round it all out with, a note to end on, but it didn't come.

Putting his hands in his pockets, Tyrone took a step back.

'Goodbye, Holly'

He watched her turn around and then she looked back. 'Merry Christmas! I almost forgot.'

Tyrone raised his hand, just briefly. He'd done it. He'd let her fly.

The carriage smelt salty, like cinema popcorn. Holly found her seat number and tried but failed to wedge her rucksack into the luggage hold.

'Why not put it at your feet?' said the woman on the opposite seat. 'I won't mind.'

'Thanks.' Holly sat down, looked out of the window and tried to steady her mind. She felt uneasy, irritated to be struggling with rucksacks again.

'The hedgerow is pretty in the snow,' said the woman, 'but think of the little birds in this weather. You wonder how they survive, don't you?'

Holly nodded in agreement but said nothing.

'Don't you wonder where everyone is going,' said the woman, 'on a Christmas Eve afternoon?'

'I guess so.'

'I think it's amazing the way everyone travels now, don't you think?'

Holly nodded again.

'It's made the world so small, or that's what my husband says.'

'Does he travel?' asked Holly, feeling she ought to make an effort.

'Oh yes, he used to travel all over the world lecturing about dairy farming.' The woman's voice was somehow reassuring. 'Argentina, Chile, all the South American countries, can you imagine? But he has dementia now, my poor love.'

'I'm so sorry,' said Holly.

The woman's eyes squinted, as if searching for positives.

'But he loves me, he tells me all the time. He says, "Ann, I'm so glad I married you." Isn't that lovely?'

Holly agreed it was and, sensing the woman's anguish, she thought of Serena and the concern she'd had for the future of Knockboden. Holly could still feel the satisfying feeling of closing the shutters to keep the cold out. She thought of Jagger and Daiquiri rubbing their heads against her legs for a snuggle. Of wet logs sizzling in the fireplace and damp jumpers in her bedroom chest of drawers.

'We are very sorry for the delay, ladies and gentlemen, but there seems to be a technical problem,' came a loud voice through the speakers. 'We know it's Christmas, and we'll ask Santy for a bit of magic to get us moving as soon as possible.'

'Oh well,' said the woman, looking at her mobile phone. 'They won't be too long, will they? I see a text message has come in from my daughter. She's having terrible trouble with her heating. Thinks they might need a whole new system, can you imagine?'

'Hold on.' Holly sat up. 'I think I'm on the wrong train.'

'Oh dear,' said the woman. 'Aren't you lucky you realised before the train headed on?'

Chapter Seventy-Two

In the drawing room, Tyrone couldn't get comfortable, and it wasn't because the snoring duo of Jagger and Daiquiri took up most of the sofa. The fire was lighting nicely; that was something. He thought about closing the shutters, keeping out the darkness and the cold, but then he'd have to think about the evening. What did people eat on Christmas Eve? He couldn't even visualise a plate of food. He didn't feel like having a drink or a bath. He thought of the madness of having the TV crew at Knockboden. Holly had made that happen. The entire experience had been like a speed date, except it had deeply altered his perspective on life. The house he'd once scorned had come to feel like the most tranquil place on earth, but loneliness had crept in faster than he could ever have imagined.

He looked towards the doorway to the hall and saw the familiar flicker of lights from the Christmas tree. Damn, he'd forgotten to ask Holly how to reset the programme. He wondered again where she was now. With a pang, he imagined her with Giles. Maybe she had booked a flight to London, but felt she couldn't say.

'I've blown it, haven't I?' he said, getting up from the sofa to throw a log on the fire. The dogs raised their heads, looked momentarily sympathetic and returned to sleep. He walked into the hall on a mission to switch off the Christmas tree lights, but from a distance, he noticed the angel toppling to one side. That would have annoyed Holly, and it strangely bothered him too.

He found a three-step wooden ladder in Serena's study and carried it out to the hall, positioning it beside the tree. He'd straighten up the angel, then turn off the Christmas lights. Maybe he'd have toast and Marmite in the kitchen, fill a hot-water bottle and go to bed. But why hadn't he told Holly how he felt? That for some crazy reason he'd decided to sell his shares in the bank and exchange his life of relentless New York luxury for this world of draughty corridors, creaky floorboards and wobbly angels. Why had he not told Holly that she was the crazy reason, that she was the one who made him realise that Knockboden was where he belonged?

The lights continued flashing and baubles dangled around his shoulders as he nudged the angel back into an upright position. The dogs must have been surprised by the sight of Tyrone leaning into Christmas tree, as they began to bark. He lightly touched the angel's head and wondered if he'd take down the tree after all, but then he realised he was meant to be turning off the lights, not admiring the ornaments.

'Tyrone?' came a voice from below. He looked down to see that beautiful face emerging from behind the branches.

'I was going to call but the battery in my phone —'

Without giving Holly time to utter another single word, Tyrone jumped off the ladder and swept her into his arms.

'I wanted you to stay,' he whispered, 'I desperately wanted you to stay.' He loved her, without question, and holding her face so gently in his hands, he kissed her beneath the Christmas tree, the lights still flickering.

'Hey, you're shivering,' he said then, darting to close the front door. He took off his jumper and wrapped it around her shoulders. 'You're like a gift from the gods, there should be a ribbon around you.'

'I'm not just for Christmas, you know?' Holly laughed, her cheeks pink from the cold.

Tyrone kissed her again, and together they floated across the hall towards the drawing room.

'I'm sorry it's so chilly, I've only just lit the fire.'

'I tried calling Edwin, but there was no reply,' said Holly, rubbing the dogs' heads as they clamoured for attention, 'but I got a lift from the charming Garda Tom.'

She stopped at the doorway and looked up at him.

'This all feels like some kind of dreamy miracle,' she said. 'Is it a dream?'

'No, Holly, this isn't a dream. This is for real and I'm madly in love you.'

He leant down to kiss her again, at which point there was a large honk from outside and the dogs began barking.

'Have you ordered a Christmas choir to serenade us?'

'Not that I know of,' said Tyrone, advancing to the front door and opening it. He could see a silver car with reindeer antlers and a red nose on the bonnet glowing through the flurry of snow.

'Merry Christmas, Merry Christmas,' came a woman's voice from the car. 'Surprise, surprise.'

Tyrone froze, and turned to Holly.

'That's not who I think it is – is it?' asked Holly, hiding behind the door, her eyes wide in astonishment.

'Oh holy night,' said Tyrone. 'This sounds insane, Holly, but do you remember the song on the radio in Turpinstown, before we went shopping for Preston's birthday party? The song that reminded you of your family.'

'Tyrone, what have you done?'

'Afterwards, I did a little detective work and I found a couple of people—'

'A couple? What do you mean a couple?'

'I rang your mum, no answer but I left a message, and I Facebook-messaged your brother, Gabe, in Australia.'

'You're actually on Facebook?' Holly began laughing. 'But, hold on, are you telling me that you invited my mum and brother here for Christmas?'

'I'm so sorry,' said Tyrone. 'I just thought that somehow, if you knew that your family were coming …' He paused, and looked at her. 'I hoped you'd want to stay here too, but I never heard back from either of them about coming here. And with everything going on, I completely forgot.'

Taking his hand, Holly stood beside him and they looked

out onto the snow as her mother revved the engine before parking at a right angle on the lawn.

'The thing is,' said Holly, 'I haven't actually told my mum and brother ... you see, they still think I'm getting married.'

'Then, why don't you tell them that you *are* getting married,' said Tyrone, getting down on one knee.

Holly gasped, with eyes sparkling. 'Tyrone, I don't know what to say ...'

Epilogue

Christmas Day, Two Years Later

Jagger and Daiquiri careered around the hall as the #Javia twins chased them, hurling Coco Pops, with a cameraman trailing closely behind. The Christmas tree looked as majestic as Serena remembered and the cool air of Knockboden a delightful contrast to the sickly sweet air-conditioning of the spacious LA bungalow she shared with Eric.

'Where are they?' asked Olivia, dressed in knee-length Uggs and a cropped fur jacket, a white muslin over one shoulder.

'Hold that pose for one second, sweetie?' Jake leapt next to her, held some mistletoe over her head and took a selfie as he kissed her cheek.

'But what about Holly and Tyrone? Shouldn't they be here by now?' asked Serena.

'My nerves are giving me heartburn,' said Juliette O'Leary, carrying a plate of reindeer-shaped cheese puffs. 'Do I honestly look old enough to be a grandmother? Surely

Holly could have waited a few years and given me time to consider the role.'

'Time waits for no man, nor baby,' said Eric, putting an arm around Juliette's shoulder. 'Have a sip of this Bloody Mary. The vitamin C will pep you up.'

The dogs began to circle Serena's legs. 'Shush!' she commanded, and everyone froze. 'Is that the gravel? Yes, I can distinctly hear gravel crunching. They're here.'

'Oh my God,' said Juliette, 'am I on camera? Should I re-apply my lippy?'

The director, so discreetly dressed she was almost in camouflage, nodded kindly, knowing the shot was all about #Javia. They had close to two hundred million followers now, not to mention all the multi-million-dollar contracts since the arrival of their twins.

The front door opened, revealing a proud father with his arm around Holly, who held the ultimate Christmas bundle in her arms. Serena instantly recognised the blanket, with its tiny sprigs of holly berries, embroidered by Edwin's Babs.

'Hashtag baby in the house,' yelled Jake, taking off his sunglasses, sweeping his lashes in the direction of the camera and taking the twins' hands with Olivia.

'Hello, everyone,' said Holly, her eyes glistening. Serena shook her head as she watched her: confident, strong and more at ease than Serena had ever imagined possible.

'Presenting Juniper Harpur,' said Tyrone.

Serena and Juliette gathered around the baby.

'She's beautiful, darling,' said Juliette, 'looks so like me when I was that age.'

'Well done to all you wonderful Christmas angels,' said Serena, reaching for her glass. 'And a special toast to our new Christmas babe. Welcome to Knockboden, darling Juniper, and . . .' Serena's voice broke, 'I never thought I'd say these words again with a feeling of such utter and genuine happiness.' She took a deep breath. 'Merry Christmas, my darling ones.'

Acknowledgements

I wrote this novel during the long hot summer of 2022, recreating the festive spirit with a miniature Christmas tree on my desk and a jolly jingling soundtrack blasting out from Alexa. Early one especially sweltering June morning, I was driving to the village shop when I tuned into Lyric FM to find *Marty in the Morning* discussing Christmas songs with Sinead Tyrrell, the AA Roadwatch presenter.

'Fair play, Marty, it's never too early for a Christmas song,' said Sinead.

Marty concurred, and the next thing I knew, with the sun rising high, I was listening to a beautiful rendition of 'Have Yourself a Merry Little Christmas' by the Mornington Singers. A Christmas song on national radio at the height of summer. What were the chances? As my eyes filled with happy tears on my journey home, I saw a black cat and two magpies at the same time. ALL TRUE.

Therefore, I would like to sincerely thank Marty Whelan, and the universe, for tuning into my thoughts and making me feel like I was on the right track.

Thanks also to Mariah Carey, as I've pretty much listened

to 'All I Want for Christmas Is You' every day for the past six months, and I still love it.

Thank you Mary Claire Rogers, especially on the day you kept me going when I thought I couldn't go on, and to Rachael Comiskey for her constant Swiss wisdom.

To the wonderous wordsmith Larry Fogg, a humungous thank you.

Thank you Dan Shaw Smith for the daily sight of peaceful doves, and to John Asaraf and Les Brown, thank you for more than you can ever know – though you probably do know.

For reminding me of the magic of writing, thank you Natasha Geary, and thank you Iliane Dingel-Padberg and Moritz for making Mulranny beach a summer highlight.

Ollie, Alfie, and Geronimo, muchas gracias for looking after Oldfort and Dilly. Many thanks to Bernard Cloney for guiding Holly and the Land Rover safely home to Knockboden.

To the marvellous Rosie O'Neill, thank you for introducing me to Margaret Marbury, whom I look forward to meeting in NYC.

I am massively grateful to the podcasts *How to Own the Room* with Viv Groskop; *How to Fail* with Elizabeth Day, and *Happy Place* with Fearne Cotton, and special thanks to Sonia Choquette, for guidance on intuition, and Amanda de Cadenet, on prioritising. All massively helpful and I recommend them so highly.

This novel gave me a delightful excuse to feed my imagination by indulging in the re-make of *Dynasty* (on Netflix) which I absolutely loved. Further research via *Love Island* and *Love is Blind* made for interesting viewing.

I am massively grateful to the Festival of Writing and Ideas for spurring me on to write this book. With special thanks to

Ciara Francis, who wisely told me to focus on the 'can do', and to Marita Doyle, who made my year by assuring me that this is the time to make things happen! And huge thanks to Alice Forde for reminding me to keep up the positive self-talk.

For underlining the wonders of Tyrone Guthrie, thank you so much, Marita Conlon-McKenna.

Thank you Suzanna Crampton for guiding me from very early on.

To Jonathan O'Grady, thank you for putting the word blockbuster (now one of my favourite words) in my mind, and thank you to Sheana Forrest for teaching me the Pomodoro.

Thank you to Ronan Sheehan for one of the best letters I've ever received, to Martin Kelly, for his beautiful vocabulary and to JC O'Mahony for inspiring Serena and Eric's romance.

I am continuously full of gratitude to Paula Campbell at Poolbeg for inviting me onto the writing highway, and thank you to Edward Denniston.

Thank you Justin Green and Anthony Jackson for Bertha's Revenge, and for Insta-Love inspiration, thank you Andy Cairns.

For sending oodles of creative confidence my way, thank you so much wondrous Dede Gold.

Thank you to the Charleston Angels: Iona Hoare, Lucy Kelly and Tiffany Black.

'Miracles do happen.' Thank you Herbie and Jacquie Brennan for all of your help, and here's cheers to a star, Lessie Forde!

Xièxiè nǐ zuì qīn'ài de péngyǒu, Dominique Patton, it feels you are near, even when you are far.

For me teaching me to be Brave, I am very grateful to Philip McKernan.

For our surroundings of organic splendour, thank you William and Emily Bunbury, and John Edwards.

Thank you John Schwatchke, the finest pen pal in the universe.

Wendy Mae Millar, the Cagney Wenson reference is for you, with happiest of memories.

From often remote I.C.A.V.I.P phone calls to Anya Hindmarch advice, I am massively grateful to Clare Durdin Robertson – I've used a serious amount of shampoo while writing this book!

My thanks also to the splendiferously elegant Valery Mahoney for keeping me in style.

To my godmother, Helen Price, thank you for the Charles Dickens characters who are right here with me as I write. And Hughie Casey, I am so proud of you.

For your bountiful encouragement, thanks to my parents-in-law, Ben and Jessica Rathdonnell.

Grazie mille to Nicola Coveney: the way you connected me with other worlds made all the difference.

Blessed are we across the fields, and so many thanks to Tom and Sasha Sykes, and Rupert Butler for all the feel-good, encouraging vibes.

I'm forever grateful to Aunt Bo for inspiring adventures, and thank you Liz Cairns, Faenia Moore and Virginia Hartley for being marvels in a multitude of ways as I wrote. And to Gilly Fogg, always at the ready to buoy me up and zap over the speediest of solutions.

Erin Van Vuren, thank you for your beautiful quote.

To my editor, Ciara Doorley, I'm so grateful to you for seeing what I see in Serena Harpur – thank you for your brilliant guidance. Many thanks also to Donna Hillyer for your eagle eye, and to Katie Green for spot-on details. At Hachette, thanks also to Joanna Smyth and Stephen Riordan. Thank you as well to typesetter, Claire Rourke, for all her tweaks to this novel – you have the patience of a saint.

My tremendous gratitude also to the following people, who may or may not realise they nudged me forward as I wrote this novel: Johnny and Lucy Madden, Alex and Daria Blackwell, Cilla Patton, Ahmed Salman, Aisling Killoran, Mary Rogers, Roly and Emma Ramsden, Adri Sanchez, Annabel Butler, Selina Guinness, Susie Tinsley, Gesa Cosby, Joanna Fennell, George and Eve Fasenfeld, Mim and Janie Scala, Charlie Murless, Brains Miller, Karmendra Jaisi, Sebastian and Ali Barry, Jacquie Doyle, Andy and Cathy Goss, Noel and Les McMullan, John Brogan, Jenny Pringle, Andreas Frank Thorsland, Nick Burma, Megan Comiskey, Cormac O'Carroll, Charlotte Capel Cure, Coibhe Butler, Freddie Durdin Robertson, Finley Gallagher, Jago Butler, Adrian and Claire Coffey, Debbie McDermot, Euan Rellie, Iris de Villeplee, Jo Patton, Kirstin McDonagh and Michael Molloy, Lenny Abrahamson, Bernard Doyle, Cathy Gilfillan, Sonia Rogers, Neil Gaiman, Larry Fogg, Charles Butler, Hugo Jellett, Lu Thornley, Marina Lawlor, Amelia Raben, Brian Morgan, Floella Benjamin, Amanda Morris, Kate Campbell, Bernard de Croix, Charlie Fowler, Tara Quirk, Nicola Bunbury, Ned Kelly, Miranda Richardson, Austin and Marti Sullivan, Phyl Herbert, Mary McManus, Roz Jellett, Jack O'Driscoll, Joanna Madden, Jane Cregan, John McDermot, Yoly Johnson, Mim and Janey Scala, Nick Wilkinson, Nuala Reilly, Noelle Doyle, Caroline Burton, Stan Ridgeway, Rachel Collins, Brian Donaldson, Nick Coveney, Sally Rooney, Louise Knatchbull, Maggie Frietag, Lemn Sissay, Breda Brown, Aileen Blackwell, Sally Gibbs, Brenda Coller, Liza Mitchell, Fish Gore, Jago Butler, Brennan's

Shop, Robert O'Byrne, Robin Fogg, Mark Boobbyer, Daisy and Nic Jacquier, Renauld Semerdjian, Sophia Couchman, David and Jan Roberts, Simon Lewis, Gillian Keegan, Matthew and Grainne Dennison, Mandy Hartley, Chris Blackwell and Adam Rynne.

To the greatest of believers, Ger Nichol, tremendous thanks for being my amazing agent, always encouraging, with immeasurable enthusiasm.

Thank you dearest Mum for cementing my self-belief as we watched over Clew Bay, and for exhilarating adventures, including Languedoc vineyards in 42 degrees. You are a brilliant mother – the best in the business.

To Turtle, I am putting an infinity symbol beside my thank you ∞, as your patience and good humour is extraordinary, plus you are an expert in guiding me out of procrastination and knowing when it is the right time for me to write, despite my temptation to curl up with you on the sofa.

Jemima and Bay, thank you both for all the love – especially that night when you told me to 'keep going' and that 'my future self' would thank me!

For Aunt Meike, who liked to read the last page first, I'm always thinking of you.

Huge thanks also to the always *Absolutely Fabulous* Sarah Beth Casey and to my favourite writer on the planet, Jilly Cooper.

Finally, I raise a coupe de champagne with love, thanks and admiration for Avia Riddell Martin, whose wondrous energy, generous nature and glamorous spirit was a gift to all of us lucky enough to have known her.